Splash

ᴬ Tiger Lily's Café® Mystery

By Kathleen Thompson

Kathleen Thompson

Splash

Volume 6

ᴬ Tiger Lily's Café® Mystery

By Kathleen Thompson

This book of fiction is not to be used as a resource when studying Native Americans. Readers interested in the subject are urged to research the topic using standard methods.

ISBN-13: 978-0-9984023-5-2

ISBN-10: 0-9984023-5-4

© Registration # TX 8-309-111

Library of Congress Control Number: 2017904564

Kathleen Thompson

A List of Tiger Lily's Café® Mystery Series Books:

This cozy mystery series has everything you seek: an eclectic cast of characters, a mystery or two, and diligent detectives on duty. The detectives just happen to be feline.

Tiger Lily's Café is set in a Midwestern town nestled into the coast of a Great Lake. The setting itself acts as a character, bringing the reader into the sights, sounds and smells of the small resort community of Chelsea.

Read the series in order, or read any book alone. While characters grown and change, each volume stands alone with a clear beginning and a clear end.

- Turtle Soup (2014)
- Boo! (2015)
- Phishing (2015)
- Holiday (2016)
- A Rock And A Hard Place (2016)
- Splash (2016)
- Chasing A Butterfly (2017)
- Pumpkin Squash (2017)
- Snowblind (2017)
- Hearts On Fire (2018)
- Morel Of The Story (2018)
- Dragon Fire (2019)
- Beach Bunnies (2020)
- Shipwreck (2020)

Kathleen Thompson

Kathleen Thompson

Cast of Characters

Annie Mack, with the help of her "kids" and a talented staff, owns and manages a bed and breakfast, a cafe and other businesses on the south side of The Avenue. She has lived in Chelsea for only a few years, but her ancestral roots to the town date to the Civil War era.

Annie's SASHET Rainbow: (sa SHAY) a model that assigns color to each core feeling. **S**adness is blue; **A**nger red; **S**care green; **H**appiness yellow; **E**xcitement orange; and **T**enderness purple.

For more information, visit Liberation Psychotherapy: www.libpsych.com/articles/sashet/sashet.html.

Ben and JoJo are college students. They work part-time all over town, including most of Annie's businesses.

Boone is the person to call if you need anything: mowing, snow removal, landscaping, maintenance, preventative maintenance, and just about anything else. He is married to **Harriet (Hilly),** who provides business cleaning services. His sons **Daryl** and **Donny** work for him. Their roots are in rural Appalachia, and they are so much more than people think.

Candice is the head waitress at Mo's Tap. A native of Chelsea, her long, thick, dark hair is the envy of most women who meet her.

Carlos is the manager and baker at Mr. Bean's Confectionary. He is a citizen of the US but was originally from Mexico. He supports his mother and younger sisters, who still live there. He is preparing to marry Isabel.

Cheryl inherited The Marina from her parents. It's a small deep water marina with basic amenities. Cheryl is married to Ray. She has known Annie since they were children.

Chris is Annie's special friend, although neither of them are ready to commit to a permanent relationship. He is the Officer in Charge of the Coast Guard Station. His stress relieving hobby is art. His sketches – in charcoal, pencil and pastel – are sold for charity.

Clara owns the flower and gift shop, Bloomin' Crazy. She is a citizen of the US, originally from Haiti, and has an ebullient personality. She keeps The Avenue decorated with fresh and silk flowers year-round.

Cookie probably has another name, but this is what he goes by. He cooks at Mo's Tap and learns what he can from Felicity at every opportunity. He's reticent at best, and he yearns to have his own restaurant. To keep him, Annie opened a fine dining restaurant, Bon Vivant Grille, on Fridays and Saturdays inside the Café.

Daniela is a former professional baker who lives in Mexico; she and her daughters are now financially supported by Carlos. She has been a mother figure to Isabel, who will soon marry Carlos. Her adult daughters, sisters to Carlos, are **Rosa** and **Valeria**.

Diana is the chief instructor at L'Socks' Virasana (Veer AHS ana). She is Mem's daughter. Diana left home right after high school and did not speak to her mother until her return ten years later. Their relationship, while tenuous, continues to grow stronger.

Felicity is the chef at Tiger Lily's Café. She is young, perky and extremely talented in the kitchen. She manages the Café, the upstairs catering facility and outside catering operations.

Frank recently moved to Chelsea to open an antique shop, Antiques On Main. He and Mem are in a relationship.

Gema recently moved to Chelsea to open Gema's Creations. There, she makes and sells unique jewelry pieces. She has space in the front corner of Antiques On Main.

George is the bartender and manager of Mo's Tap. He is a top-notch bartender and can be counted on to keep confidences. He is a volunteer with the local Coast Guard.

Georgia and her daughter Frederica **(Little Fred)** recently moved to town. She manages the kitchen at the Bon Vivant Grille on weekends, coordinates catering for the Café, and cooks part-time at Mo's Tap. Her father, **Fred Calendar**, comes to town on occasion.

Geraldine was the leader of the "it" crowd in high school, and somehow, life didn't turn out quite as she expected. Everything Annie isn't – perfectly dressed, perfectly coiffed, and perfectly awful – Geraldine is more than a thorn in Annie's side. **Everett** is her on-again-off-again husband.

Ginger is the daughter of Pete, the Chief of Police, and Janet. She works part-time at L'Socks' Virasana. Because she moved to town as a teen (when her father retired from the Marine Corps), and because she is one of the few African American teens in town, she sometimes feels like an outsider.

Greg is a progressive realtor in Chelsea. His goal is to get the right property to the right owner, always moving Chelsea forward.

Gwen is Annie's accountant. A motherly figure, her financial acumen is hidden from all but those lucky enough to have her in their corner.

Hank is a former member of the Town Council. He opposes Annie in every way.

Harry is the regular driver for the rental company used almost exclusively by folks on The Avenue.

Henrie manages the KaliKo Inn in an elegant manner. He does not invite confidences and speaks little about himself. Always formal in tone, people have difficulty pegging his accent. Is it French? Cameroon? Rwandan?

Holly and Jolly, twins, own DoubleGood, an electronics and hardware store. Holly lives in a wheelchair. Natives of Chelsea, they used to hate the names given them by their parents. Now, they enjoy the novelty of it.

Ian is a childhood friend of George. He coordinates local sporting and team events. He is light-hearted and fancy-free.

Isabel is going to marry Carlos. She has moved from Mexico to plan the wedding.

Janet is Pete's wife. She spent twenty years as a Marine officer's wife. She traveled the world and is now living in Chelsea. She is an outsider, not having grown up here like Pete. She is the ultimate community volunteer.

Jennifer and Marie, sisters and nurse practitioners, own The Drug Store and The Clinic. Folks call the sisters before calling nine-one-one. Chelsea natives, they know everyone. And their secrets.

Jenny is an attorney who focuses on family law. She enjoys taking on cases that will right an injustice. She is always ready to engage in battle with those who don't believe a woman, much less a woman of color, can dance with the big boys.

Jerry learned how to make candy in a minimum security federal prison. He was not an employee. Jerry works hard to overcome his shyness, particularly around women.

Jesus manages Sassy P's Wine & Cheese and also selects the wines. His family, famous vintners in the Napa Valley, owned, farmed and made wine for generations before California became a part of the United States.

Joan is a member of the Town Council. She opposes Hank in every way. Clara's pet name for her is "Joan of Chelsea."

Laila owns Babar Foods. A traditional Pakistani, she is raising her children without the assistance of a husband. Her children are **James**, **Ava** and **Carl**, who lives with Autism.

Marco is a police officer in Chelsea. He is "second in command" because he was the only officer that didn't go off-kilter during a hostage situation. Marco prides himself on being one-hundred-percent-eye-talian-American.

Martha used to own a bed and breakfast. The cottage was renovated to add an apartment suite, now occupied by Georgia and Little Fred. Martha is retired and enjoys spending time at the Inn.

Mem owns the health food store and cyber café, CyberHealth. Her wisdom is reassuring to everyone, including her daughter, Diana. She teaches the safe use of social media to all ages and has equipment and technology that is helpful to the small-town police department.

Minnie chooses perfect cheeses to accompany the rotating wine selections at Sassy P's Wine & Cheese. She comes from several generations of cheese makers in Wisconsin.

Nancy and Sam are Annie's mother and step-father. They have been married since Annie was a child. They come for extended visits in Chelsea and have learned to call this town their second home.

Pete is a native of Chelsea. He retired from the Marine Corps and is now the Chief of Police. Like Annie, his ancestors arrived in the Civil War era. His, however, came up via the Underground Railroad. He and his wife Janet have three children, the eldest of whom is Ginger. Clarice and Tamara are in high school and junior high.

Ramon (ra MONE) is Clara's boyfriend. A Jamaican by ancestry, he plays saxophone with a jazz fusion band called Bergamasco (after the breed of his dog). He and Clara work hard to maintain their mostly long-distance relationship.

Ray owns and operates The Escape, a yacht fashioned into a cruiser for fishing, diving and pleasure. He is married to Cheryl; Chris is his best friend.

Teresa is a newcomer to the area. She came to this community to serve. She pastors a small church, Soul's Harbor, and pastors the community through her outreach.

Terrence & Jerald Timmer-Schmidt have just moved to town. Terrence is a heart surgeon; Jerald is a psychiatrist. They have opened a medical office building in town.

Trudie is the barista at Tiger Lily's Café. She is from Jamaica and ended up in Chelsea when a former boyfriend dumped her at the campground. Felicity saved her, and they have been the best of friends ever since.

Annie's Cats

Annie has seven cats. Most people would call them "rescue kitties." From Annie's perspective, each of them rescued her.

Tiger Lily is a beautiful tabby cat with soft green eyes. She is the titular manager of Tiger Lily's Café, the main gathering place for Chelsea. She is generally calm and logical.

Little Socks is a bright-eyed black cat with white socks. She has a commanding personality and is small and sneaky enough to serve as a cat burglar. She spends time at the yoga studio, L'Socks' Virasana (Veer AHS ana).

Kali, Ko and Mo are litter mates. They shared a secret language as kittens; Kali and Ko now speak "cat," but Mo still speaks "secret." Kali and Ko can be found at the KaliKo Inn, a lakeside bed and breakfast. Mo spends time at Mo's Tap, an upscale blues bar.

Sassy Pants is aptly named; it's difficult to keep this little girl's attention. She is overly sensitive and will react out of emotion instead of reason. She entertains at Sassy P's Wine & Cheese.

Mr. Bean is the baby of the family and is mostly gray with traces of tiger. He has two speeds: fast and love me.

Other Companions

Claire is a blue point Himalayan cat whose human is Frank. She's beautiful and loves people. She is stand-offish with other cats.

Cyril is an English setter whose human is Pete, the Chief of Police. Cyril is friendly and calm. He is an excellent hunter.

Fiamma is a Bergamasco. Dreadlocks cover her face. In fact, her entire body is covered with a combination of long dreadlocks and mats of hair. She is an outrageous flirt.

Honey Bear is a large, golden, long-haired mutt of a cat who believes it is his perfect right to be anywhere. Other cats hate him.

Jock is a Portuguese water dog whose human is Ray, the captain of The Escape. Jock is spirited and affectionate; he loves children.

Oscar McMurphy was a stray, named Scaredy Cat by the kids. Despite the name, she is a girl who now lives with Holly and Jolly. She claims Holly as her very own. She is often in and out of the Inn and other places on The Avenue with her brother, Simon Finnegan.

Simon Finnegan was a stray, named Fat Cat by the kids, who now lives with Holly and Jolly. He claims Jolly to be his mom. He is often in and out of the Inn and other places on The Avenue with his sister, Oscar McMurphy.

Speckles is a tortoise shell cat, named for her orange speckles. She belongs to Georgia and is Little Fred's chief nanny.

Tillie came to live on The Avenue with her dreadful family from England. She is a Jack Russell Terrier and now lives with Carlos and Isabel above the Confectionary. She has free run of The Avenue, including the Inn. She is small enough to squeeze in and out of the cat doors.

Guests at the Inn

Valerie and Evie have come for some early-summer beach time.

Clark, Bryce, Monte and **Kim** will compete in the Chelsea Grand Prix, a bicycle tour that includes a metric century ride.

Collin and **Celeste Curtis** have come to go on day cruises during the week.

Grant and **Erika** will celebrate their wedding. Their friends **Tom** and **Denise** will witness the nuptials.

Others In Town

Brad, of Brad's Buoys & Gills, a shyster, always out for the most money he can get for the least outlay. He uses The Marina when he picks up clients, but keeps his boat at home.

Cycling Teens

- Girls
    - Alena – Brendan's younger sister
    - Carol
    - Jessie
    - Renee – also a lifeguard
    - Traci
- Boys
    - Bill
    - Brendan – also a lifeguard
    - Eddy
    - Eric

1

Henrie had a light morning. One guest. Her room, the back bedroom on the main level of the KaliKo Inn, had access to the beach. Henrie knew she went for early morning walks and that she would return in about a half hour.

She was not just a guest; she was a friend. On days she was the only guest, Henrie served breakfast in the kitchen.

Henrie paused to look out the kitchen window. The cloudless sky was as blue as sapphire. He could almost feel the cool June breeze on his face. He promised to walk to the lake himself after breakfast. It was time to splash around barefoot at the edge of the lake.

Henrie heard Annie come from her apartment on the third floor to the second floor landing. He assumed she sat down at the computer to check email or Facebook.

Henrie was an enigma. He came with the highest recommendations from a five-star hotel in New York. Yet he seemed quite content to live in this small resort community and work at this Inn, where he was chief cook, bottle washer, toilet bowl cleaner and concierge.

He did not invite confidences and spoke little about himself. Most people, townsfolk and tourists alike, came away thinking, what is that accent? French? Cameroon? Rwandan? They also went away with the eerie feeling that he could read their minds. Indeed, whatever was needed or desired, he offered before a request was made.

Today, breakfast would be French toast stuffed with cream cheese and fresh strawberries, oatmeal with walnuts and cranberries, coffee and juices. And bacon. He had to make bacon for another reason, so he made enough for breakfast.

Henrie heard what could have been a herd of wild horses come down the stairs. Annie was already at the kitchen door. Seven cats and a little dog came in at a run. They pranced around Henrie and looked up with expectant, adoring faces.

"Do you ever feed them?"

"Yes. They've had breakfast. Well, I didn't feed Tillie. I expect her own momma fed her, but the cats have eaten."

"I do not believe you." The stern look on Henrie's face didn't match the smile in his voice.

He walked to the dining room with a small bowl and a platter of shredded bacon. A table beside the door had a covering over it and a sign that proclaimed this to be the Seven Cats Detective Agency. Henrie picked up a corner of the table covering, leaned over, and dribbled bits of bacon into seven little cat dishes, one for each cat. Henrie put the last of the bacon into the small bowl and put that on the floor for the little dog.

Bacon gone, the eight friends pranced around, asked politely for "more, please," but eventually realized that was not going to happen.

Tiger Lily looked up at Annie. Annie looked down at Tiger Lily.

"It's Monday. Don't you have someplace to be? I imagine the breakfast rush is in full swing at the Café."

Tiger Lily gave Annie a quick blink, then whirled to bop a few cats on the nose. With the exception of two dilute calico cats – two very large dilute calico cats – they turned and ran to the front door, out the cat door, down the porch steps, and up The Avenue on their way to work.

The little dog, Tillie, looked confused. She made up her mind and followed the herd outside.

The two large cats flicked their tails and walked sedately to the library, where they jumped to the windowsill, cleaned their paws and faces, and curled up to take a nap in the sun.

This was Chelsea, a resort town on the eastern coast of one of the Great Lakes. The town was snuggled into the lake on one side and the wooded acreage of a state park on two other sides. It had the feel of a village separated from the rest of the world.

Annie, Henrie and the cats lived at the KaliKo Inn, a bed and breakfast with beach-front access to the lake. The Inn was just one of the businesses owned by Annie, who had inherited this building and another building, long enough for five storefronts, just to the east of the Inn.

Each business bore the name of a cat – or two – who acted as the titular managers. Heaven help the human managers if they ever thought they were responsible for the places. The cats themselves knew better.

Tiger Lily, a pretty tabby cat, reigned at Tiger Lily's Café, the gateway to Sunset Avenue and the premier gathering place for Chelsea natives and tourists.

Little Socks, black with white markings, sometimes called a tuxedo cat, "managed" a yoga studio, Lil' Socks' Virasana.

Mo, litter mate to the two dilute calicos, was a handsome long-haired gray. He spent his days at Mo's Tap, an upscale blues bar.

Mr. Bean, the youngest, a muscular gray kitten, danced in the windows to bring customers into his Confectionary, where the best baked goods and chocolates in the state could be found.

Sassy Pants, whose maker apparently took a paint palette and threw it at her, played with whatever fell on the floor at Sassy P's Wine & Cheese. Usually, what fell on the floor was a wine bottle cork that one or another employee would "accidently" drop. Or throw.

The two calicos, Kali and Ko, stayed right here, at the KaliKo Inn. Here, they greeted guests, sniffed luggage, made sure Henrie cooked a proper breakfast, tested the chocolate truffles left in guest rooms every evening, and slept.

Tillie, a Jack Russell Terrier, was a regular guest of the Inn. She belonged to Isabel, but until Isabel came from Mexico a few weeks ago, Tillie lived with Isabel's fiancé, Carlos.

Carlos managed Mr. Bean's Confectionary. While Tillie lived with him, he took her to work every day. Tillie now lived with Isabel at the Inn. She still loved to go to Mr. Bean's during the day to dance in the windows, competing with the kitten for attention.

Annie helped Henrie set the table, which was ready just as Isabel came in from her walk on the beach. She smiled and said, "Good morning." Annie and Henrie, instead of responding, looked at one another, then back at her.

Henrie spoke first, using the formal tone everyone knew so well. "Sit down, let me pour coffee, and if you would like, please tell us all about it."

Isabel sat on one of the tall chairs set around a butcher block table. Her English had a beautiful Mexican lilt. "There's nothing to tell."

Annie sat beside her. "Don't mind us. You don't have to tell us everything. You're getting ready to be married. You have a lot on your mind."

"I don't mind that you ask, really. I just don't know what to say. How to say it."

Silence reigned as the trio ate breakfast. Henrie and Annie were of the same mind in this regard. Sometimes, silence is golden.

Isabel sighed. "It's, well, it's Daniela and the girls."

Daniela lived in Mexico. Not only was she Carlos' mother, she had been a surrogate mother to Isabel. "The girls" were hardly girls anymore. Rosa and Valeria, sisters to Carlos, were young adults with jobs.

"Do you want to talk about it?"

"It's…it's so difficult. Carlos and I both want her to move here, but she won't."

"It's her home. It has to be hard to consider moving."

"It hasn't been her home for more than a decade. The cartel took everything she owned, including the life of her husband. They took her home, her business. They put her in a hovel and they 'allow' Rosa and Valeria to work. I haven't even been able to tell Carlos that they take a percentage of everything he sends as payment for their largesse."

Annie and Henrie looked at Isabel, eyes wide. "What? All these years, and he's been paying the cartel without knowing?"

"All this time. And because she's been such a good little soldier, they 'allow' her to visit Carlos every now and then. I guess that's their way to assure the money keeps coming."

"Why won't she move?"

"She doesn't think they will let both of the girls come."

"How can they stop them?"

"They have their ways. If someone won't stay willingly, then...well, then they resort to more compelling measures."

"Why do they need the girls to stay?"

"They have some education, and their jobs pay as well as any in the country. They have been able to stay out of 'the life' by paying a percentage of their salary to them. Carlos thinks their jobs are low-paying. He doesn't know how much goes into the pockets of someone else."

Annie thought about the previous December. "They were all here for Christmas. You, too. Why didn't they stay then? Why didn't you all stay?"

"It's not so simple. Daniela lives better than most because of Carlos, but the whole town lives in poverty. No one else can afford to travel freely. She has family there. Sisters, brothers, nieces and nephews, and all of the relatives of her late husband. They can't afford to move. If Daniela and the girls were to disappear, come here and not return, the extended family would pay the price. And the price would be steep. Arms, legs, even their lives would be taken in payment."

"Carlos was able to move. How did that happen?"

"He moved before the cartel moved into town. He was already out of reach."

"Is there anything we can do?"

"Only if you have enough money to move the entire town at one time. Under cover of darkness."

"And you haven't talked to Carlos?"

"What would I say?"

Henrie, who had remained silent throughout the exchange, spoke up. "You would say, 'Carlos, we need to talk.' And then, tell him everything. Allow him to be a part of the solution."

"He'll go down there and start trouble."

"This has been going on for years? No one is in imminent danger. Start with that."

Isabel sighed, pushed her plate away and stood. She looked at both Henrie and Annie. "You have no idea how often I've thought that very thing. It has to be done. We have to talk. Right now, I need to think. Thank you for breakfast, and thank you for being my friends."

Isabel left the room, headed down the hallway to her own room. She stopped and turned, "By the way, have you seen Tillie this morning? She left as soon as I fed her."

"She's small enough to use the cat doors. She's probably at Mr. Bean's, dancing for customers."

Isabel smiled sadly and shook her head. "I wish we were all that free to move around."

Annie left the Inn and walked up The Avenue. It was a beautiful early summer day. Having heard Isabel's news, she didn't enjoy the sun on her face and the breeze in her hair nearly as much as she should. Even the smell of the lake and the flowers on The Avenue failed to lift her heart.

She read articles and watched television news about life in Mexico. She knew the story about the bakery, how it had been taken over by what Carlos called a "gang." Well, maybe it had been a gang at that time. Isabel said Carlos got out before the cartel came in. But certainly, Carlos kept up with the news. Was he aware how deeply the cartel had its hooks into his family?

Annie was an unassuming woman. Today, she was clothed in a typical outfit, a colorful, flowing top, capris and sandals. Her hair grayed uniformly, but it was hard to tell her age. High cheekbones gave just a hint of Indian heritage. She only recently learned a bit of the history behind those cheekbones.

Annie took this walk up The Avenue most mornings, going first to one business, then the next. This morning, she considered skipping Mr. Bean's, but that wouldn't do. She would have to make sure the conversation didn't go near the danger zone.

Her first stop was Sassy P's Wine & Cheese. Jesus, the manager, had his back to the door, filling bins with wine. He was in the dry red section. Her favorite place.

Jesus grew up in wine country in California; generations of his family were vintners. Jesus loved the industry but was not interested in making wines. He preferred to choose wines rather than make them. Living in this resort area, in the middle of a region bursting with wineries, both new and established, Jesus was in his element.

His partner in life was also his partner at Sassy P's. Minnie grew up in Wisconsin cheese country, and she further educated her palette in Europe. Her inventory of cheeses continually changed to match the selection of wines that came and went.

Annie sat at the tasting bar close to Jesus. Sassy Pants, jumping from high bar stool to the bar, dropped to her back and offered her stomach for rubbing. Annie complied.

Jesus turned slightly. "Good morning. I have something I want you to try."

"Wine?"

"Yes."

"It's pretty early."

"You'll want to try this."

Jesus walked to the refrigerator holding white wines for tasting.

"I have an excellent summer white. It's a crisp Sauvignon Blanc. It tastes like pink grapefruit, honeysuckle, and lime."

"Perfect. Now I don't care what time it is."

"I'm just giving you a taste! This is the wine we'll have on special for the rest of the month."

Annie tasted the wine offered. "Wonderful. This would be great with sushi."

"Exactly. Felicity has placed orders for us along that line for our small plate specials. We're going to stick with sushi, spicy Asian cuisine and fresh seafood through the end of June."

Minnie came out of the kitchen area. "I'm having a little trouble choosing just the right cheese."

Jesus laughed. "Oh, yes. I forgot to tell you that our compromise on the cheese front was to have sake as a special also, because, as Minnie informs me, sake and cheese pairings can be explained as…what was that again?"

"Umami, the Fifth Flavor."

"There are five flavors?"

"In the east, there are five basic flavors: dryness, sweetness, acidity, bitterness and astringency. In the west, we have only four: salty, sour, sweet and bitter. What we're going for is a fifth western flavor, something more savory."

"And I thought your training was in Wisconsin and Europe. Where did you learn this?"

Minnie smiled. "This isn't new. Actually, this theory was first discussed in 1908. Still, pairing cheese and sake can be tricky. Do you want to try?"

Now Annie laughed. "I'm not drinking sake at this hour of the day, but why don't I pick some up this afternoon? Henrie and I are spending the evening together. We're going to watch the sunset and moonrise."

"I'll put three small bottles of sake and the cheeses I would pair with each in a double cooler. One side will keep the sake warm; the other will keep the cheese cool."

The three friends chatted a bit more, Annie's hand on Sassy Pants' stomach the entire time. And then, it was time to go. Next stop, Mr. Bean's Confectionary. Annie gave an inward groan. She was a rotten liar, and her face never cooperated when she had something to hide.

Fortunately, Carlos was out of the building. Jerry, the candy maker, worked the front counter. People traveled for miles to purchase boxes of truffles, and he now had standing orders from restaurants and specialty grocery stores throughout the region.

Jerry learned his trade in a federal prison. He wasn't an employee. A private person, he did not talk about the reason for his incarceration, but not too long ago, a police officer with a mean streak – this particular police officer, Marco, was making an attempt to reform – spread the rumor that Jerry was incarcerated for murder.

Jerry's offense had been to help his mother, in tremendous pain with terminal cancer, commit suicide. In his home state, this act resulted in a murder charge. He was kicked into federal court and received a light sentence at a minimum security facility. He chose Chelsea as his do-over hometown.

Jerry reached behind the door leading to the kitchen and brought out a plate of colorful truffles. They were in all of Annie's rainbow colors: blue, red, green, yellow, orange and purple.

"These are the featured truffles until the end of the month."

"They're beautiful! What's inside? What are they called?"

"Since the end of June is our Pirate's Cove party, these are Tiger Lily truffles. Peter Pan's Tiger Lily. I don't want your girl to assume we named the truffles after her, so you'll have to explain it."

"I will!"

"The party will be big on kids and kids' games, and this is something they'll like. They're s'mores truffles, with dark chocolate, graham cracker pieces and marshmallow. Not necessarily something you would like, but, you know, I can't always go around pleasing you."

"You could try."

"I could, but…"

Inwardly, Annie cheered. A few months ago, Jerry would not dare tease her in this fashion. In a way, Marco's bullying brought him out of his shell. He was more comfortable in Chelsea and more comfortable on a personal level than ever before.

Out loud, she said, "Well, just this once, it will be alright."

Annie asked to have a box ready when she walked home that afternoon, purchased a cat treat and a dog treat, and gave them to the two little munchkins that had been at her ankles since she walked in the door.

Annie left to continue her walk, thanking all the puffy clouds in the sky that she had missed seeing Carlos.

At Mo's Tap, she found George cleaning the bar, getting ready to start his day. George was a Chelsea native. A handsome, happy-go-lucky kind of guy, she realized he was as surprised as everyone when he impulsively married Candice a couple of months ago.

The floor manager, formerly an off-again, on-again girlfriend, now his wife, didn't seem as surprised as she seemed, well, amazed.

Their relationship, always professional at work regardless of their status, continued to be professional. Annie could tell they worked through a few bumps along the way, but she had no doubt they would work it all out in time. George had a large apartment above the Tap; Candice had given up her apartment in town and now lived there as well.

Mo apparently felt helpful this morning. As George cleaned each section of bar, including the glasses and bottles in the vicinity, Mo inspected his work. He sniffed the bar, pawed glasses, curled his beautiful fluffy tail around stems, and left a trail of long gray hairs in his wake.

On occasion, George stopped to stare at Mo, who graciously stopped to stare back.

Annie, after watching the dance for a minute, said, "You know, I used to make Mo go somewhere else until you opened up. You could actually get ready without his help then."

Mo looked at Annie with an unreadable expression.

Annie continued, "Do you want me to do that again?"

George laughed, drawing Mo's stare back to him. "No. I kinda like having him around. A few cat hairs here and there add to the ambiance."

Candice came out of the kitchen. "Oh, hi, Annie. Sorry, I have to interrupt. George, Cookie said he's going to have to take off both Thursday and Friday; he's having some issues with the menu of the new place, so he has to make a couple of buying trips around the region."

Annie asked, "Why would he have to do that?"

"He insists on getting local meat and produce if possible, and for some reason the Marsh Haven farmer's market is closed this week."

Annie said, "Oh, yes. Some construction work is going on, and they don't have access to water or electricity this week. I forgot about that."

George asked, "Is Georgia scheduled to work?"

"Cookie said she agreed to work both days, and he's sure she can handle it."

"Okay." George walked over to the service window, put his head inside and said, "It's alright, Cookie. Annie's here right now, so she knows about it, too."

Annie could hear Cookie's muffled voice, then he popped out of the kitchen door.

"Hey. I was gonna call, but I needed to make sure I could get the time off first. Everything's under control."

Cookie, well, he had another name but no one knew what it was, had cooked for Mo's Tap for a long time. While he still did, Annie gave him a shot at his dream, a fine dining restaurant. The Bon Vivant Grille was open Friday and Saturday evenings – at least until the end of this summer – using Tiger Lily's Café. They would evaluate the success of the venture in August and make plans from there.

For now, a new young cook in town, Georgia, helped out at Mo's Tap and was Cookie's right hand person at the Grille. Isabel, shortly after arriving from Mexico, joined

Cookie's staff as the hostess and floor manager. This gave her a part-time job, and she seemed to shine in the role.

"Do you need help picking up produce?"

"Thanks, but you know, this is kind of a blessing in disguise. I can go to the farmer's market and think I'm getting the best produce around, but I like to take a look at the actual farm or garden. I want to see if things are clean, well maintained, and if they actually come from a plot of land here in the region. Now I have an excuse to travel to their bases of operation."

"Good thinking. Well, still, if you need anything…"

"I'll let you know."

"Are you ready to share your menu for the weekend?"

"I want to be sure I can get the meat and produce first, then I'll let you know."

Annie walked around the dining area for a while, not because she wanted to see anything in particular, but because she wanted to drape Mo around the back of her neck, pull his tail and scratch his cheek. He liked it best when she walked around at the same time.

She finally settled him onto a bar stool and left, headed for the next to the last place, Lil' Socks' Virasana, the place in which she should really spend more time. And not just talking.

Diana was behind the counter. One of her part-time instructors, Ginger, led a class. Little Socks was curled into a black pillow on the windowsill, all white parts carefully tucked out of view. She believed herself to be invisible.

Annie sat close to Little Socks, which was also close enough to the counter to carry on a conversation. She leaned back in order to have a hand on the back of the sleek little cat as she talked. "Have you found instructors to cover your vacation time?"

"Yes. Everyone is confirmed. I'll leave right after the block party and be back by the sixth."

Diana had not taken a vacation since coming "home" to Chelsea a few years earlier. She lived with her mother, Mem, across the street in an apartment over her mother's shop. She now had a long-distance relationship with, let's face it, a rich man she met while he vacationed in Chelsea.

It was time for Diana to take some time for herself.

Annie had her fingers crossed she would come back.

"That's not a very long vacation." Annie looked at the calendar on the wall. "It's less than a week."

"I don't want to be gone longer than that. And no, Annie, it doesn't really have to do with work. I know the studio will be fine. Ginger is actually going to step up and manage it. I would rather have a reason to leave after a few days than to stay too long and have to leave early."

"Believe it or not, I understand your thinking."

"When are you going to take a vacation, Annie?"

"A vacation? My whole life is a vacation. I love it here. I have no reason to go anywhere."

"How about to go with Chris to visit his family?"

Annie stared at Diana. She didn't really know what to say. It was as if Diana had listened in to yesterday evening's conversation. Chris, her special friend, had gone beyond asking her to do so and was beginning to have a demanding tone in his voice about it.

"I'm sorry. I didn't mean to intrude."

"Oh, no, I'm sorry. I just was struck by, well, by something. Actually, Diana, I am kind of thinking about it. Maybe."

Diana laughed. "Believe it or not, I understand your thinking."

Annie's last stop of the day, at least of the first half of her day, was Tiger Lily's Café. She would spend the rest of her morning here, staying through the lunch rush. If needed, she would help behind the coffee bar or on the floor, serving or bussing tables. If not needed, she would visit Tiger Lily or have lunch with whatever friends came in.

Today was a light day. She had lunch with her friends Clara and Mem. Tiger Lily stayed with them at the table for most of the meal, hopping down whenever someone new – generally a tourist – came in. She had a job to do. She had to greet new guests and suggest appropriate meals. How else would they know what to order?

Tiger Lily left their table to greet a group of tourists. From a ledge – build especially for her and on every side of every table in the Café – she placed a paw on the menu to recommend a strawberry and spinach salad with poppy and sesame seeds and a Worcestershire vinaigrette, a grilled chicken Caesar wrap, and baked lemon butter tilapia. She was pleased to have one hundred percent participation in her suggestions. This table had taken three hops in order to reach the menu in front of each guest.

As she settled into the sunbeam at Annie's table, one of her best human friends walked in. She sat up to watch until he was seated. She jumped down, trotted to his table and leapt softly to one of her ledges.

Ian turned to use both hands on Tiger Lily. This is why she liked him so much. He stroked both of her cheeks at the same time with his thumbs. After a sufficient period of time of cheek-stroking, he moved one hand to stroke her from the tip of her head to the tip of her tail, and cupped her chin with the other hand. Tiger Lily was in cat heaven.

While Annie watched, Felicity came from the kitchen and sat with Ian. She had paper and a pen and made notes as they talked.

Annie brought her attention back to Clara and Mem as the women rose to leave.

"Breakfast tomorrow," said Mem, dropping a tip on the table. "Laila said she could join us this time."

Ray reached to pick up the radio. Cheryl called from The Marina. "Where are you?"

"About a half mile out."

"Turn around, and keep an eye out for Brad. He just used our dock for a pick-up again today. I swear, Ray, I'm gonna call the police next time…"

"I'll give him a call."

"Don't bother. He's either not answering, or his radio doesn't work again."

Ray swore under his breath, gave The Escape a slow swing back toward land, and called down to his passengers, "Have to do something. Don't worry; you'll still get in a full day's fishing."

Ray kept his eyes on the boats headed in his direction from Chelsea. There it was. One of the worst excuses for a rental boat – well, any kind of a boat – headed his way. As he watched, the boat turned. Ray wasn't surprised. The Escape was visible for miles around, painted in vivid rainbow colors from end to end, top to bottom. Ray powered up and quickly overtook the boat. Thing. Contraption.

He glanced at his charter guests. They watched, wide-eyed, as he made the approach. Pulling alongside, he yelled, "Brad! Brad! Pull over!"

Brad, the man at the wheel, pretended not to see or hear. Ray tried the radio. Nothing. Cheryl was right. It was either turned off, not working, or being ignored.

Brad's Buoys & Gills kept chugging out, and Ray finally let him go. Brad's passengers looked with what Ray could only assume was longing at The Escape, now pulling away and heading once again to deep water.

2

Annie bussed a few tables as the lunch crowd thinned out. She motioned to Felicity and found a table in the corner.

Felicity and Trudie brought lunch for themselves and sat with her. Tiger Lily joined them and curled into a ball in front of Annie, who didn't have a plate, after all, and the sun was shining right there. It was the perfect spot. Until the sun moved on, that is.

Felicity, the manager and chef of the Café and their catering venue upstairs, was young and perky. Sometimes, she was just too perky, but then again, she remained lighthearted through all of the angst that comes with running an eatery in a tourist town. Servers and cooks coming and going. Health department reviews. Grill fires. Turtles. Whatever.

Trudie was from Jamaica. She ended up in Chelsea by accident when an abusive boyfriend dumped her at the state park's campground. She wandered into the Café and was "adopted" by Felicity, now her best friend. They shared side-by-side apartments over the yoga studio and worked more as a team than as manager and employee. Trudie was a manager in her own right, with the coffee bar as her domain.

"This was a slow Monday," observed Annie.

"Not really. As soon as we rest our tired little dogs, we have several catering jobs to fill. It only looked light from the dining room."

"I could have been doing something for you, then."

Felicity looked at Annie. "Annie, you know we love you, but frankly, I would actually have to be on my death bed to ask you to help in the kitchen."

"Really?"

"Really. Don't act so surprised. Sometimes I think you pretend to be a rotten cook so you can get out of helping any of us in our kitchens."

"Well, at least you smiled as you said that."

"What's up with Mem and Clara? The three of you looked pretty serious over here."

"Oh, nothing, really. Clara has this new relationship…"

Trudie cut in, "He is the hottest thing to hit The Avenue in years. I mean, really, he's hot!"

Felicity chided her, "Hands off. But hey, you need to ask him about that drummer in his band. Did you meet him when they played here?"

"No, I didn't. I wanted to introduce myself, but I was busy. And, well, you know, men and I usually get along better when I keep my hands off."

Annie laughed. She stroked Tiger Lily for a few seconds, then asked, "Do you have any cruise catering this week?"

"Kind of. Ray got some meals for today, but the rest of the week is iffy, because of the storms headed this way."

"How do you prepare for that?"

"Ray ordered frozen meals for a couple of day cruises, so if he doesn't take off, he doesn't have to get them. And that moonlight wedding, well, we're just going to have to see about that."

"You must be catering for Ian again this year."

"Yep. This Saturday is the Chelsea Grand Prix. We'll have snacks and drinks for his volunteers at each of the SAG stops, and we'll make sure to have enough for bikers that need to rest."

"Is he going to work the SAG stops or ride this year?"

"He's going to ride the metric century again this year. He's been training a group of teenagers, and he'll ride with them to make sure they learn how to ride for something like this and stay safe."

Felicity laughed and continued. "The kids love him, but when he's coaching them, well…they have a different opinion altogether!"

Tiger Lily was bored with the conversation; she showed it with a thump of her tail. The thump reminded Annie she had somewhere else to be.

"Oh! It's almost time for my shift at the lighthouse!"

There were two lighthouses in Chelsea. One was a historic site on the breakwater. Visible from anywhere on The Avenue, this was a focal point of the vaunted sunset views. Many locals and tourists made the mile walk – roundtrip from the beach to the lighthouse and back again – at all times of the day, and nearly every time, no matter what time of year, fishermen worked from both sides of the breakwater.

Another lighthouse was nestled into the State park. Still town property, this lighthouse boasted a museum in the house portion of the structure, and visitors were allowed to go to the top of the lighthouse as well.

Annie volunteered in the museum for the local historical society. Recently, wifi had been added, so Annie often took a laptop with her. She stopped by the Inn on her way to pick one up.

Since she was running late, she dashed up the stairs to her apartment without stopping to introduce herself to their most recent guests. She would make up for her faux pas this evening. And besides, Henrie had everything under control.

When Annie arrived, five minutes late, she was shocked to find Geraldine behind the desk. Geraldine was a perfectly coiffed, perfectly dressed, perfectly made-up, perfectly obnoxious woman. She had tried so many times to make Annie's life miserable that the last time she tried, Annie slapped Geraldine and her friends with a lawsuit. This was currently pending and, in the meantime, a restraining order kept Geraldine and her friends 500 yards away from any of Annie's businesses, which effectively kept them all away from The Avenue.

Annie didn't miss seeing her at the Café. In fact, she enjoyed going into the Café even more, knowing Geraldine would not be there.

"Geraldine. I didn't know you volunteered here."

"Why, yes. I heard this was a lovely volunteer opportunity, and here I am."

Annie didn't know what to do. The restraining order was specific to Annie's businesses. She couldn't force Geraldine to leave the premises.

"Well, I'm here now. I'm sorry to be a little late. I'm sure you have other things to do."

"As a matter of fact, I do not. I called my husband and told him my replacement was late and I would have to take another shift. I'm afraid he won't be back to pick me up for a couple of hours."

Annie mentally kicked herself. She was only five minutes late, which was not good, especially for volunteers who counted on being able to leave on time. But she was sure Geraldine knew Annie was her replacement, and she played right into Geraldine's hands. Annie thought quickly.

"Well, if you prefer, I can leave so you can have this shift to yourself."

"Oh, no. I'm sure there is much you can teach me."

Annie groaned. Just as she lamented her fate, crafted in part by her own hand, a busload of tourists trooped in from the parking lot.

Geraldine blanched.

Annie, seeing the change of attitude, said quickly, "Just watch and listen to me. There's a script in that drawer there. Read it while I give the introduction to the lighthouse and museum. Eventually, you'll know it by heart like I do."

Annie got through the introduction easily then invited the group to climb to the top of the tower, tour the museum or visit the gift shop.

When they had moved on to see other parts, Annie put on her training hat. She turned to Geraldine.

"This is the introduction we give to most tourist groups. On occasion, teachers will bring students to the museum. They usually give us a heads up so we can gear our presentation to the need. For example, at the beginning of the next school year, I'm going to give a lecture on Lake Scott. Often, Pete and I give a synopsis of our family histories in the area. It makes for a unique point and counterpoint lecture."

"Why would that even be interesting?"

Annie stopped herself before her eyes rolled. She continued as if talking to a ten-year-old. "The differences of our beginnings here in Chelsea make it interesting. My ancestor was a lumber baron; Pete's family arrived via the Underground Railroad."

Geraldine made a face that probably meant, "Whatever." Out loud, she said, "I was not aware we actually had to do something."

"Volunteers usually do things."

"Talk, I mean. Running a dust cloth over some books is one thing. Actually talking to people, well, that just wasn't something I counted on."

"They didn't tell you before they scheduled you here?"

"No, they did not." Geraldine didn't bother to say that they had spoken to her about all manner of boring items and she had not bothered to listen.

Annie groaned. Audibly this time.

"I'm going to go to the other room. If you are determined to stay, you can handle the tourists while I do some research."

Annie let Geraldine assume she was doing research for the museum. Instead, she logged onto Facebook and settled in to catch up.

Henrie greeted the Inn's newest guests, Kali and Ko beside him like bookends. He walked to the head of the porch steps to greet them as the girls walked beside him, tails held high in the air. When Henrie stopped walking, they sat in regal poses befitting their status as hostesses of the best B&B in Chelsea.

They looked at two women, younger middle aged, dressed in fashionable clothing and with hairdos, finger and toenails that looked freshly done. They smiled. They giggled. They turned around several times, taking in the ambiance of The Avenue.

Henrie waited until they stopped spinning to say, "Welcome to the KaliKo Inn. Please, leave your bags here. I shall retrieve them directly and take them to your room. I am Henrie, your host. These lovely cats are your hostesses, Kali and Ko."

"They are so pretty!" "Ooh!"

As Henrie turned to allow the guests access to the house, Kali and Ko moved to the side. They typically let the guests get into the door before they started sniffing the luggage.

Today, though, something inviting emanated from one of the bags and Ko couldn't help herself. She darted in between the legs of the guests and made a beeline to a small cloth bag. She sniffed and pawed in earnest.

One of the guests stopped to watch, and she asked Henrie, "Will our bags be okay there?"

Henrie looked at Ko, clapped his hands twice to gain her attention, and pointed to the foyer. Ko, usually noncompliant, like a cat, gave Henrie a look that said leave me alone. But she left the bag and went into the house, growling a little, just enough that he could hear.

Inside, one of the new guests made introductions. In a pretty, tingling voice, she said, "I'm Valerie, and this is

Evie. I doubt you'll see much of us. We might come in to grab snacks, and of course we'll have breakfast, but we're looking for sun and sand."

Valerie was the owner of the interesting cloth bag. Ko wrapped herself around Valerie's legs as she completed the paperwork. She signed in using her name and address, listing Evie, first name only, as a guest. Evie walked around the downstairs rooms, sticking her head in and making appropriate cooing noises.

While the paperwork was in process, Kali used the cat door to take a closer look at the bag and have a sniff or two herself.

Henrie invited his guests to refresh themselves in the downstairs restrooms and to make themselves comfortable in the chairs and sofas of the foyer. Being Henrie, he did not consider any welcome proper if he did not offer a beverage. He offered, made and served iced tea in tall, clear glasses. A silver tray bearing the glasses also held two silver teaspoons, sugar, fake sugar and lemon.

When Valerie and Evie were seated and comfortable, Henrie placed himself in front of them and described the accommodations.

Evie looked around as he talked. She caught the important points. She knew they would be in the carriage house, but she understood the common areas in the main house were available to them as well. She couldn't wipe the smile off her face. She was really here! What a beautiful town, and a perfect Inn.

From the foyer, she could see into both the library and the dining room. Furniture was both elegant and comfortable, upholstered in shades of slate blue and gray.

Tables, bookshelves and other wooden furniture were of light-hued walnut. The walls of each room were a different color, but all were a light pastel. The entryway was blue; the library lavender and the dining room rose.

The house was bathed in light from the windows, which had minimal coverings. The entryway had a large welcoming bouquet of fresh blue blooms, and a smaller but similar bouquet in the dining room could be seen from the foyer. From his position, Henrie turned slightly and pointed out the coffee and snacks corner and the reading areas in the library, the foyer, and the second floor landing, quickly mentioning the televisions and computers in each area.

"Of course," he continued, "you will be in the carriage house, which has many of the same amenities. But these are available to you as well."

"Tell me again why we're in the carriage house?"

"Every other room of the Inn has been reserved for the week. Placing you in the carriage house may not be optimal, as you will have to walk here for breakfast. I trust, however, that you will find the room to your liking."

Valerie turned to Evie. "When he explained the room to me on the phone, it sounded like we could invite almost everyone we know, and it's private." Henrie thought he caught a wink in Evie's direction as Valerie turned to face him again.

Henrie pointed to the back hallway. "Down this hallway is an all-season porch. From your room, there is a walkway through a garden to the beach, I will show that to you directly, and there is a door beach-side to the all-season porch."

It was at this point of the conversation that Annie dashed in, gave a quick wave and a smile to the women as she went upstairs at a fast clip. They watched as she hit the second floor landing then rounded a corner and, they could tell from the sound, went up another flight of stairs.

Henrie continued, nonplussed. "The carriage house is not an optimal place from which to view the sunset. You are welcome to come through any entrance to get to the porch. If you prefer the beach, you will note all manner of tables and chairs and a cabana at your disposal. This is a private beach, which means that you and individuals you may invite have access to it, but the general public does not."

Valerie cut in. "We can go to the public beach, though, right? If we want to meet people while we're here?"

"Certainly. The public beach is an easy walk from the front of the house. Access to the beach is at no charge. If you prefer, you can start at the private beach, which is separated from the public beach by a partial fence. You need only walk around it."

Henrie waited while Annie made her dash in reverse, once again smiling and waving at the guests.

"Every afternoon a snack will be available here in this Keurig area. Depending on the selection, it will be on the counter or in the refrigerator. May I entertain questions before taking you to your room?"

Valerie and Evie had nothing to ask. Henrie retrieved a luggage cart and led the way to the porch. The women assisted as he loaded luggage. Evie did a little dance as she walked down the steps.

Valerie asked, "Is it possible to take the cart to our car? We went on a shopping spree on our way here, and we have lots of shopping bags."

Henrie complied. When the bags were loaded, he rolled the cart to the carriage house and the stairway that went to the second floor.

"Please go up. I will bring the bags in a few trips. This is the only room that is not accessible by elevator or ramp."

The women refused his offer and each grabbed two pieces of luggage and a few shopping bags before going upstairs.

Evie looked around the room. This was – by far – the best room yet! She vacationed with Valerie every year, trying to have a good time on a budget. These few days a year were the only happy days of her life, and she was able to take them only as long as her mother could babysit the kids. And only if she took less than one hundred dollars per trip.

Valerie paid for everything.

This room was large. Sleeping and living areas were delineated by furniture groupings. Windows brought daylight in from every direction but the back. That wall was painted in bright colors. Evie didn't realize that one change to the carriage house – the removal of windows from that wall – maintained privacy for the honeymoon suite below.

There were three queen-sized beds with room for additional cots, an eclectic mix of seating for ten people, a gaming table, and an outside balcony that faced the front lawn. A large television and wifi access were also available.

Dressers and a large locking armoire allowed for several guests at one time. The room featured a kitchenette with a coffee and tea corner and a medium-sized full bathroom.

Evie looked at Henrie with a smile. "This will do nicely."

3

Nine cats and one little dog sat under the covered table in the dining room. Henrie put afternoon snacks here at the same time he put snacks out for guests. Today, Tiger Lily invited their friends from across the street, Simon Finnegan and Oscar McMurphy.

The two cats were dumped at the campground at the end of last year's bitter winter. Through the best of luck, they found their way to The Avenue and relative safety. They lived on the street, finding shelter where they could. Eventually, they found a fur-ever home on the other side of The Avenue.

Like Tillie, they took advantage of cat doors all over The Avenue.

Unlike Tillie, they were known to the cats by other names. When they were dumped, they had never been given names other than, "Here, kitty, kitty." Tiger Lily and her siblings named them Fat Cat (Simon Finnegan) and Scaredy Cat (Oscar McMurphy). Their current names were courtesy of their new fur-ever humans.

Despite her name, Oscar McMurphy was a girl. Well, a fixed girl. Frankly, all the cats and dogs on The Avenue were little "its," but they identified as male or female.

This evening, Tiger Lily asked if anyone had anything to report, suspicious activity around The Avenue, new people or evil deeds. No one had anything.

"*Oh, wait.*" Ko looked at Kali. "*We need to tell them about that bag.*"

"*Oh, yeah. Ko found a bag with a weird smell. I smelled it, too. I don't know what it is.*"

"It didn't remind you of anything?"

Kali and Ko looked at one another, then at Tiger Lily.

Kali said, *"It had lots of smells. There was some oily smell, and something metal, and something that smelled like icky chemicals."*

"All of that together?"

"Yeah, but separate, too."

"What are their names?"

Kali and Ko spoke together, one at a time, remembering the names. *"That one with the bag is Valerie." "And Evie."*

"They must be in the carriage house. Are they upstairs or down?"

"Upstairs. Henrie has a couple coming in for the downstairs one."

"They're going to spend all day, every day at the beach."

"At the beach? It's barely summer."

"But it's hot outside."

"Not every day."

"At least they'll track their sand into the carriage house, not here."

Oscar McMurphy said, *"This is boring. Is this all you do at your detective agency?"*

"No!" "We have real cases!" "We do exciting stuff!" "We duz brave tings!" "Trill!"

Tiger Lily asked, *"Do you want to hear some stories?"*

"Yeah!"

They gave up their afternoon naps to relive past glories. It was interesting how their friends, the dogs Cyril and Jock, didn't show up in the stories they told.

Cyril, an English setter, lived with his human, Pete, the Chief of Police. Jock, a Portuguese water dog, helped on the cruising yacht, The Escape, with his human, Ray. They were invaluable in solving every mystery in which the cats were involved. Today, the tales got longer and taller and only the cats got credit for inventive, heroic or deductive actions.

Mr. Bean said, *"Let me tell the first one!"*

He told the mystery of the turtle in the soup at the Café and other problems the Café had. *"There was a bug, and honey on everything, and then that turtle…then your mommy Holly was nearly killed!"* Through the investigative skills of the cats, Mommy's not-friend Geraldine and her partner in crime, Hank, were found to be at fault. They were trying to ruin the business at the Café, so Geraldine's copycat restaurant would succeed.

Kali and Ko said together, *"Let me tell the next one!"* *"I want to tell the next one!"* Speaking on top of one another at times and around one another at others, they told another tale.

Four people stayed at the Inn for a few days before a scheduled several-day cruise on The Escape. Before the Escape took off, they murdered a server from the Café. She, the server, knew them from before and probably threatened to tell the police bad things about them. If not for Mo and Mr. Bean, her body would never have been found.

But that was only part of it. Right before they left on the cruise, before the body was located, Little Socks was able to cat-burgle one of the guest rooms. She found a clue that told Mommy Ray was in trouble, but Mommy, even though she is very nice, was too stupid to get it until after The Escape was long gone. *"And then, when Mommy finally got it, she called everybody, and we had to help the police and the Coast Guard and all the humans." "But it wasn't quick enough. Ray got thrown off the boat!"*

If not for the cats, Ray would still be floating around in the middle of that big body of water. And Jock, too.

Sassy Pants said, *"My terns! I tells da next one!"*

Little Socks covered her head with her hands. She couldn't stand to listen to the young cat mangle the English language.

Sassy Pants chose the story about the murder mystery cruise. Ray and Henrie wrote a murder mystery to be performed by guests of the KaliKo Inn. The first act was done at Sassy P's with a local audience. The second was at a restaurant in another town after a day cruise on The Escape, and the third was in the middle of the lake on The Escape itself. *"An dey had funny names an everyting, an it was real confusing, an some of dem didn't like cats!"* Before they left for the last act, one of the cast members killed another one and left the body in the basement of the Inn.

If not for the heroism of the cats, they would never have been arrested.

Mo said, *"TRILL!"*

Tiger Lily groaned. Mo and his litter mates, Kali and Ko, used to speak in a secret language. Kali and Ko now

53

spoke cat; Mo still spoke the secret language. Tiger Lily had never learned to understand him. With the help of his translators, Kali, Ko and Sassy Pants – who for some unknown reason could read minds – Mo told the story of people staying at the Inn at the same time as the murder mystery cruisers.

During a storm, they took hostages in the basement of the Inn. Had it not been for the heroism of the cats, the police would have found nothing but dead bodies. Instead, they found knocked out and trussed up bad people. *"And the cats caught all of them!"*

Little Socks said, *"If everyone else is telling a story, then let me tell one, too."*

She told the relative newcomers to The Avenue about the spearfishers and catfishers that stole lots of money from Mommy's businesses by doing something – *"I don't know what it was"* – on the Internet – *"I'm not sure what it is, but it's like magic"* – and if not for the cats, the phishers would never have been caught. And then, Mommy's friend from the FBI was hurt and left in an old house to freeze to death.

If not for the cats…well, you get the picture of the tale that was told.

Tiger Lily hoped the newcomers would never retell the stories to Cyril or Jock. Without the two dogs, the cats would not have succeeded. But, she decided, what the big boys didn't know wouldn't hurt them. As long as no one told….

She tried to wrap up story-telling time by saying, *"And then, the two of you and Tillie came to The Avenue, and you know all the rest of the detective stories."*

But the others didn't want to leave just yet. Fat Cat and Scaredy Cat relived their heroic actions that saved cat-napped Little Socks and Sassy Pants from certain death. They also neglected to relate the smart thinking and strenuous efforts of Cyril and Jock.

Tillie sat back and listened to everything, soaking up the history and reliving the part of the recent stories that belonged to her. Including the part where her former owners, those mean people from England, had master-minded the cat-napping. Best leave that be for now.

Mr. Bean said, *"Let me tell another one! Let me tell about the burglaries and that ring we hid until we could get it to Pete!"*

Sassy Pants agreed. *"I wants to tell bout da guy wots got killded wit da white rock!"*

Tiger Lily bopped the younger cats on the nose. *"They were there! They know those stories!"*

They heard Annie. "Kids, we're going to the beach. Come on!"

A herd of wild elephants ran from the dining room to the all-season porch and out to the white sand.

4

Valerie and Evie walked The Avenue. Sunset Avenue, known simply as The Avenue by locals, ran from the town building to the lake, one long city block. The KaliKo Inn, anchoring The Avenue at the lake, was on the south side.

The women, exploring the area that would be their universe for the next few days, left the Inn and walked toward the Café. They took their time and soaked in the atmosphere. The day was perfect. Blue sky, soft breeze, temperature in the low seventies.

The Avenue was wide, deep enough on either side for angle parking from one end of the street to the other. Today, The Avenue was filled with bicycles and their riders in town for the Chelsea Grand Prix.

Bikers were on the sidewalks, in parking places, on the median. The median, wide and attractively appointed with benches, game tables and a brick walkway, allowed walkers and bikers to mingle without effort.

As Valerie and Evie left the Inn, they turned back to look at it. Bright blue awnings with narrow stripes in a multitude of colors surrounded the lower level of the building, setting off a long, wide front porch. That porch had café table and chair sets as well as settings of wicker furniture, including gliders, rocking chairs and Adirondack chairs, cushioned in every color imaginable.

The carriage house, their home for the next few days, sat back from the house and matched the Inn in color and tone.

As they walked up the sidewalk toward Main Street, they noticed a rainbow of colors, red, green, yellow, orange and purple. The long, two-story building that started next to the Inn and ended at the Café was well-kept. The original brick façade was offset with colorful awnings and wrought iron café tables and chairs painted to match the awnings. Each table was in use, some by four or five people, others by one or two.

They passed and looked into the windows of the winery, bakery, blues bar, yoga studio and, finally, the Café. As they walked, they talked about when they would check each place more thoroughly.

They crossed The Avenue and walked toward the lake on the north side. They stopped in front of each place to look into the windows. This side of The Avenue had one long, two-story building that somewhat mirrored the building on the other side. The brick façade had not been as well maintained over the years and was now covered with paint.

The church, Soul's Harbor, was pale lilac. They looked in the window of the gift shop that supported charity. Then came a tea shop and cyber café, CyberHealth, painted pale peach.

Evie said, "She has kitchen gadgets. If I had money to spend, I'd spend it on gadgets like this."

The next storefront was a grocery store, Babar Foods. The exterior was painted butter yellow. A look inside the window brought an enticing view of fresh fruits and vegetables with the promise of an exciting deli in the back.

The next store, DoubleGood, was a combination hardware and electronics store. The store was painted mint green. As they looked inside the windows, Valerie said, "I need a new laptop. Before we leave, I'm going to stop in."

They did more than look in the windows of the flower and gift shop, Bloomin' Crazy. Before leaving, Valerie purchased a ring and bracelet for herself and a necklace and earring set for Evie, all from a fair trade vendor.

The last business had a double storefront. The Drug Store and The Clinic were painted light slate blue. Valerie gave a droll smile. "If we hurt someone, accidentally or on purpose, I guess we'll have to bring him here."

They chose to eat supper at Sassy P's Wine & Cheese. When they entered, they met Annie on her way out. Annie stood just outside the door, holding it open.

"Hi. I'm Annie. So sorry I ran in and out without introducing myself today. I was running late."

"That's okay. I'm Valerie, this is Evie. We're staying in the carriage house for a few days."

"Are you here for supper?"

"Yes. We want to try as many places as possible and thought we would start here and work our way up."

"I don't want to tell you want to do, but as you can see," Annie held up both hands, filled with bags and thermos containers, "I'm carrying supper out. Tonight is the summer solstice and the full strawberry moon. Henrie and I – and probably most of the people who live and work on The Avenue – will be on the private beach watching the show. It starts real soon; the solstice hits sometime after 6:30."

"Oh. That's a good idea. Evie, what do you think?"

"I think a bottle of wine and whatever they have to carry out sounds like a great idea! Thanks, Annie. We'll join you on the beach."

Annie left and the two women entered the winery. A pretty woman behind the bar said, "Did I hear Annie talk you into take-out?"

"Yes. Do you have suggestions?"

"I do. I have boxes of cheese, sausage and artisan crackers ready to go, or I can put some sushi in a small cooler. We can pair either with wine."

Valerie and Evie looked at one another, then back at Minnie. Together, they said, "Sushi!"

Evie added, "If we're going to the beach, can you open the bottles for us?"

"I can't do that, but I have an inexpensive set here, glasses and an opener, that would work. I can set up a tasting for you, and you can decide what you want to take."

While they sat at the bar, waiting for the wines to be set up, Evie looked around.

She could see a garden dining area in the back. They were in the main tasting room, a bright and modern room with wooden touches. Display counters, shelving and the bar had a light walnut finish, and the bar had what appeared to be delicate hand-carved trim.

The wall behind the tasting bar was painted cranberry red; the other walls were lavender. At the end of the bar were a few café tables; she and Valerie sat on highly polished wooden stools with seats resembling hollowed out wine barrels.

If the food and wine were half as good as the winery was pretty, it would be more than worth the trip.

Annie had rainbow-colored truffles, sake, a bottle of wine, and cheese. Henrie had two turkey bacon cheddar wraps from the Café. He put fresh vegetables and fruit into a chilling bowl. Cat food, dog food and dishes for water found their way into the picnic basket.

They were on the private beach with their picnic by 6:00. Tonight was the summer solstice, making this the longest day of the year. The full moon would begin to rise before the sun had set, allowing both the sun and the moon to be visible at the same time. The solstice would happen shortly after 6:40; the sunset would end around 9:45.

This moon, the Strawberry moon, could actually look like a strawberry if the weather would only cooperate.

It did. The sunset and moonrise were brilliant, glowing coral and orange. To the far north and the far south they were treated to a lightning show. A few hours of driving time in both directions would put them in the middle of the storms. Here, though, the lightening only punctuated an already brilliant, cloudless sky.

Almost all of their friends joined them on the beach. By acknowledgement, they were part of the "private" in private beach.

Valerie and Evie were excited to be here, on this day, at this time, with uninhibited views of the evening sky. Evie whispered to Valerie, "I'm going to do more of this from now on."

Annie and Henrie watched and organized tables and chairs as more people arrived. Everyone brought picnics of their own, or bottles of wine, or coolers with water and beer. The few children that lived on The Avenue invited school friends. They made a giant sand castle, only to kick it down as the sun and moon reached the peak of their color.

Cyril and Jock were here with their humans. They ran up and down the beach, chasing balls and sticks thrown by Pete and Ray. When they were given permission to do so, they helped destroy the sand castle, running through the turrets with wild abandon.

The cats and little Tillie were more sedate. They found interesting rocks, bugs and shells, and they dabbled their feet at the edge of the water. For the most part, though, they stayed close to Annie and the picnic basket.

Henrie pulled one of the long, low tables from the Inn out to the beach. Several people joined in the sake and cheese tasting, giving their opinions about their favorites.

One pairing was of a gamey sake with basil and olive oil asiago and crusty French bread. Another was a more complex and cloudy sake with blueberry infused cheddar cheese dipped in honey. The third pairing was a chilled, sparkling sake, creamy artisan Mt. Tam cheese and pear slices.

After tasting all three, Annie didn't care which she liked the best.

Annie wished that Chris, her special friend, could be here. He was on duty at the Coast Guard Station. For the moment, Annie enjoyed a relaxing evening with those whom she was lucky enough to call "friend."

The sun was down; the moon was up; their friends were gone; their guests were in the carriage house; even Tillie went to bed with Isabel. Henrie and Annie moved to the front porch, the better to see the moon. Annie's cats called dibs on their favorite pieces of furniture. With many ups and downs, a few hisses and bops on the nose, each one finally had a place.

Henrie and Annie positioned their chairs to better see the sky. They leaned their heads back, and, faces looking at the moon rather than at one another, they talked about the week to come. It would be a busy one.

Henrie asked, "Did you have the opportunity to meet our current guests?"

"Yes. Nice women. And yes, Henrie, I apologized for running through the house earlier without saying hello."

Henrie smiled. "Thank you. We must maintain some civility. I only hope our lake is not too cold for them this time of year."

"I think they'll be fine. We just entered summer according to the calendar, but the weather folks have been calling it summer for weeks. And that's really all they want to do? Go to the beach?"

"That is their stated intention."

"Who's coming in next?"

"The entire town is expecting arrivals, in fact, some contestants are already here, for the Chelsea Grand Prix."

"I thought there were a few more bicycles on The Avenue today. How many are we getting?"

"Four. Three men and one woman. I gather they are avid bicyclists. They plan to do the metric century. They arrive tomorrow."

"I hear that goes through some rough country. Ian is training some teenagers, and he'll ride with them to make sure they stay safe."

"That is wise. There are dangerous curves around the tip of the lake, and all of the routes are off the proverbial beaten path. I have heard this particular metric century is one many bikers want to get on their resume."

"Why is this group coming so early? The Grand Prix isn't until Saturday."

"They want an advance look at the route. I gather they will take part of the route one day and another part of the route the next. And they may walk part of it, because they cannot cycle all of it."

"Every year the bikers get here earlier." After a moment, Annie asked, "Who comes in next?"

"On Wednesday, a couple arrives for what the gentleman called a second honeymoon."

"Is that the couple in the honeymoon suite?"

"Not this couple. They will be in a room on the main guest floor. They hired Ray for two day trips, to fish. However, there may be a problem."

"Not The Escape? Is it in dry dock again?"

"No. Ray finally understands he is not the master of his universe. He telephoned to say he expects the weather will not be conducive."

"That's right. Felicity said something about that. What have you heard about the weather?"

"Hot, humid, thunderstorms, hail and high straight-line winds."

"How bad will it get?"

"Our local weathermen and women have been swooning over the likelihood of 'events' to occur this week. One used to be able to rely on future-casts. Now, it appears one station tries to outdo another in prophecies of doom. Here is my prediction: your guess is as good as mine."

"I guess I'm not going to worry." Annie gazed at the sky. Then she asked, "We still have another group coming? Who's going into the honeymoon suite?"

"They arrive Thursday. There is to be a wedding ceremony this weekend on The Escape. The happy couple will take the suite; their friends will have a room on the main floor."

"Felicity told me about the wedding. I didn't know they would be guests of the Inn."

The two fell silent. Finally, Annie sighed. "I could stay here all night, but I think I have to get up in the morning. The kids and I should go to bed."

Henrie sighed. "I suppose I should as well."

They remained on the porch for quite some time.

5

Henrie loved a full dining room; with Isabel and two additional guests, he was on his way. It would only get better as the week went on.

Today, Tuesday, Henrie served a simple egg casserole made with herbs and cheese, and rosemary roasted potatoes, bacon, sausage, ham, French toast, steel-cut oat groats with brown sugar and fresh berries, English muffins, wheat and rye toast, fresh strawberries and blueberries, and, of course, a variety of juices.

Isabel, Valerie and Evie arrived at the same time. Lively conversation ensued, especially when the two new guests learned Isabel was here to plan her wedding.

Valerie asked, "Who's the lucky guy?"

"The baker – and manager – of the Confectionary up the street, Mr. Bean's. His name is Carlos."

"Carlos. Is he handsome?"

"Very."

"Rich?"

"In spirit."

"Even better!"

Henrie moved in and out of the dining room, nearly invisible, as he refilled platters, took dirty dishes, replaced coffee carafes and cast stern looks at Kali and Ko.

Henrie listened with half an ear as Isabel told the women about the best places on the beach.

"Start out here at the private beach. When you want to be alone, just stay here. But for some company, walk along the shoreline from here to the city park's beach."

"What kind of company? Men?" The women looked at one another and giggled.

Isabel laughed as well. "If you want to hook up with men, it's not going to happen at the city park during the week."

"Oh, well, really, we just like to look."

"You'll be able to look, but mostly at teenagers, at least this time of week. And mothers with smaller children."

"What if we want to explore? Are there interesting places further on?"

"You can keep going past the city park and you'll pass the beaches of the state park. You might see more interesting folks there, people that are camping or exploring. You can walk to where the lake starts to curve around, and you'll come to a rocky area. I've been there. Just make sure you take some tennis shoes or some other kind of shoe if you want to climb. You don't want to do it with bare feet or flip flops."

"How far up is that?"

"Maybe a mile. If you are up to the walk, and if you take something to eat and drink with you, it can be enjoyable."

Kali and Ko rubbed against the legs of the women, looking up with expectant faces. They hoped for treats. Henrie finally shooed them away; they went to the library windowsills to sulk.

While Henrie took care of their guests, Annie met Clara, Laila and Mem for breakfast. It wasn't often they could all get together. This summer, Laila insisted that her oldest child, James, work in the grocery store in the morning. His afternoons could be spent being a teenager with other teens on the beach.

James wanted to participate in the Chelsea Grand Prix. Several of his friends were training with Ian. They spent their mornings riding, sometimes on bicycle trails in the region, sometimes on public roads, sometimes off-road on a farmer's property.

James understood why he had to work. His mother wanted him to learn responsibility, and she had worked far too long without respite. And saving for college, he couldn't afford a good bicycle. He swallowed his disappointment and vowed to be upbeat when his friends talked about their bicycle training.

Laila enjoyed the bit of freedom these mornings brought. She had begun to consider hiring someone to work with her part-time. She knew James would prefer to be training, like his friends, but this was the last summer she could encourage him to take responsibility. At least the last summer before he went to college.

Laila was Annie's best friend. She owned a grocery store on The Avenue, Babar Foods, and filled her deli section with Pakistani and Indian dishes. She was a single mother to James, Ava, who would start high school this fall, and Carl, a boy living with autism and still in grade school.

Mem and Clara had regular part-time help. The part-timers didn't work every day, but they worked often enough to allow the women to have a bit of freedom during the workday.

Clara, a dark-haired Haitian beauty, owned the local flower and gift shop, Bloomin' Crazy. Mem, whose daughter Diana managed the yoga studio, owned a combination cyber café, health food store and tea shop, CyberHealth.

On most of the mornings the four were able to get together, they solved all the problems of the world. Unfortunately, they didn't have a pipeline to the world's rulers, so their words of wisdom did not reach the appropriate ears.

Today, the topic of conversation was a little closer to home. It was about Clara. Again.

"I have to tell you, I love living with Ramon. When he's home. When he's not, not so much."

Ramon played saxophone in a jazz fusion band. His relationship with Clara was young, and it was Ramon himself who urged Clara to consider what a relationship would bring. He was gone at least half of the time, playing all around the country.

Mem was the woman every woman on The Avenue approached when they wanted sage advice. She was mature in every way. She asked, "Have you established some ground rules?"

"We have, and you know, Mem, it was hard for me to sit down and do that. I kinda shoot from the hip."

The women laughed. They knew well how Clara shot from the hip.

Mem continued. "Tell us some of them."

Clara opened her purse and pulled out an iPad. "I have them right here. I have to look at them every now and then to make sure I'm following the rules. The first one here is to avoid excessive communication."

Three women looked at her with blank faces. Annie asked, "You mean, you need to shut up every now and then and let him get a word in? That has to be hard. For you, I mean."

Clara made a face. "That's not quite it. It means that we don't get all clingy on one another and call or text or message all day long. We pick one time a day, unless there is something that just can't wait, and have a conversation."

"How do you know when to do that? He could call when you're making deliveries, or you could call when he's got a meeting with a venue."

"That's part of another rule here. Let me see…oh, yeah. Know each other's schedules."

"So that's part of the daily communication? Telling one another what you're doing the next day?"

"Oh, no, we don't waste our talking time on that. Every morning, I send him a text and let him know my plans for the day, and he does the same. We just don't, you know, have a conversation about it."

Laila summarized. "So, you communicate regularly, you know what one another is doing every day, and that's working, right?"

"Right. And let me tell you, I have to keep up with him. He's got some creative ways of communicating."

"Like what?"

"Well, we had a video chat the night before last, and he was ready for me. He was in bed, well, he was lounging in bed, and he had candles lit all around him, and a bottle of champagne and fresh fruit. I could feel it, smell it, taste it."

"Was he naked?"

Clara laughed. "Believe it or not, we have a rule about that, too. Either one of us could take a screen shot, and what if one of us got mad at the other, or our phones or computers were stolen? Absolutely nothing goes on during a video chat that we would be embarrassed about if someone else saw it. Which means he doesn't see any new negligees until we're looking at one another face-to-face."

"Do you know his friends?"

"I know the guys in the band, but I'm getting to know more about all of them and more about anyone he knows, because we follow each other on Facebook, Snapchat, Instagram, Tumblr, you name it."

"I didn't know you did all of that."

"I have to. He has a younger audience, so he needs to stay current. So, now, I have accounts out there also."

"I'm lucky to get onto Facebook once a day. And get off it. If I get on it, I get sucked in, and all of a sudden I've lost a good chunk of the day."

"I mostly do that at night. I get ready for bed – or whatever, it could be a video chat – and tuck myself in with my iPad. Sometimes it's early in the morning before I realize how much time I've spent."

Mem finally asked, "So what is it, Clara, that has you worried?"

"Worried? I'm not worried. It's just that I'm not as happy without him. When he's there, it's perfect. When he's not, I, well, I'm not as happy."

"You probably communicate with him more than I communicate with Frank."

Annie added, "And more than I do with Chris. What are you missing?"

"Sex."

Three dumbfounded faces looked at Clara. Then they burst out laughing.

After a pause, Laila asked, "Have you all been keeping up with the weather reports?"

"It's not going to be good."

"I know. I worry about the kids. James and most of his friends spend every afternoon on the beach. I talk to him all the time about the dangers of a rip current or getting into trouble in the water before you realize you're in trouble. He's a responsible kid, but I still worry."

"He'll be fine. He's a bright young man."

"A bright young man who, like everyone his age, can sometimes be driven to bad decisions by peer pressure."

"His friends are good folks, right? He and Ginger are good friends, and I've met lots of the kids they hang out with."

"I know. I just worry."

Mem said, "Come by the shop and I'll give you a couple of bags of Passionflower Tea. If it works for you, you can buy a box."

"What will it do? I give it to James and he stays safe?"

"You drink it and stop worrying so much about your almost-adult son. And, by the way, ladies, have you seen my flyers around town?"

The women laughed. "They're hanging up everywhere we go, including our own places of business."

"Then I can count on seeing you, right?"

"Right." The women had just committed to Mem's Saturday morning seminar on the healing aspects of tea.

Isabel's morning was not as pleasant. She went to the Confectionary and asked Carlos if he could join her. They went across The Avenue to Mem's teashop, where a young man served English breakfast tea and scones.

Isabel began the conversation by saying, "Carlos, I need you to listen to me carefully. Let me get through it before you say anything. Keep breathing while I talk. Above all else, know this. No one is in danger. No one." And then she told him what he should have been told years ago.

Ray pulled the skiff into the pieces of wood that served as a dock for Brad's Buoys & Gills. The poorly maintained boat was there. Sagging in all the wrong places. The paint – what was left – was a dingy gray. Mostly, the wood showed through, cracked, out of shape and moldy. He did manage to keep the name on, in thin, black creaky lettering.

Ray stepped out gingerly and tied his skiff to the piece of wood that appeared to be the most sturdily attached to…something. He walked up the yard – not grass, not weeds, not gravel, not asphalt, just a patchwork of all of the above – plus trash – and knocked on the door.

And knocked. And yelled, "Brad!" And knocked again.

Finally, a bleary-eyed man appeared. Brad spoke with a mixture of midwestern slang and southern drawl. "Eh? Awful derned early, Ray."

"You have to stop using The Marina to pick up your clients, Brad."

"Water's free. Cain't keep me frum bein' in the water."

"Water's free. Dock space isn't. And don't even think about it; I've told you before I won't rent space to you. Not for a month, a week, a day or even an hour."

"I's tole ya I'd git the money up front from my payin' customers. Give ya ten bucks ever time. Heck, I'll give ya twenty. Ten to pick up an ten to throw off."

"No. No. No. How many times do I have to tell you? Someone sues you and that deathtrap of yours, and they get any notion The Marina has something to do with it, I'll be sued right along with you. Maybe charged with a crime. I told you a hundred times. I'm going to the police department this morning to swear out a complaint."

Ray made a quick turn and didn't bother to reply to the string of vile words that followed him to the skiff.

Ian gathered his group of teens at a vineyard north of Chelsea. The fields provided several miles of hilly countryside, safe from traffic and hard on the legs. There were nine youth, each with a bicycle they had worked to earn the money to purchase. Ian and his employer, a local bank, purchased the tools and other items needed for bicyclists to compete: helmets, shoes, a set of wrenches and screwdrivers, chain tools and spoke wrenches. Ian would carry extra zip ties, duct tape and an air compressor.

He could be counted on to chair athletic and community events that involved the entire town, like the Chelsea Grand Prix. As marketing manager, the bank saw a value added opportunity whenever he could be involved, wearing a polo shirt with the bank logo, and offering opportunities for local financial support.

He had worked with this group of teens for a year. He started with ten, five boys and five girls. One of his prized students, James, had to bow out due to work and family commitments. Ian was sorry to lose him, but made every effort to include James in other activities.

This group of teens had worked out together since the late days of March. They were used to riding a metric century – sixty-three miles – but Ian would not tire them out with that trip every day this week. "Today, we're going around the vineyard three times. That will be a little over thirty miles. Are you up for it?"

"Yes!" "Bring it on!" "When do we do sixty?" "Let's go!"

Ian smiled, not answering the question, which had been asked and answered several times before. "Head out!"

As they went up and down the hills, following the country roads surrounding the vineyard, Ian sped or slowed, making sure to speak to every teen.

He sped to the front of the pack to Alena and Carol. "Hey, slow down. We aren't racing today."

"You never let us race!" This was from Alena, a strong young woman, both in body and in spirit, who was generally quick to argue when told to slow down.

"This year, you'll do it my way. Next year, you can make your own decisions."

"But, Ian…"

Carol cut in. "Let's just slow down. Look. We're way ahead of everyone, but we're still in front."

They slowed, and Ian coasted until the next two students met him. Brendan, Alena's older brother, and a lifeguard at the town park, and Renee, a fellow lifeguard.

"She didn't want to slow down, did she."

"No, not really. I forgot to ask earlier. What are your schedules like this week?"

Brendan said, "I work every afternoon except for Saturday."

"I only work two days. I don't remember which two. My heavy week is next week."

"With the weather reports, I'll probably have to schedule some time at the community building, and I can only get in during the afternoons this week. If you're working, you'll miss a session or two, but I'll give you a workout to do in the morning."

And so it went, checking in, moving on. What Ian didn't hear when he moved on were the complaints. He was aware of them, but with the natural noise of his bicycle, once he was away from them, he didn't hear the specific words. Words like, "He needs to get a life." "He's going to kill us, practicing every day." "We need to do the whole metric." And "When is he going to let us race?"

Collin pulled into the condominium complex in his cherry red Toyota Supra. When he emerged, his tailored suit impeccable, he brushed a piece of lint from the top of the car and looked backward at is as he walked to the unit. What a beauty.

Celeste opened the door before he knocked. "That's the new one? Pretty. We'll break it in this week, won't we, honey? Here, take my bags."

Collin looked at the pile of luxury luggage in the entryway. Two large rolling bags, a medium case, also on wheels, and two personal bags. Matching. "Think you have enough for a week?"

"Oh, honey, I'll have at least one more on the trip home. Our first stop better be to buy a matching piece for the clothes and jewelry we'll buy."

He looked back at the car. "Where do you suppose all of this will fit?"

"You'd better find room for it, or find yourself someone else to go on vacation with."

Collin sighed, took the two large bags, and wondered how....

Celeste clicked down the walk in her three-inch stilettos, Givenchy handbag over the shoulder of her Gucci spring dress. Her gold and diamond Chopard earrings, necklaces, bracelets and rings screamed Look. At. Me. "Don't forget to lock the door!"

He turned around. She had taken nothing.

He wondered when he should tell her his financial ruin may be imminent.

6

Valerie and Evie walked to the Confectionary to get box lunches. They sat at a table in front of the counter and ordered from the special board.

Evie ordered a sandwich of thinly sliced ham and prosciutto with pepper jack cheese on a jalapeno bagel. Valerie ordered a farfalle pasta salad with roasted chicken.

Evie looked around while they waited for the order. Of course the most prominent features were the dancing cat and the bouncy dog. The décor was bright. Most of the walls were painted lime green with the exception of a bright white accent wall behind the counters. The accent wall was strewn with lime green and sunburst orange shapes.

"Bright," she said. Valerie agreed, but she really wasn't paying attention. Her nose was pressed against the pastry and chocolate counter. As Jerry brought their sandwiches, in boxes with handles that would carry easily to the beach, Valerie ordered two cookies and a selection of truffles in rainbow colors.

Ray and Jock left the Confectionary. Ray carried a cardboard container with two cups of coffee, two cinnamon rolls and four dog treats. He'd seen Cyril napping under the tulip tree before nipping into Mr. Beans; he was certain he would find Pete there.

Jock ran ahead of him, knowing where they were headed, and dropped to the ground under the tree. Ray placed two treats on the ground in front of each of them, received the grateful "Woofs" and went in. Marco sat at the front desk.

"Where's your dispatcher?"

"Out to lunch. Pete's in his office."

"Thanks. Oh, and Marco, I'm going to be making out a complaint against Brad's Buoys & Gills for continuing to use The Marina without payment. Actually, without permission. I won't take a cent from that guy. Not that you patrol the docks, but…"

Marco laughed and leaned back in the chair. "Good idea to get it on record, Ray. Just in case."

Pete came to the door. "What's that? Brad is still using your docks? It's a wonder that leaky sieve can get from his place to yours."

"It's a wonder anyone gets on it when they see what they've rented."

"Have you seen his ad? It's splashy." Pete opened a drawer at the front desk and pulled out the yellow pages, leafed through and found the right page. "Here. This is what it looks like in the book, but you should see it online."

Ray couldn't believe it. He had the name of his boat in one section, the name of The Marina in another, and a listing underneath the appropriate categories, like fishing, deep water rentals, lake cruises and others. He couldn't afford anything splashy like this. It was a full-color picture of a well-equipped yacht, much like The Escape. A crew of people were on deck, holding a day's catch of deep water fish.

"Isn't there a law against this?"

"Probably, but that's beyond my jurisdiction. We're not in the truth-in-advertising business. We're in the catch-a-killer-that's-staying-at-the-KaliKo-Inn business."

"That'll keep you busy, alright."

Ginger, Pete's daughter, drove to The Avenue and parked behind the grocery store. She entered the back of the store, carrying a backpack with a blanket, towel, sunscreen, a book, bottles of water and some rings to toss. She was followed by her younger sister, Clarice. Clarice carried a similar backpack.

Pete's ancestral family arrived shortly before the Civil War, coming from the south via the Underground Railroad. Generations of roots helped Pete as he re-acclimated to the small town, but Ginger and Clarice, moving in as teens, were outsiders. Ginger naturally gravitated to James, another outsider. He moved here with his mother a few years before, and in the small public school, he stood out as both a newcomer and a Pakistani.

Ginger, a dutiful daughter, drew the line at having to cart her younger sister to the beach. Because her mother pushed her over the line, she moved quickly, forcing the younger, shorter girl to almost trot to keep up.

James looked up at them from behind the counter. He smiled at Ginger, then gave a knowing wink to Clarice. He said to Ginger, "Don't worry. I have to bring my sister, too. Ava and Clarice can keep one another company."

Ava ran down the back stairs from the apartment at that moment. "Don't leave without me!"

Laila, from the deli counter, said, "Be careful. There's only one lifeguard on duty during the week. James, keep an eye out for Ava. And Clarice."

"I will, Mom." To Ginger, he whispered, "Let's get out of here!"

The four teens walked quickly, the older two in long, easy strides, and the younger in shorter, quicker steps to keep up. The beach was at the end of The Avenue and on the far side of the town park, less than five minutes on foot. It was a walk they made often, all year round.

This summer, they made it every afternoon. Today, the beach would be filled with teens from the high school. Many were friends, others not so much. For the most part, the afternoons were sun-filled and presented an opportunity to just be teenagers. Too old to be supervised every minute of every day and too young for adult responsibilities.

It did not take them long to find their particular groups of friends. Ava and Clarice ran to be with teens their own age with instructions from both of the older teens. "Don't leave the beach unless you tell me." "Don't go into the water without letting me know."

And then, the older teens forgot all about their supervisory responsibilities and lost themselves in fun with their own friends.

James met a group of bikers who talked about their training session this morning. They were still pumped with energy. Brendan, one of his closest friends, was at the lifeguard station, but Bill and Eddy did not have afternoon jobs.

"How's the training going?"

"It's rough, man. Good for you that you aren't doing it."

James looked at his feet. He wanted to be involved, but he couldn't do that and work for his mother at the same time. Plus, he didn't have the money for a bicycle that was appropriate for this kind of race. He was saving his money for college.

Bill and Eddy kept talking, paying no attention to Jame's change of attitude. "That Ian, man, he's working us every day this week."

"And he won't let us race, man."

"We have to ride like little babies…" "Up and down those hills…" "And the rules…" "Yeah. We have to eat certain things, get to sleep at a certain time…" "And no dates on Friday night!"

James looked up at this. "No dates?"

"He thinks we won't get enough sleep if we go out. You know, if we go to a movie or anything, there's always something afterwards…" "Like ice cream…" "Yeah, ice cream…"

James found his sense of humor again and joined in the fun.

Ginger loved the water, no matter how cold. She ran to the lake and joined others in the one thing teens on a lake can't live without: the ultimate splash game. She turned often, catching the eye of the handsome young life guard, Brendan. He was in her class at school, and he was mighty fine. She was pleased to see he was typically looking back.

Ava and Clarice found a group of friends and joined in a game of ring toss, then Frisbee. Soon, the girls followed others out to the water, where they alternately swam, dove, dog peddled out several feet and back, and played water dodge ball.

Shivering, they made eye contact and headed for the beach at the same time. They huddled under their towels on the sunny sand until they were warm enough to talk.

Clarice looked around. Ginger was google-eyeing the lifeguard. James played volleyball. She turned to Ava. "Want to walk up the beach to that cliff?"

"Mom doesn't want me going there. She says it's dangerous."

"It'll be fun. Come on. They aren't paying any attention. We'll go there, climb up, and be down before they ever miss us."

"We'll get in trouble…"

"No we won't. It'll be fun!"

Ava finally said, "Okay. But not today. I don't have the right shoes. Tomorrow, let's bring our tennies. We can leave when we know they aren't looking.

Valerie and Evie dropped to their blanket after a healthy dose of water-time. The early afternoon sun was warm; the sand was hot. The water was another story. Evie, shaking with cold, wrapped a towel around her shoulders. "The water's still awfully cold!"

Valerie laughed, "No, it's not. It's definitely sixty degrees."

They shivered for a while, then Evie suggested, "Why don't we take a walk up the beach like that woman suggested this morning?"

"Good idea. The walk will warm us up. We can eat lunch when we get to the rocks."

They gathered their personal items and packed them into over-sized shoulder bags.

"Let's at least walk along the water. It's not so cold we can't wade in and out of it."

They walked and splashed their way up the coast.

Evie lived in a medium-sized town in Indiana. Valerie lived in a larger town just a half hour or so from Evie. They had been best friends since college. Swim team members, they bonded the year they both tried out and barely missed making the Olympic swim team.

They vacationed together often. Their shared love of swimming usually took them to a beach or a resort with a fabulous pool. Both were still strong swimmers. The vacations were always Valerie's treat.

This week, they had an ulterior motive for their visit to the lake. That they went away together every year worked in their favor. When Evie asked her mother to babysit, the request didn't raise a red flag. It would be easy duty; the children had vacation Bible school all week.

Evie, with three children, discovered her marriage was in crisis. To be honest, it had been in crisis for years. Now, though, it was at a critical juncture. She found herself in a position of having to make a decision. Did she want a divorce or did she want her husband?

She decided on the divorce. She had not yet told her husband. She wanted to make it hurt. Her husband, an attorney, was much in demand in their small town. She knew he had to make more money than his meager allowance to her would indicate.

She was allowed a used junker car. Every car she owned dropped dead before her husband would replace it with another junker. His own cars – late model Japanese sports cars – were "necessary" for his image. He couldn't afford two upscale cars, and she, as the wife, would have to make do. She knew, having taken a message from the dealership, he would pick up the latest model this week. He probably had it by now.

She shopped for clothes and shoes, both for herself and her children, at Goodwill. His suits and shirts came from a tailor. They were impeccably made, from the finest silks and linens. His clothes never wrinkled. Again, image was everything.

She made menus and grocery lists for a month and shopped at the bargain grocery store. She and the children ate out once a month, at McDonalds; he ate lunch out every day and often had business dinners with partners and clients. Of course, this was another necessity.

She had a garden in her back yard and preserved vegetables and fruits for the winter. She made jelly, jam, spaghetti sauce and salsa. She baked her own bread. She didn't purchase junk food or frozen foods. In fact, she purchased very few prepared foods, making everything from scratch.

With all her frugality, at times she was forced to ask her husband for more money. Those conversations were the absolute worst. His emotional abuse, hard to handle at any time, became exaggerated. Lately, the episodes threatened to elevate to physical abuse.

Valerie had never married. A career advertising executive with a hefty salary, she moved in circles Evie only dreamed about. Valerie hated the life her friend was living, but she didn't judge. Now, Evie had asked for a favor. A big one. Valerie decided to put that hefty salary to good use this week.

The first thing Valerie did for Evie on this trip was to take her to a salon on their way to Chelsea. Evie now had a new short haircut and a color treatment. They both got manicures and pedicures. They went to several boutiques to purchase new lingerie, outfits, swimming suits, shoes and sandals. Valerie purchased luggage for Evie. No more ratty-looking second hand, unmatched pieces for her. They felt like a million dollars, and from a distance, even Evie's husband wouldn't recognize her.

On the walk to the rocks, they talked about their plans for the week. Just talking about it brought a sense of new purpose to Evie.

The walk to the rocks didn't take as long as they thought. When they thought they needed a rest, Valerie spied the outcropping in the distance, and they pushed forward without stopping.

When they reached the area, they dropped their bags on top of a large flat rock and found smaller rocks upon which to sit and eat lunch.

Valerie looked up. "This looks kind of dangerous."

"It does, but I can see a path to the top. We can do it."

"What are we going to do when we get up there?"

"Just look. I'll bet we'll be able to see for miles. What do you think?"

They both looked up. Finally, Valerie said, "Let's do it tomorrow. We see how it looks, and now we know how to dress for it. We can pack our bags differently."

"Okay then. Let's eat lunch, swim a little, and go back to the beach."

"We still have to figure out how to find him."

"Let's make some calls this afternoon. We might get lucky and figure out which charter he's hired."

Henrie, a cat on either side, greeted his new guests from the front porch. "Welcome to the KaliKo Inn."

The four guests, three men and a woman, headed straight to the Inn without responding. The woman, talking into a cellphone, at least met Henrie's eyes and smiled.

Henrie turned to the limousine driver. The limousine was actually a small bus used by the regional airport in Marsh Haven. The driver had placed most of the luggage on the sidewalk and had begun to struggle with the last items.

Checking the clients were out of earshot, he complained to Henrie, "I hate this time of year. If it ain't one thing it's ta'other. This week it's these danged bicycles."

Henrie took the first bicycle from the man, walked it to the sidewalk next to the porch's ramp, and pushed down the kickstand. He did this three more times, listening to the driver complain the entire time, looking toward the door on occasion to assure himself the guests were safely away from the tirade.

"These here are rich people. Know how I can tell? They's used to being waited on. And do you think any one of 'em thought to give me a tip? No. Not a single penny. They's probably used to having 'their people' take care of that, but they left 'their people' at home this time."

When the bicycles were out, the driver gave a final disgusted wave, got into the little bus and drove away.

Henrie walked each bicycle up the ramp and to the right of the front door. Here, Henrie had placed the rack he purchased three years ago. The Inn had guests attending the Chelsea Grand Prix from the first year of its inception. Now a standard bicycle event, Henrie was happy to have this stand to allow guests to leave their equipment on the porch.

The first year, Henrie blanched to see riders walking bicycles through the Inn, putting kickstands down on his beautiful hard-wood floors. Never again.

Henrie wondered at the audacity, or perhaps it was presumption or entitlement, that allowed four presumably healthy adults to leave the work to one person. Thank goodness for tools. Always prepared in advance, Henrie took hold of the luggage carrier he had left beside the bicycle rack, rolled it to the end of the sidewalk and filled it with luggage dropped by the driver.

Henrie opened the door to see all four sitting or walking around the room, bottles of water in hand.

"I am Henrie, your host. Kali and Ko," he pointed out the cats now climbing over the luggage on the carrier, "are your hostesses. They assist me in looking out for your every need."

One of the men scowled at the cats, getting a low growl in return. The woman said, "Monte, cut it out."

The man turned his scowl to her but stopped looking at the cats.

Henrie addressed the woman. "You requested two rooms. The rooms are across the hall from one another, one lakeside and one overlooking the winery and the side garden."

The woman answered, pointing as she spoke. "Clark and Bryce normally stay in the same room." She looked at Henrie. "Monte and I do okay together. I'm Kim."

Henrie proceeded to tell the four guests about the amenities of the Inn. He finally pointed down the hallway to the all-season porch. "The all-season porch and the beach are delightful vantage points from which to watch the sunset. As the Inn is full this week, you may prefer to take your breakfast to the all-season porch or the front porch. You will find trays in the dining room that will assist you should you so desire. Before I escort you to your rooms, do you have questions?"

Kim asked, "What time is breakfast?"

"I can serve you at any hour you desire. What will work best for you?"

She looked around at the group then back to Henrie. "7:00 would work best. We need to get in some practice runs this week, and we may have to get going earlier on Saturday."

"Certainly. That can be arranged. By the way, I have altered our typical breakfast menu to supply your energy needs. There will be scrambled eggs, fresh fruit, high-fiber breads, peanut and almond butter, fruit smoothies and steel-cut oat groats made with walnuts and berries."

This was met with no response, but Bryce asked, "The website said a car might be available?"

"Yes. You may use one of the vehicles belonging to the Inn. Do you need it this afternoon?"

They looked around at one another, communicating silently. Bryce looked back at Henrie. "I think so. We have a map of the course. I understand we can't ride it completely until Saturday, and we can't drive the route completely either, but we thought we would scope out what we could."

"Certainly. Please let me see your map. I can pinpoint your current location."

7

Annie spent the lunch hour and most of the early afternoon at Tiger Lily's Café, working through the lunch rush. This week would be a busy one with regular customers, the typical summer tourist crowd and bicyclists who had arrived early.

Several touring boats had followed Ray's lead and this year made regular catering orders for their day trips and multiple-day cruises. Felicity had to hire a new week-day catering coordinator; she chose Georgia.

Georgia was a recent addition to Chelsea. She rented a suite in what used to be a bed and breakfast. With luck and a little help from Henrie, Georgia found this home, and the elderly owner of the former B&B, Martha, was finally able to retire. Martha helped Georgia care for her baby, Frederica.

A marvel of energy and efficiency, Georgia managed to cook part-time at Mo's and to cook and help with management details of the Bon Vivant Grille on Friday and Saturday nights. She had become so indispensable in a short period of time that she was now a full-time employee. Technically, she worked for Mo's Tap, but her time was split three ways.

Today, even during the lunch rush, Annie saw Georgia in the kitchen, working on meals that would be frozen, then delivered to cruising boats at The Marina. She had a compact working area consisting of a stovetop and convection oven with a small counter to the left. These pieces of equipment were new purchases designed to allow a person to work separately while the main kitchen was in use.

The Café's business was expanding, and with that came a few growing pains, but nothing that couldn't be handled.

Simon Finnegan and Oscar McMurphy hit the Café at the peak of the lunch rush. They loved the lunches placed behind the hostess stand for companions on The Avenue.

Tiger Lily, who had already eaten, motioned with her head to the dishes on the floor. *"There's still plenty here. Help yourselves."*

"Thanks!"

Holly hit the automatic door opener with her left hand as she leaned over to peer into the window behind the hostess stand. As she wheeled into the Café, she first went behind and looked at the two big cats, who looked up with full mouths and "oops, we got caught" facial expressions.

Holly and her twin sister Jolly – as adults they were no longer angry with their parents about their names – owned DoubleGood, the combination hardware and electronics store. Holly, since an accident at a young age, lived in a wheelchair. Together, the twins were the fur-ever parents of Simon Finnegan and Oscar McMurphy.

"You are going to eat Annie out of house and home someday. It's a wonder she doesn't send you packing."

The cats managed to swallow and they both sat down, eyes still on Holly.

Holly laughed and wheeled around to join some friends in the middle of the room. Before she got away from the hostess stand, three men and a woman walked in. One of the men looked down at Holly with a dismissive facial expression.

As a server approached the hostess stand, she looked first at Holly and started to speak. She was interrupted by the man, who said, "There are four of us." This surprised the server, who looked first at the man, then at Holly.

Holly gave a slight shake of her head and smiled. "It's alright, Kate. I'm going to join Jennifer and Clara at their table."

Kate seated the four.

Holly wheeled herself away and Tiger Lily looked down at her friends. *"I'm going to go over there and say hello, see what I can find out."*

Tiger Lily jumped down, trotted to the table and hopped to one of her ledges, the one in between the woman and the man who had spoken. The man took his arm and, with a fairly strong movement, shoved Tiger Lily to the floor.

The dining room went silent. Tiger Lily, surprised but not hurt, stood her ground on the floor and hissed.

Annie hurried from the coffee bar to the table, leaned down to pick Tiger Lily off the floor, and looked at the man. Holding her temper in check – this was, after all, a customer – and with her "this is a customer" smile on her face and in her voice – this was often misinterpreted as her syrupy-sweet-viper-coming-out-of-the-woodpile smile and voice – she said, "Welcome to Tiger Lily's Café. I'm Annie. This is Tiger Lily. I'm sure she won't bother you again."

Tiger Lily kept a low growl going as Annie talked. Her tail flicked back and forth. Annie held on, wanting to protect both her cat and her customers.

Annie took a deep breath, nodded at Kate, who appeared at her elbow, and continued. "The specials today are a field-fresh tomato stuffed with cottage cheese and surrounded by fresh fruit, a grilled peanut butter and jelly sandwich with a cup of soup of your choice, and vegan meatloaf with mashed potatoes, made without milk, of course, covered in a spicy tomato sauce. Kate will be your server today. Let me know if there is anything I can do for you."

She nodded at the table, turned and walked to the hostess stand, where she set Tiger Lily, holding on to her for a while and petting her. The dining room, which had hung on her every word, came to life again with the soft hum of voices, whispering rather than talking.

After the server took their orders, the woman looked at the offensive man. "Well, that's just great, Monte."

"What?"

"That woman? Annie? She owns the Inn where we're staying. She owns all these places on Sunset Avenue. I told you about her and I told you about the cats. It's all on the website."

"Well, that darned cat shouldn't have jumped on the table."

"She didn't jump onto the table. She jumped to her ledge. Look at this." Kim pointed to the ledge. "They're all over the place. Look around. I told you about them."

"I told you, I don't like cats."

"Apparently you don't like women in wheelchairs either."

"I didn't say anything to her."

"You didn't have to. You can be rude without opening your mouth. I told you that if you couldn't mind your manners you could find someplace else to sleep. It's not our fault you can't pay for your own room. Or meals, for that matter. Any more attitude like this and I'll forget about footing your bill."

Bryce and Clark muttered something under their breaths to one another.

Monte, angry, said, "Speak up. You weren't talking about me loud enough."

They both looked at him, then Kim. Clark spoke first. "Neither of us wanted you tagging along in the first place. When Kim asked us to help you out, we said you could take a flying leap."

Bryce added, "The only reason you're here is that Kim is paying for you one hundred percent. She may have told you we were helping out, but we're not. I wouldn't pay a dime for you."

Monte, face red now, spluttered, "I didn't ask you for anything."

Clark shot back, "That's right. You just asked Kim, and she can't say no to you, her darling baby brother. The one that squandered his entire inheritance in two years."

Bryce joined in. "Tell me again what happened this time? Whose fault was it that you lost this last job you had? And how long ago was that? Six months?"

"I should be able to rely on family."

"We're cousins by blood. We stopped being your family years ago."

Monte stood up, shoving his chair back in the process. The dining room was beginning to go quiet again. He looked around at the three at the table, broadened his look to everyone in the dining room, looked down to give Kim a hard stare, and stalked out.

He didn't even glance at the hostess stand on his way out the door. Tiger Lily stood her ground, sitting tall with an inscrutable cat stare.

Of course, she had back-up. Simon Finnegan and Oscar McMurphy, cowering behind the hostess stand, would have jumped out to help if that man started anything. Well, that's what they told themselves, and what they told Tiger Lily later.

After lunch, Clark and Bryce took the car to check out Saturday's route. Kim walked up and down Main Street, window shopping. There were few tourist shops on Main, but she found an antique shop with a jewelry store in the front corner.

After window-shopping, she stepped in and was greeted by a cute, artily-dressed young woman. "Hello. Welcome to Gema's Creations."

"Are you Gema?"

"I am she. Let me tell you that you'll see mostly silver here, but I make everything. I work in gold and platinum, and I can use any stones you would like."

"Do you make everything to order, or are these for sale?"

"Both. If you see something you like, you can have it, or you can tell me you like it but would prefer another stone or metal."

"I saw this one, and I like it. Can I try it on?"

Gema drew out a magnificent one and a half carat emerald ring, one of the few gold pieces in her display case, with an offset band, each side containing seven diamonds. As Gema described the ring, she had to stop herself from making a "deal" on the price. No longer on the rock and gem circuit, she had her own storefront. The price was the price. She had overhead now. She ended the description with, "And it's a steal at forty-two hundred dollars."

Kim didn't quibble. She left with a new ring.

Kim turned the corner to walk down The Avenue. First, she walked the north side of the street, looking into windows of a charity shop, a tea house and cyber café, a grocery store, a hardware store with electronics, a flower and gift shop, and a drug store. She would shop later this week.

Kim turned around, crossed The Avenue and walked back toward the Café. The last storefront before the Café held a yoga studio. She looked in; a class was in session. What she saw was mesmerizing; she went inside to sit at a bench and watch.

The woman in the wheelchair was taking the class. Her chair was in the middle of the floor, back and sides removed. She used her upper body and arms to follow the poses. The woman in the wheelchair doing yoga was not mesmerizing. The little black cat was.

As Kim watched, Little Socks – she was certain this was the name of the cat – stood on the woman's legs. She faced the woman and stretched her front legs to the ceiling, sometimes one at a time, while she placed a paw on the woman's shoulder, sometimes two at a time. She seemed to raise to her toes with each position change.

The woman's pose changed; the cat jumped nimbly to her shoulders. Facing the woman's back, she stretched her right hind leg out, then her left. Her tail and her left hind leg softly brushed the face of the woman.

The woman leaned forward; Little Socks moved to the middle of her back, balancing on all fours. She stretched her tail and hind end to the ceiling, then shifted and stretched her head as high as it would go.

As the woman rose in the wheelchair, Little Socks put her hind legs on a shoulder and her front legs on her head. From here, she twisted her upper body backwards and forwards. Finally, she jumped to the woman's lap and finished the routine. She kneaded the woman's legs, turned around three times and curled up in a ball on her lap for a nap.

The class ended. The woman wheeled her chair to the bench where Kim sat. The cat roused herself and jumped to the bench, then to the windowsill where she repeated the kneading, turning and curling up on a black pillow.

Kim said, "I'm Kim, the sister of the man who was so rude to you in the Café. On his behalf, let me say how sorry I am."

Holly laughed, a bright laugh. "Thanks, but it wasn't a problem. I'm Holly."

"It was a problem, Holly. Well, it wasn't as big a problem as what he did to Tiger Lily."

Little Socks, without appearing to, perked up.

"That was pretty bad. We all noticed that you let him have it."

"As if that's enough. I was embarrassed to say anything to Annie."

"Don't be. She's easy to talk to."

"I'll speak to her tonight. He won't. He'll never apologize. But I'll let her know if he does anything like that again, he'll have to go."

"She'll appreciate that. You can see that all the cats belong, really, to all of us on The Avenue. We won't let him – or anyone – hurt them."

Later that afternoon, as the cats gathered under their table with an afternoon snack, Tiger Lily told her siblings the story. She finished it by saying, *"The other people at the table didn't seem to like him too much."*

Mr. Bean said, *"A man came into my place and acted like he was going to hit Tillie and me, or kick us or something. Jerry came out and took us behind the counter."*

"No!"

"Yes. He must have been the same guy."

Little Socks added, *"That woman came into the yoga studio. They didn't like what he did to you."*

Kali said, *"I'll bet those are the people staying here. They have those bicycles on the porch."*

Ko added, *"That one guy was mean. He's staying with the woman in the room on the lake side."*

Tillie said, *"I can go into the room and chew up some stuff. Would that help?"*

Tiger Lily looked at her in amazement. *"We don't do things like that, Tillie. If we need to, we can spy on people, or maybe, if we have to, steal something from the room. But we don't ever do anything bad like that."*

Mo said, *"Trill!"*

Sassy Pants translated, *"Cept for dat time dat Little Socks peed on da luggage."*

There was a murmur of agreement.

"But there was a reason for that, and they were leaving. It wasn't going to start to smell until they were long gone."

"An den, it smelded really bad!"

The cats laughed at the memory.

Tiger Lily looked at Tillie. *"Thanks, Tillie. If there is ever a need for something to be chewed up, we'll call you first."*

8

Valerie and Evie decided on an early supper and a DVD from the Inn's library. They dressed in casual clothing and walked up the street to Mo's Tap.

Each ordered a hamburger, Evie a black and bleu and Valerie a mushroom and Swiss.

"This is pretty boring," remarked Evie. "On vacation, and we order burgers?"

"We'll top it off with an artisan beer. Then we can say we had something unique."

Their server, her name tag said her name was Candice, recommended an appetizer of Portobello mushrooms stuffed with spinach and goat cheese. "That way you can say you had something a little different. And if you get the fried sweet potatoes and onions instead of fries, you can really talk about something unique."

Evie said, "Deal." Candice left and Evie looked around. This was an upscale blues bar. Casual but not tacky. Blues music played softly in the background. Loud enough to hear, soft enough to allow for pleasant conversation. The walls were a buttery yellow color with light taupe on the accent wall. The tables were burnished oak with comfortable oak chairs. The booths were also oak with dark taupe cushions. On the other side of the room she saw several private areas with overstuffed chairs and accent tables. A few areas had oaken barrel tables.

Valerie looked around as well, but at people, not the atmosphere. "I don't expect them to arrive until tomorrow, but just in case, we need to keep our eyes open."

Annie walked quickly up the sidewalk. She knew she would be late, so she told Chris she would meet him and their dinner guests at Mo's Tap.

Mo, who typically liked to be carried, followed Annie up the street at a sharp trot. He was going to need a nap when he got there!

When Annie arrived, she waited for her eyes to adjust and looked around the room. Mo had already spied Chris and was on his way to the table.

As Annie reached the table, Chris and two middle-aged men stood up to greet her. Terrence and Jerald Timmer-Schmidt recently moved to Chelsea to open a medical practice. A psychiatrist and a heart surgeon, they stayed at the Inn several months ago and fell in love with the town. They decided to move and open a practice that could wind down to part-time as the years went on.

Terrence spoke with the slow drawl of the south. "Good evening, Annie. It is always a pleasure to see you."

"Terrence, hello. And Jerald. How are you?"

Jerald's drawl was just as soft. "Very well, as ever, now that we're in our new home. We are nearly settled. You must come visit."

"I've driven by countless times. I can't wait to see the inside."

The two, married for a decade, purchased one of the lakefront homes in what Annie called the hotsy-totsy section of town. It was huge. And beautiful. Annie had never been inside any of the homes on the lakefront, with the exception of Boone and Hilly's home, and she couldn't

wait to see how the rich really lived. Boone and Hilly lived
a bit north, after all. Not really in the hotsy-totsy section.

Chris came from old money. His parents lived on the
shore of another Great Lake. He attended private school
and, later, Yale. He could have gone into the family
business and lived a life of ease on the family estate, but he
chose the Coast Guard. He was familiar with and
comfortable in the kind of house Terrence and Jerald had
purchased.

Candice waited on the table, double checking that the
little hood was on the table candle. She stared at Mo and
said, "Don't you dare try to take off that lid. You'll catch
yourself on fire."

Mo closed his eyes in a long, soft blink and almost
smiled. He was in one of his favorite places. On top of a
table with a lighted candle. Perfect for dancing and
swishing his tail.

Sandwiches and artisan beers ordered, Chris, Terrence
and Jerald talked like old friends.

Watching the men communicate, Annie thought again
about her reservations of meeting Chris's parents. She was
not from money at all. Her mother and step-father,
comfortable now, had to work hard for everything.

Annie herself, even after an inheritance that included
trust funds and these properties and businesses, was not
what anyone would call rich. And she wouldn't know how
to act if she became rich. She was certain she would pick
up the wrong spoon or fork, wear the wrong kind of outfit
or shoes, and say something totally midwestern and
hickish. Probably all at the same time.

Yet Annie felt truly at ease with all three of these men, who were totally without airs.

Terrence and Jerald were committed to this small town, even though a call for psychiatry and heart surgery were not heavy here. They realized they could help the rest of the community by drawing patients from the region. Their new office was established on Main Street in a building located by Greg, a local realtor.

Terrence and Jerald intended to work closely with Jennifer and Marie, owners of The Drug Store and The Clinic, to spell them every now and then from their constant on-call status as the local first responders.

Annie realized she had been daydreaming when Jerald said, "Annie, I asked what you thought about a housewarming party a week from Saturday."

"Oh, really, whenever you have it, I'll be there."

"Well, you'd better be there, because you'll be catering. Or Tiger Lily's Café will be catering. We asked Felicity to make sure to contract some of the side dishes out, so we'll have Indian and Pakistani dishes from the grocery store. And we've already talked to the winery and Mo's Tap. We want to have the best drinks around."

Terrence added, "And Jerry promised to make some special truffles to go along with the desserts Carlos will make."

"So you've already got this planned?"

"Everything but the date itself. We wanted to make sure it would work with everything else going on in town."

Annie thought for a minute. A week from Saturday was the second of July. It would be two days after the block party, always held on the last day of the month, so there would be no conflict with that fundraiser.

"You know it's in the middle of the Fourth of July weekend. Will that be a problem?"

Terrence laughed. "Jerald is so excited to have a lakeside home. He can't wait to blow up a thousand dollars' worth of fireworks. Lots of people on the lake will set off fireworks all weekend, but believe me, no one will have spent as much as Jerald. It will be spectacular, and a perfect way to end the open house."

"Well, then, I think a week from Saturday is perfect!"

"We have invitations ready to go. We'll just put that day and date in and start walking around town delivering them to everyone, even people we've never met. We're going to plaster the town in paper."

"When will you have the time?"

"Our offices won't open until the middle of July, so we can slide by a bit. And really, the house is nearly finished. Your staff will do all the cooking and set-up, so we have plenty of time."

"We even hired your landscapers and cleaners, Boone and Hilly; they'll have everything shipshape. We've got nothing but time on our hands."

"That's great news for Boone and Hilly. The folks in your neighborhood will see what good work they do, and they will never lack for steady jobs. You may drive up the price for me, though." Annie thought about that negative thing for a second.

"Oh, I don't think so. They are loyal to you. They almost didn't take the job with us because they thought it would interfere with what they do for you."

"They finally hired some new people for both cleaning and landscaping. They're training them and supervising them fairly closely."

"Tell me, why did you hire them?"

Terrence and Jerald looked at one another. Jerald answered. "Remember when we stayed at the Inn?"

"How could I forget?"

When the two men were guests at the Inn, someone kidnapped two of Annie's cats, Little Socks and Sassy Pants. Obvious attempts had been made to get all of the cats, but luck and circumstances prevented that from happening.

"When we returned to the Inn that day, Hilly was protecting the cats that had not been taken. She was a regular bulldog. Boone came in to be with her, and he was just as protective."

Terrence took over the reasoning. "We figured anyone that would be that loyal to someone they worked for would be just the people we would trust to have in our home. So we didn't even consider anyone else."

Annie talked in between eating fried portabella strips. "Is there anything I can do – I mean, me, personally – to help you?"

"No, really, everything is under control."

"We have to stop by Bloomin' Crazy and give her the date."

"Did you know we're on her regular Thursday route now?"

"No. How did that happen?"

"We like the way you get fresh flowers in each of your places every Thursday. It says a lot about your commitment to the town and to your customers."

"And we like Clara's taste."

"We've given her free rein. She can decide, every week, what to put in the foyer."

"And Thursday's the perfect day."

Annie laughed. She was happy these two men chose Chelsea. Everyone would be a little bit better off because of them.

In a back booth, Carlos and Isabel continued their conversation. Annie saw them but did not interrupt, not even to say hello, because they looked to be deep into their discussion.

Carlos had the look of a man betrayed. It was obvious he was not angry with Isabel. That was a good sign. But he had a lot to think about, and Annie didn't want to intrude.

She noticed Valerie and Evie in a booth. They seemed to be having a great time, laughing and talking, but they seemed to look around a great deal.

In another booth was the group of bikers. Annie's gaze turned a little cold.

Chris said, "Annie, what is it?"

She looked at him and shook it off. "Nothing, really."

"Annie."

"Well, there is a group of bikers staying at the Inn. They're at that window table. Today, at the Café, one of the men shoved Tiger Lily to the floor."

The men at the table stiffened and asked for a full explanation. Mo stopped dancing. He listened to everything Annie said, but his gaze was on the window table. He found the man that looked mean enough to do it and committed the face to memory.

As Annie finished the story, the woman got up from the table and walked over. She smiled at the men and turned to face Annie.

"Excuse me, Annie. You may recall we met, sort of, at the Café today. My name is Kim. I'm here to apologize for the behavior of my brother. He, well, he doesn't always behave well in polite company. My cousins and I let him know we expect better of him. He won't bother your cats again."

"Thank you, Kim. I appreciate that." Annie thought she should say more, but her heart was still angry. She pushed the anger down and added, "I understand you're in town for the Chelsea Grand Prix."

"Yes. We're riding the metric century."

Annie's eyes were drawn to a man who had just entered Mo's Tap. He looked around the room and his gaze seemed to land on Annie's table. He walked straight toward them.

He stopped, nodded congenially to the humans, and took Mo's head in his hands, stroking his cheeks then giving the same tip of the head to tip of the tail stroke that Tiger Lily received earlier. Mo loved the attention.

Ian let go of Mo and said hello to the humans, turning to Kim to say, "I'm Ian."

Annie laughed. "This is Kim. Kim, Ian is the coordinator of the Grand Prix. You might want to get to know him, and maybe he can teach your brother how a cat can fall in love with a human."

Kim smiled, a hint of interest in her eyes. "Care to join my family at our table, Ian?"

As Kim walked away, Annie noticed, as an accessory to very casual clothing, an expensive emerald and diamond ring. Wowzer.

9

It was the middle of a perfect week. At least a perfect week weather-wise. Let's be honest. The first part of the week was perfect, but from this afternoon on, the weather was going to take a turn for the worse.

This morning, Annie woke up with a good deal of energy. She and Chris watched the strawberry moon until nearly midnight and this Wednesday morning was gorgeous.

After feeding the kids, Annie went downstairs to help Henrie with breakfast. Henrie wisely kept her busy carrying food to the dining room and fixing a bacon treat for the cats. Like Felicity, Henrie didn't allow Annie to do any more in the kitchen than he had to. To be polite.

Annie chatted with Valerie and Evie, getting to know them a bit more. Isabel made a quick appearance, taking a to-go coffee and a cinnamon roll. She kept her eyes to the floor; Annie barely made eye contact and got only the merest good morning from her.

In the kitchen, Annie was grateful to hear from Henrie that the bikers had eaten early and had gone to check their route.

"Henrie, I didn't get a chance to tell you about that biker and what he did to Tiger Lily."

Henrie, cooking another pan of bacon, turned from the stove and looked at Annie. "Which biker, and what did he do?"

"It was Monte. Kim, the sister, approached me at Mo's last night to apologize for his behavior."

"Annie, please tell me what he did."

"Tiger Lily did a tabletop hop and he shoved her to the floor."

"He did not!"

"He did, and it took a great deal of energy for me to allow him to stay and order. But he didn't."

"He did not order?"

"He didn't stay. They argued about what he had done, and he stomped out."

"Oh, I see. He must be the gentleman that went to the Confectionary for lunch. I saw Jerry, and he told me of an overbearing man that made a lunge at Mr. Bean and Tillie. Against regulations, Jerry took the two of them behind the counter until he left."

"He lunged at them?"

"I believe he feigned a lunge, intending to scare them. It worked. I did not realize the man in question was a resident of the Inn."

"Kim apologized for his treatment of Tiger Lily. I don't think she knows he continued to be abusive."

"I will keep an eye on the gentleman."

Tiger Lily and her siblings were already off to their respective places of work. Annie grabbed her bag, filled with her laptop and a charger, just in case she worked too long, and left.

Her first stop was the office of her attorney, Jenny. After meeting Geraldine at the museum, Annie wanted to know the status of the lawsuit and how far the restraining order would go.

Jenny was ready with a cup of coffee, some almost good news and some bad.

"It looks like the attorneys on the other side are ready to make a deal, rather than go through the courts and further tarnish the 'good names' of their clients."

"Good names? They haven't had good names for years."

"They apparently don't realize that, and frankly, they still command some respect here in town."

"You're kidding!"

"No. There's no figuring why people still look up to them. Geraldine and Hank have made the local news more often than our current presidential candidates, and their personalities are just as polarizing. For as many people that hate them, there are a similar number of people that love them and believe everything they say. And the B&B owners, even though most of them had to sell, have family in town. Blood is pretty thick."

"There's no accounting for taste. So, how good is this almost good news? What are they willing to do?"

"I don't have specifics yet. It sounds like they are willing to come up with a sum of money, but they also want complete secrecy about the agreement, and, well, here's a little bit of not-so-good news, they want a public acknowledgement from you that they were not in error for trying to take over the management of your businesses."

"What? Privacy on the acknowledgement of their guilt but a public apology from me?"

"That's just their opening salvo. Believe me. They are not going to get either one. I'm still out for blood."

"Well, okay, that's good news. But there's bad news, worse than we've already discussed?"

"There's nothing I can do about Geraldine volunteering at the museum. We were specific in our request to the Judge. We wanted to keep her away from The Avenue, and we have succeeded in that regard. However, you always knew you could run into her anywhere else in town, and we didn't think to include things like 'where Annie volunteers' when asking to hold her at bay."

"I can talk to the director and see if she can make sure I'm not scheduled right before or right after her."

"That's the best you can do."

"Okay, Jenny. Thanks."

Annie went to the library for her next two tasks. She decided to do the easy research first. She went to the local history section, found a table for her laptop, and found some books to start. Her intent was to write a narrative about Lake Scott that would appeal to high school students.

The subject was fascinating to Annie. Her ancestors moved to Chelsea shortly after the Civil War to become involved in the lumber business, and Lake Scott figured prominently in the lumber industry.

Annie took notes about the founding of the town of Scottsburg, the damming of the river and the birth of the huge lake. Tragedies filled the history, including more than one occasion when the dam burst and had to be rebuilt. The town of Scottsburg no longer existed. After the most devastating break, the entire town – then and to this day – lay at the bottom of the lake, destroyed by rushing water.

After an hour of research, Annie got sidetracked into the geography of Lake Scott and the land around it. She had not taken the time to explore the area and was unaware of the topography. Because she had bikers at the Inn who were getting ready to ride the metric century around it, her interest was piqued.

Annie went to the main desk of the library to flip through the brochures. She found what she wanted, a brochure about the Chelsea Grand Prix. The ten-mile route began at the city park and went into the state park for five miles. Bikers would hit that mark and return to the city park.

The thirty-mile route took bikers along the same path, but they rode forward through the state park for another ten miles. The trail was scenic, but typically it was a walking trail. It was used for biking one time a year, for this event. The trail had some rough spots for bikers, including exposed roots, downed branches and limbs, and closed-in spaces that could be difficult even for walkers.

The metric century route continued through the state park, exited on the other end, followed Lake Scott's coastline and went back to the city park. It wasn't a perfect metric century; in order to set up a route, the trail was almost seventy miles long.

A significant portion of the route around Lake Scott was on rough ground used mainly by hikers. This section was rocky with treacherous turns. Annie had heard of bikers walking part of the course rather than hazard the trail on two wheels.

Once bikers made it around the lake, public roads brought them to the city park where they could check in. SAG stops – support and gear stops – were peppered throughout the race route. It was not possible to get a

SAG station into the treacherous part of the route, but there was a stop before and one after.

Annie went to her laptop and pulled up information about biking in general. This was a serious sport. Bikers carried what appeared to her to be a lot of gear, like extra footwear, raingear, a cotton scarf, energy bars and water. And while the SAG stops would have a variety of tools, bikers themselves would carry hex wrenches, Phillips and flathead screwdrivers, a chain tool and a spoke wrench. Prepared bikers also carried zip-ties and duct tape.

Annie looked at the time and realized she had let the morning get away from her. She needed to get to the Café, and she hadn't finished her two projects. She had a decent start on the Lake Scott research, but her personal project – the discovery of who she was – had not even been broached.

Well, Annie thought, I'm always going to leave that for last. I know who I am. I'm a big old chicken. Bawk!

As Annie left the library, she received a text. After reading it, she thumbed in quickly, "coming call henrie bring car." She ran.

Henrie waited for her, car double parked, at the Winery. Annie threw her bag into the car and ran in. Minnie waved her behind the tasting bar.

Sassy Pants lay there, breathing at a very slow rate. Minnie said, "One of the customers asked what was wrong with her, and when I looked, she was walking like a drunk person on four legs. She fell down and peed on herself, and she's just been lying here. I texted as soon as she fell, so, at least since someone saw her acting funny, it's been about ten minutes."

Jesus knelt beside Sassy Pants with two towels. "That sling worked out well for Mo last time. Let me put her on it and I'll help you carry her out."

Henrie held the door to the Winery and the front seat passenger door as Jesus and Annie settled the little girl in. "I will call the clinic and alert them to your arrival."

Annie nodded, got into the car and gunned it up The Avenue, on her way one more time to the emergency veterinarian clinic in Marsh Haven.

Ian and his group were biking around the vineyard again. For this trip, he held Alena to the back of the pack. He held her there by riding with her. Every mile of the way. They were about halfway through, and he could tell she was just about to burst with energy and impatience.

"If it kills me, I'm going to teach you to pace yourself."

"It just might!"

"Just might, what?"

"Oh, never mind. Do I have to go this slow all afternoon?"

A gust of wind hit them in the face. Ian wasn't heartless. Not all the time. He turned to her, raised his voice to be heard, and said, "We're done after this lap. Your folks would kill me if I kept you out in a storm! How about racing up to tell everyone else?"

Alena smiled and took off. Ian smiled to himself as he watched her go. She would be a star someday. He didn't know what she would star in, but it would be something.

10

In the early afternoon, Henrie met his newest guests, Collin and Celeste. Collin, when making the reservation, told Henrie they would be on their second honeymoon. He had asked for and received a referral to a yacht for day fishing trips. Henrie referred them to Ray, knew the reservation was made, and wondered if Ray had yet to mention they would not go out. He kept that information to himself.

Henrie took the luggage cart to the cherry red sports car. From the back seat, he unloaded two large rolling bags and two personal bags. Expensive, matching luggage. From the trunk, he took two garment bags and a canvas bag, an expensive matched set, an additional rolling bag and a medium bag on rollers, both matching the set from the back seat. The third large bag, from the heft of it, was only partially full. A price tag was still attached to the handle. Henrie glanced and nearly had a coronary.

Henrie was astute. More astute than most. He thought to himself that if this couple was on a second honeymoon, he was an uncle to a primate. But he said nothing. He welcomed them and wished them the best as they celebrated their wedding vows for a second time.

He showed them to their room, the front room overlooking The Avenue. Kali and Ko were excellent hostesses. They sniffed every piece of luggage, jumped on the bed to show the couple how comfortable it was, and danced on the balcony so they would come out to see the view. Kali made sure to put a significant amount of hair on the man's pant legs.

Before Henrie left the room, Collin asked, "What's with all the bicycles? We couldn't find a parking place for lunch before we got here, and, well, you can't turn around without whacking someone walking a bike."

"They are in town for the Chelsea Grand Prix. Since this is the beginning of summer, and Chelsea has a reputation as a resort community, many bikers come early."

"Well, Celeste, maybe we can get our act together and do the bicycle ride next year."

Celeste gave him a cold stare, then turned and smiled at Henrie. "He's joking, of course. You wouldn't find me on a bicycle unless a jewel thief was chasing me."

Henrie took note of the gold and diamond jewelry around her neck, in her ears, on her arms and fingers and privately wondered if she would be able to get the weight of them onto two wheels. Out loud, he said, "My sentiments, exactly."

He then remembered his manners. "Have you had the opportunity to lunch?"

"No. We still need to do that. We decided to find a parking place here. I guess we can walk somewhere."

"On this block alone there is a wine and cheese shop with lunch selections, a confectionary that serves sandwiches, a bar with excellent sandwiches and meals, and of course, the Café on the corner. Across The Avenue is a tea shop with lighter fare."

Celeste, primping at the mirror, said, "Let's just go to the Café, and then see if we can't find a jewelry store or something. You promised me a gift."

Henrie, ever helpful, said, "The Café is at the corner of Sunset Avenue and Main Street. From there, walk left on Main. Two doors in that direction is an excellent jewelry store, Gema's Creations. She is new to town and has space inside the antique shop. As the name implies, she makes her own jewelry. Each piece is unique."

"Does she work with that glass stuff?"

"Not that I am aware. She works with silver, gold and platinum and will craft anything you desire with precious and semi-precious stones."

Celeste seemed to perk up. "Well, now, that sounds like just the thing. Come on, Collin, let's get some lunch and go shopping. Tell me you love me with jewelry."

At the front door, Celeste looked at the gathering clouds. She turned to Henrie. "Are these for anyone to use?"

"Certainly."

She grabbed a large rainbow-colored umbrella as they walked out the door.

Valerie and Evie sat on their blanket, once again invigorated by a quick swim in the cold lake. The sun was not as warm today, and the clouds threatened rain. The wind had picked up and cast a chill on their bodies.

Valerie finally said, "Okay. We've put this off long enough. Let's go."

Evie looked up at the clouds. "We might get caught in the rain."

Valerie laughed. "It's not going to rain for hours. The weather reports said it would start to rain sometime tonight."

They picked up their bags and once again walked up the beach to the rocks. When they arrived, they rested for a few minutes, then went up, one at a time, Valerie first.

They had to be careful. Most of the rocks were big, and they could find places to hold on as they pulled themselves up to the next level, but there was plenty of loose stone, and smaller rocks made the way treacherous.

By the time they reached the top, they were more jittery than winded.

At the top, Evie walked as far inland as she could. "I didn't realize I was afraid of heights."

"Since when?"

"Since now, I guess. But wow. What a view."

"And private. This must be a corner of the state park. One that isn't visited very often."

"And look down there." Evie pointed to an inlet that had been hidden to them from ground level. It looked like a deep water cove. "That looks like a great place to pull in a boat. I'll bet people do that a lot, to fish or swim."

Valerie looked at Evie with a meaningful glance. "I'll bet they really do. How much do you want to bet that's where they will pull in?"

"Really? Could we be this lucky?"

"Well, look at the weather. Certainly they're coming today, and they would be going out, when, tomorrow and the day after. What fishing charter is going to go out in the middle of the lake with the current weather reports?"

"I'll bet you're right." Evie looked around. "Well, let's do some exploring while we're up here. We might be back tomorrow."

"Let's walk into the park and see how far we can go."

As they turned to walk into the park, Evie heard voices and turned to look down the rock trail. "Hey, look. We're not alone. Looks like a couple of teenagers coming up."

Valerie looked. "Looks like they're a little more agile than us."

"They're what, twenty years younger than us?"

"More like twenty-five. Come on, let's go."

Ava and Clarice kept an eye out for the right moment. Finally, it came. Ginger was google-eyed with Brendan, who should have kept a better eye on the water, and James played volleyball, teaming up with his bicycling buddies.

"What's up with that? Why do they play the same game for hours and hours..."

"It's not the game, Ava, it's, you know, girls and boys showing off."

"Ick."

"Look. Your brother seems to be joking an awful lot with Traci."

The girls watched for a while. It was true. Traci was on Ian's bicycle team. She and James seemed to be watching one another more than they watched the ball.

They looked one more time at Ginger, who was still google-eyed at Brendan.

"Come on, let's go."

They ran, laughing, up the beach toward the illicit rocks.

Down the beach, two groups of teens enjoyed a sunny early afternoon in and out of the water. This would probably be the last day of the week they could go into the lake, given the weather reports. Rip currents would take over, probably by this evening.

James and Ginger kept a tepid eye on their younger siblings. They were both good kids, but it was summer, and each hated to be saddled with the responsibility.

Ginger, after a fast game of beach volleyball, walked to the lifeguard stand and chatted with Brendan. She did not mind that he continued to look at the lake while they talked, because the few times he looked at her, he looked in a manner than made her heart jump.

While she stood there, she glanced around for Clarice. She didn't see her. Brendan had to leave to handle a few unsupervised, fighting boys. She took the time to walk to her backpack. She fished out a bottle of water. After a long drink, she looked around again.

No Clarice. No Ava. James was on the volleyball court, not looking out for the girls. He was paying more attention to Traci. Should she be worried? How long had it been since she made eye contact?

She stared at the teens in the water, walking closer to make sure. It would be easy to spot them. One black face, one brown. She couldn't see either Clarice or Ava. She went to the volleyball game and said, "James, where are Clarice and Ava?"

James missed a shot and glared at Ginger. "What?"

"The girls. When is the last time you saw them? Where are they?"

James looked around and walked out of the game to shouts and catcalls.

"To be honest, I haven't been watching," he said. He looked around the beach. "How about you? When did you see them last?"

"The last time was before my volleyball game. Let's go look for them."

"Where?"

"I don't know. Maybe we need to ask people if they saw them."

"Let's split up. I'll go toward Annie's beach; you go the other way. Do you have your phone?"

"I'll get it out of the bag."

The two took off, almost at a run, hearts beating fast.

Ginger asked every adult and family group she came across if they had seen two teenaged girls, one black, one Pakistani. No one had seen anything, until finally, at the edge of the city beach, a woman with two young children said, "Sure. They were headed that way, wading in the water."

The woman had gestured to the north, toward a barren stretch of lakefront that led to a rocky area. Teens liked to go there to climb, but adults didn't want them to go alone. The area was too remote, and the climb could be dangerous.

Ginger called James and waited as he came on the run. Together, they headed toward the rocks at a fast walk.

When they reached the rocks, at least a mile away, they stood at the bottom and gazed up. Ginger saw a flash of red. It was Clarice's swimsuit cover. It was on top of a dangerous-looking outcrop of rock. And Clarice was wearing it!

"Clarice!" she shouted. "Ava!"

The two girls turned, saw their older siblings and waved.

Ginger turned to James. "They are in so much trouble."

When the girls reached the bottom, the smiles on their faces were gone. Ginger and James glowered. In a voice low enough to be that of a thirty year old father, James said, "Let's go. We won't make it home before it rains. We will never be able to explain this one."

Valerie led the way into the trees of the state park. They walked for what she guessed was a quarter of a mile through trees and undergrowth, looking back every now and then to make sure they knew how to return.

Valerie finally held up her hand, every bit the scout telling her troops to halt and be silent.

Evie kept her voice low. "What is it?"

"People. They're coming up the trail, and listen."

The women listened. Voices, male and female, getting louder, and no one sounded happy.

Soon, a man came into view from around a curve, then a woman, then two more men.

The women crouched where they were, invisible to the people on the path because of the undergrowth and trees.

The man in front was angry. "I told you this path would be rough. We won't be able to make speed here, and there's room for maybe two bikes abreast at the most, one when you go around these curves. If someone gets in front of us, we'll be stuck."

He stopped right in front of their hiding place. "And look, right here, if we don't keep low enough we're going to be wiped out by branches. What kind of a bicycle trail is this?"

The woman said, "Monte, I told you, it's a walking trail. Bikes aren't allowed except for this one day of the year. They won't let walkers on the path that day."

"It's too rough. I told you I needed a new bicycle. Mine won't make it."

"I told you I would cover your expenses. I never promised to buy you a new bicycle."

"After everything I've done for you!"

The other two men, talking at the same time, said, "Give it a rest, Monte!" "Oh just shut up!"

One man said, "Kim, I've seen enough. I'm going back the way we came."

The other man agreed.

The woman, Kim, looked at the man called Monte. "I'm going with them."

"Fine! I'll check the rest of it out myself. Maybe I'll tell you about it, maybe I won't."

As he turned to walk forward, the women heard him say, "Family. What deadheads."

The others stood for about half a minute, watching after him. They looked at one another and turned to go back.

Valerie and Evie gave them a minute to get out of earshot, then turned to look at one another. Valerie started it. She let out a gasp, then a giggle. Soon, Evie joined in.

Eventually, Valerie said, "Well, I don't want to walk the trail, do you?"

Evie, not liking the thought of going down those rocks at all, said, "Actually, running into those clowns on the trail sounds better to me than going down the rocks."

"Chicken?"

"Oh, all right. Let's get it over with."

When they got to the rocks again, Evie remarked, "Those kids must have only come up part-way. They're already gone."

Valerie started down. "At least they aren't stranded here with broken legs. I doubt we would be able to carry them."

They continued, backwards and very carefully. When they reached the bottom, Evie said, "Okay. We've had this adventure. We don't have to do this again. Right?"

"Only if this is the only way of spoiling their vacation."

"Let's hope there's another way to do that. I know. If we think they'll be in that cove, we'll go through the park."

As they started up the beach toward the city park and the Inn, the rain started.

Annie was not allowed to go into the examination room with Sassy Pants. She paced the waiting room and texted Chris to let him know where she was and why.

She called Minnie. "What have you found out?"

"The customers that told me about her said they saw a man with her a few minutes before that, but he left."

"Did you get a description?"

"We didn't have a lot of customers. I served him. I think he was one of those bikers. He ordered sake – a large one – and he sat in the garden near the back tasting bar. No one else was back there until those customers got here."

"So, what do you think? Did he hurt her somehow?"

"The woman said it looked like he was holding Sassy's head to his sake cup, but she said she could have been mistaken. When he saw them, he let go of her and she shook her head and jumped down. The man left, and in just a minute or so, Sassy started acting funny."

"Thank goodness they said something. Would you know the man if you saw him again?"

"Oh, yes."

Shortly after the call ended, Doctor Ralph came out with Sassy Pants in a cardboard cat carrier. She appeared to be resting comfortably, curled into a fluffy towel.

Doctor Ralph sat down and motioned for Annie to do the same. Sassy's carrier was placed on a seat in between them.

"I'm pretty sure this is alcohol poisoning. She had many of the symptoms: loss of coordination, slow breathing, slow heart rate, low temperature, she couldn't control her urination, and she didn't respond to anyone. It could have been a lot worse. Her blood chemistry wasn't altered. That could have led to long-term consequences, and it could have killed her."

"But it wasn't that bad? She'll be alright?"

"Yes. You'll need to keep her quiet tonight, and make sure she drinks a lot of water. Keep her separate from the other cats. If you notice her water doesn't go down a little every hour, use the syringe in the carrier and squirt a little water into her mouth. Not too much, until you know she can handle it and swallow it."

"Is she asleep or medicated?"

"She's asleep. I've cleaned her out, given her a charcoal treatment and some water. She'll sleep a lot this afternoon and tonight."

Annie thanked the doctor and got up to leave.

Doctor Ralph stopped her. "How is Mo? Did he heal from that accident a few months ago?"

"He did. Thanks for asking. Every now and then I catch him feeling his scar with his front paws, but he doesn't scratch at it. I think he wants to make sure it didn't mar his good looks."

"All the hair grew back?"

"Everywhere but on that strip where the stitches went. It's invisible, covered up with the rest of that long gray mane."

Doctor Ralph held the door for Annie as she left, holding the carrier carefully.

Collin, bored with the talk of jewelry, wandered through the antique store. The proprietor, Collin learned his name was Frank, worked on a display with antique office furniture: roll top desk, filing cabinets, book cases, tiffany lamps, desk and side chairs and a rocker. Collin sat in the rocker to chat.

"So, what's it like to have a place in a small town like this?"

"This town has marvelous business opportunities. We have the tourist traffic, and many come here because of the shops, and the residents are very supportive. They tend to shop local."

"But antiques? Can you make a good living?"

Frank laughed. "I can tell from your suit that you make a very good living. If that were my goal, I would be disappointed. But it meets my needs. Pays the bills. Keeps me reasonably entertained."

"I live in a small town. I'm an attorney. I guess we professionals can expect to be paid more." Collin didn't appear to notice the reticence on the part of the proprietor to respond. "So tell me, this woman, her stuff seems pretty expensive. Is it good? Worth it?"

"I believe so. I'm not an expert in the field, but on occasion I purchase estate pieces. The quality of her work rivals the quality of anything I've seen, and the prices seem appropriate."

"Estate pieces? Jewelry?"

"Yes."

"Got any I can look at?"

Frank rose. "Follow me. I keep the jewelry in a locked case by the cash register."

Collin gazed at the case, leaning in, crouching down to get a look at pieces on the lower shelves, and eventually called to Celeste. "Hey. Come look at this. I think it's a ruby. It's huge."

Celeste turned, threw a hard look at Collin, said something to the woman and walked over. "I have found a perfectly nice set already, Collin. We're just discussing details."

"Details?"

"I want diamonds. She will have to fashion something."

"Oh. Well, maybe you don't want this ruby, then."

Celeste looked into the case. "How much is it?"

Frank answered, without looking, "This is a two and a half carat round ruby set in eighteen karat gold, surrounded by twelve one half carat diamonds. It is a vintage engagement ring that would retail for $8,500. I picked it up at an estate sale, and it's priced at $5,000."

"Let me try it on."

"Certainly."

The ring was a bit large for Celeste's hand, but she turned to Collin and said, "Buy it for me. We can have it resized when we get home."

"But…"

"And then, come over here and look at the necklace she's going to make for me."

11

Kali and Ko were hard at work, checking that Henrie had sufficiently prepared the rooms for the evening. They used the cat doors to go into each room, jumping to the side tables that held the small dishes of truffles.

Ko could never help herself. Before leaving the rooms for which she was responsible, little teeth marks or cat-sized bites were visible on at least one truffle per room.

They also took time to sniff anything that was visible in the room, clothes, luggage, books, keys, wine bottles and glasses, computers, shoes. One could learn a lot with an educated sniff.

The Inn was so full, Mr. Bean offered to check the carriage house. He stood on the edge of the porch and realized he had been far too noble. He hated going out in the rain. But he did. He ran through the wet yard and up the outside stairs to the entrance, pushing the cat door open with his head.

Inside, he jumped to the table beside the door to check for truffles. He realized how wet he was and shook himself, getting more than a few drops of water on the reservation papers and brochures on the table. He looked around; no truffles. He broadened his search and saw the plate on one of the dressers. That would be his next stop.

He jumped off the table, bringing a few brochures with him to the floor, then up to the dresser. He sniffed each truffle to make sure they were the good kind. He didn't need to take a bite. He could stuff himself with truffles every day of the week if Jerry would let him. A few fell off the plate while he sniffed. One rolled to the floor.

Oh, what's this? What a pretty hair brush! That went onto the floor and was pushed to the end of the nearest bed, because it looked better there.

Mr. Bean remembered what Kali and Ko said about the small cloth bag with an interesting smell. He found the luggage under the beds. Darn. They had emptied the bags into the drawers and didn't leave them out so he could crawl in. Mr. Bean loved nothing more than to crawl into a purse or a bag. People surely loved the hair he deposited, and you could smell such interesting things!

He looked underneath the furthest bed. There, he thought. That looks like the right one. A small cloth bag was pushed into the middle under the bed on the headboard side. He crawled under and worked his way around the bag.

They were right. It smelled like some oily cleaner or something like that. Oh, and there was that icky chemical smell. And something else.

Mr. Bean hated a mystery. He took the handle into his strong teeth, braced his feet and pulled. He was a strong kitty, and he succeeded in getting the bag to the edge of the bed when he finally had to stop and rest.

He was going to work on it some more, but he heard a commotion outside. The windowsill suddenly was more interesting. He jumped up and looked out. Ray and Jock stood in the rain on the sidewalk; Ray was talking to those two people that had just come to the Inn today. The man's voice was raised and he pointed his finger at Ray as he talked.

The woman carried a big umbrella, and she had to struggle to keep it from blowing upside down. Ray, Jock and the man just stood there getting wet.

Ray didn't seem flustered, but Jock stood at attention, just in case. Ray shook his head and moved his hands as if he was stopping something, then he ended the conversation. He turned and walked toward the lake. Jock stayed for a few seconds, staring at the man, then he turned and walked with Ray.

Then, oops, there were the women! It looked like they had been hiding behind some bushes in the median. They looked pretty soggy. Mr. Bean jumped to the floor, out the door and down the steps just as they crossed the street. He jumped behind a bush, hoping he hadn't been seen. Once they were safely upstairs, he ran back to the house and the warmth of the Seven Cats Detective Agency.

Mo, Sassy Pants and Tillie weren't there. Tiger Lily had promised to save some snack for Mr. Bean. After all, he volunteered to help out. The plates were empty.

Mr. Bean's bottom lip trembled a little. He trotted into the kitchen and wrapped himself around Henrie's legs, over and over, looking up with his huge kitten eyes. He had a very small voice, hardly able to be heard by humans, probably as a result of his bad start in the world, screaming to be found before he was crushed.

Henrie falsely assumed Mr. Bean wanted attention. He leaned down to pet the kitten's head, scratching his ears just the way he liked. Mr. Bean was having none of it. He wanted a snack.

Henrie finally gave up. He stood still, looked down with a serious expression, and said, "You're going to have to go to the detective agency or I might accidentally step on you."

They stared at one another for a while. Mr. Bean finally returned to the dining room, being careful to stay away from his insensitive siblings.

Tiger Lily had just asked, *"What does anyone know about those women?"*

No one had anything to say. Mr. Bean, realizing they waited for him, finally said, *"I wanted to help, so I went out in the rain, and it was still raining when I came back, and no one could save some snack for me, so why should I tell you anything?"*

Tiger Lily got up and walked over to him. She stood in front of him, leaned in and licked his right ear, then, when he moved his head, his left. She sat. *"I'm sorry. I'm the one that ate your snack. I couldn't help it. It was fresh salmon and tuna. Henrie put out sushi."*

Mr. Bean looked at her with tears in his eyes. *"Sushi? And you couldn't save any for me?"* He turned to walk away, then turned back. *"I didn't learn anything."* Then he turned and ran upstairs to the second floor. He didn't want anything to do with his family for a while.

Tiger Lily watched after him sadly. She should have tried harder, but frankly, she couldn't resist the fresh, raw fish. She turned to the other cats. *"Well? Has anyone else seen them or heard anything about them?"*

Everyone shook their heads. Kali said, *"They go somewhere and get stuff for lunch, and they spend all day at the beach."*

Mo sauntered in as Tiger Lily asked, *"What about that new couple?"*

Kali and Ko spoke at the same time. *"Their names are Collin and Celeste." "They told Henrie they are married, but Henrie doesn't believe them." "She's not very nice." "He's handsome." "They were mad when they got back this afternoon." "Ray isn't going to take them out on The Escape."*

Tiger Lily always had to back up and breathe while the big girls talked. If she didn't concentrate on either one, she could hear both of them. Almost.

Little Socks, almost to herself, said, *"I wonder what they'll do, since they can't go out on the lake?"*

Mo said, *"Trill!"*

Kali and Ko looked at him. *"How do you know that?"*

"Trill, trill, trill, trill."

Kali and Ko looked at one another in amazement, then Kali translated. *"They called someone else with a boat and they'll be going out on the lake anyway."*

Tiger Lily asked, *"Where did he hear that?"*

Ko answered this time. *"Mo was loving up the woman while they looked up charters in the telephone book and made calls."*

"So, they're going to go out on the lake in this bad weather. That won't be good. I wonder who's taking them out."

"Trill."

Kali said, *"He doesn't know."* Ko said, *"He only heard 'Brad's Buoys & Gills.'"*

"Huh. I wonder what company that is? Sounds like they have several boats."

"Why haven't we heard about them?"

"Don't know. We'll have to find out about them."

Little Socks looked at Tiger Lily. *"What about those bikers? Were they in town today? I didn't see them."*

"They didn't come into the Café. I doubt they'll be back there."

Kali said, *"I saw them walking toward the state park this afternoon. I don't think they're back yet."*

"That one guy is mean. What about the rest of them?"

"There's nothing interesting in their rooms, and they haven't hung out a lot."

Tiger Lily looked around. *"Has anyone seen Sassy Pants?"*

All the little heads shook in the negative just as Tillie walked in. Walked. Didn't trot. Didn't hop. Didn't gallop. Walked. Her head and tail hung down.

"Tillie! What's wrong?"

Tillie told them about Isabel and Carlos. They wanted to get Daniela and the girls into the States without the extended family being harmed, but they couldn't figure out how to do it.

"It's very sad," she said. *"They haven't come up with a plan yet. Isabel is ready to say she won't leave them to marry Carlos until they can figure it out."*

Tillie lay down on a pillow and put her head on top of her paws, looking around by moving her eyes only.

The siblings talked softly or slept, not wanting to step on Tillie's feelings by talking about anything else. Thus they passed the time until Annie got home. She carried a cardboard cat carrier, and Sassy Pants was inside.

Annie placed the carrier on the floor beside the cats so they could look in. Sassy Pants slept peacefully, but she didn't wake to acknowledge her siblings. Even Tillie stuck her nose in to see.

Henrie came out to see for himself that the girl was going to be okay.

"She'll be fine, but tonight I'll leave her in the tent upstairs. You children will have to be quiet around her until she feels better."

Annie looked at Henrie. "Think you can get a photo of Monte and take it over to Minnie? She served the man who did this."

"What did he – or whomever it was – do?"

"Forced her to drink sake. She had alcohol poisoning."

"I will do a Google search now. If I cannot find a photograph, I will find a way to secure one tomorrow."

Tiger Lily growled deep in her throat.

12

Annie busied herself in the kitchen of her apartment, putting a meal together for Chris. She didn't cook the meal; she plated sushi she had picked up from the winery and returned it to the refrigerator. She heated a bottle of sake and placed it in a thermos, sliced crusty French bread, and selected a bottle of ginger and soy infused oil for dipping.

The afternoon rain was long gone. In its place was the calm-before-the-storm. Clouds over the lake came slowly. They looked ominous. Annie's favorite kind. Perfect for a meal on the deck, awaiting the storm's arrival. Tonight's sunset would intermingle with the storm.

Annie didn't hear the elevator arrive on the third floor, nor did she hear the door unlock and open. She heard six cats run to greet Chris like a long lost friend.

Chris came to the kitchen, Mr. Bean draped across his chest. "He gets bigger every day. Where's Sassy Pants?"

"She's in the tent in the living room."

Chris headed for the living room to take a look. He would have picked her up, but she was sleeping. And Mr. Bean wouldn't let go.

Back in the kitchen, he said, "She looks fine. Alcohol poisoning?"

"Yes. And it may have been done by the same guy that shoved Tiger Lily."

"You don't know for sure?"

"Henrie is going to get a photo to Minnie. Then we'll know for sure."

"Are you going to press charges?"

"We have everything we need to do that, I think. Minnie has contact information for the customers that saw him do it, and we have the doctor's records. Help me out here. Carry the tray to the deck."

Chris picked up the tray with one hand while he clung to the soft, slippery Mr. Bean with the other. The rest of the cats followed, walking around the ankles of their humans all the way out the patio doors.

Annie's patio faced the lake. Her apartment was on the third floor of the Inn, and this view was the best afforded by anyone at the Inn. As she put the sushi on the table, she heard a guest from the room below, Monte or Kim, open the patio door. She leaned over the railing to see who it was. It was Kim. She could be friendly. Kind of.

"Hello, down there. Are you going to watch the sunset from your deck?"

Kim turned to look up. "Oh, hi. No, we're going to Mo's for dinner and then to bed. We need to get an early start tomorrow."

Annie heard a loud hiss from behind. She knew the hiss was for Monte. Tiger Lily had amazing restraint. She wasn't howling like a banshee.

Monte walked onto the balcony. He looked up but didn't say anything to Annie. Instead, he turned to look over the lake.

Annie kept eye contact with Kim. "By the way, did you go to the Winery today?"

"No, I haven't been yet. I think Monte was there today, weren't you, Monte?'

Monte grunted.

Kim looked at him, which meant that she looked at his back, then looked up to Annie. "Why do you ask?"

"Oh, I just wondered if you saw anyone there that you recognized. I had to take Sassy Pants to the vet today. It seems someone – a man – force fed sake to her, and she got alcohol poisoning. We were lucky, really. He was interrupted, so she didn't get as much as she could have, and her symptoms were recognized quickly."

"She's okay?"

"She's resting. She should recover."

"You aren't sure who did it?"

"No, but there are witnesses, and with their cooperation and the doctor's records, I plan to prosecute."

"Really? That's great. What would the charge be?"

"Animal cruelty. I understand, from our chief of police, that someone convicted of an offense as grave as the one committed on Sassy Pants could count on jail time, a hefty fine and a few hundred hours of community service."

"You don't say," said Kim. Then, with a voice directed up toward Annie but a message directed toward her brother, she said, "I hope you catch him."

"I believe we will. Hey, have a good evening."

Kim started to leave but turned back. "So, that's your apartment? Where you live?"

"Yes, the cats and I."

"I've not noticed any sounds from up there. Can you hear us down here?"

"No, only when we're both on the balcony. And generally, with the baffles on my balcony, you would rarely hear me unless I stand up and talk to you like this."

Monte turned and went inside. Kim looked up at Annie again, shook her head sadly and waved a hand as she went inside.

Chris served from the ceramic sake set, one hand still on Mr. Bean's back. The little boy did not release Chris from his grip. In a low voice, he said, "So that's where the cat abuser is staying?"

"Yep. We're keeping our enemies close this week."

"Good for you. I might lower Tiger Lily down there a little later and see if she can scratch his eyes out."

Tiger Lily purred and rubbed an ankle. To let Chris know how much she appreciated him, she lay down on top of his right foot, leaning against his ankle and shin. By now, Chris was used to the gesture. He relaxed until Mr. Bean jumped down to the floor, swiped at Tiger Lily with both paws, hissing and spitting. Tiger Lily didn't hiss back, just kept backing her head out of the way, until she finally turned and ran.

Mr. Bean jumped back to Chris's lap, turned around three times and curled into a ball.

After recovering from the shock, Chris, Annie and Mr. Bean spent a relaxing evening watching the storm roll over the Lake, getting closer to Chelsea by the minute.

The bikers walked to Mo's Tap. While they walked, Kim told Clark and Bryce about the incident at the winery. She turned on Monte.

"Don't deny it. It was you. Those witnesses will identify you, and we're all going to be run out of town on a rail. Except for you. You'll be in jail, and don't think I'll come bail you out. You can rot there!"

For all the times that they disagreed, the four realized they were the only family left to one another. Their fathers, brothers, founded a successful printing business, JaxCo. The business was still a going concern; three of the four maintained positions on the board of directors.

Monte and Kim's father, Franklin Jax, was the majority partner with fifty one percent of the stock. The father of Clark and Bryce, Charles Jax, held forty nine percent. In later years, each gave ten percent to two investors who also served on the board.

This left Franklin with forty one percent, Charles with thirty nine percent, and four nonfamily members with five percent each. If a significant disagreement arose, the solution would rest heavily on the four additional board members.

If two aligned with Franklin and two with Charles, Franklin's opinion would hold sway. If just one more went with Charles, leaving only one aligned with Franklin, Charles would have the majority of votes.

Franklin, Charles and their wives were killed in the crash of a private airplane nearly seven years previously. The cousins, "orphaned" in their early twenties, drew together for comfort. Kim, Clark and Bryce were able to get through the pain. It was not so easy for Monte, who had drug and alcohol issues since his teens. Indeed, his problems were significant enough that Franklin left all his shares in the company to Kim.

Monte received a modest financial inheritance and a trust fund that would supply him an income of at least $35,000 a year. He blew through his inheritance and found that $35,000 was not enough to maintain himself in the style to which he was accustomed.

Kim, Clark and Bryce graduated from college and had careers. Kim was a realtor; Clark and Bryce used a portion of their inheritance to open a sporting goods store. They managed the store in a manner that did not drain their inherited resources.

Close in age, the four had grown up in the same neighborhood and attended the same private school. Kim, Clark and Bryce attended the same college. For the most part, they saw eye to eye on the management of the printing company in which they were now the majority shareholders.

Kim alone held her father's forty one percent. Clark, the older of the brothers, held twenty percent and Bryce nineteen percent. The other board members, at five percent each, were Evan, Courtney, Ryan and Susan.

To date, the three had not had to sway individual board members to vote one way or another, as business had held steady. Now, however, the situation was changing.

Kim saw great advantage to purchasing an entrepreneurial company with a cutting edge resin printer. The young owners were receptive to the idea of selling the company to JaxCo. Clark and Bryce agreed with the concept of getting into resin printers, but instead, they wanted to take over another company with an established reputation. This company did not want new ownership, so any takeover would be hostile.

The trip to Chelsea, planned months ago, came in the middle of intense negotiations. Being cousins and lifelong friends, the three decided to go forward with the trip. Before leaving, however, they didn't let up on making their cases to the board.

In a two week period, Kim arranged private dinner parties with the individual board members and the young entrepreneurs, allowing them to sell each board member on the merits of their company. At the same time, Clark and Bryce put together an action plan for a hostile takeover and met individually with the board members to persuade them on the merits of their plan.

When Kim thought about it, she put the scorecard thus. Evan was firmly in her corner. He would vote her way no matter what he believed, because he intended to win her over and marry into the rich Jax family. She would let him down gently after the vote. If she loved him, she would not be so attracted to Ian.

Susan would vote with Bryce. Or Clark. Susan couldn't make up her mind which of the two was a better match and had decided to take the one that offered marriage first. She thought, wrongly, that both were interested.

Courtney and Ryan could go either way. Kim had to have the support of at least one of them. She was reasonably assured both of them would vote with Evan, but when she got home, she would have to touch base with them. Again.

Dinner was over; Kim sipped a beer and thought with half her mind about her plan. With the other half, she listened to her brother and cousins, for once getting along like they all used to do, talking about baseball one minute and the latest piece of exercise equipment the next. Part of her wished this would never end.

Evie sat in the all-season porch with a plate of sushi. She had selected two pieces of each kind, one for her and one for Valerie, who was…where was she? Evie didn't like hanging around in the main house. Not when she knew certain people were here.

She heard someone walking down the hallway toward the porch. She rose and walked outside and around the corner toward the carriage house, plate in hand. She stood outside, out of sight but in earshot, and heard two voices.

She looked around the corner carefully. It was Isabel, and the man with her must be her fiancé. She walked back in.

Isabel looked up. "Hi. Are you enjoying your stay?"

"Yes, and thanks for the suggestion about walking up the beach. We've walked there twice now. Today we climbed the rocks. That was, well, it was an experience."

At that moment, Valerie walked around the corner, coming to the porch straight from the carriage house. Evie couldn't read the look on her face.

As Valerie opened the door, she gave a brief wave to Isabel and Carlos and motioned to Evie to leave.

"But I have this plate of sushi."

"Can we take the plate with us?"

Carlos went to a cupboard and pulled out two disposable plastic plates. "Henrie doesn't want guests to know that he knows what a disposable plate is, so he keeps them hidden."

Carlos, using Evie's chopsticks, divided the sushi onto the two plates and handed them over, picking up another set of chopsticks for Valerie.

"Thanks!"

"Yes, thanks. Sorry we have to run."

They didn't run. They walked, eating sushi as they went and keeping an eye out for everyone walking on the street. They went into the first building past the carriage house, Sassy P's.

Valerie and Evie settled at a table sheltered by a flowering bush. They ordered a bottle of Sauvignon Blanc and asked for two menus.

It was mid-week. The afternoon rain and threatening storm kept locals at home, apparently, and few tourists were in the winery. They had the place practically to themselves with the exception of an older man, an older woman and a younger woman sitting together in the other corner.

This garden area was casual but elegant at the same time, with regular dining tables in the center and taller café tables around the edges. A second tasting bar was available, unused at the moment.

Potted plants, miniature trees and flowering shrubs were available in abundance, sitting around and near load-bearing beams, lending an air of privacy to most of the tables.

Only the section under the ceiling was in use tonight, as the rain made sitting closer to the edge a bit wet.

They ordered three small plates to share: Korean fried chicken, tofu in a hot bean chili sauce and mixed vegetable tempura. When the meal came, they would dig into dishes with their chopsticks, sharing each, family style.

Valerie leaned in. "Just before we left to come here, I saw a couple of things that disturbed me."

"What?"

"Did you notice that some things had been moved around while we were gone today?"

"I went straight to the shower. I didn't notice anything."

"I picked up some brochures, they'd gotten wet somehow and were on the floor. And I picked up your hairbrush and some of those chocolates."

"What?"

"I thought it was a sloppy maid or something, but just as I was leaving to meet you, I thought maybe I should check the bag."

"What bag?"

"THE bag."

"Oh. Was it there?"

"It was there, but someone had moved it."

"Who would have done that? What would anyone be doing under the bed?"

"I don't know."

"Do you think it was opened?"

"I couldn't tell."

"Maybe we need to stay in the room. It's obvious we can't go over for breakfast anymore. That's too bad. Henrie makes a killer breakfast."

"I know. I've given it some thought. We can run across the street to the grocery store first thing in the morning and get some things for meals. We can cook right there in the room."

"We should have thought about that earlier. We knew they would be coming. Now we risk running into them."

"We can be smart about it. They won't get up early, so we will."

"We have to get over to that marina before they do tomorrow, figure out where they're going."

"Do you really think they'll be able to go?"

"You know him. He does not accept the word 'no.' He'll find some way to go."

"Why don't we call the marina in the morning, try to find out what's going on."

"That's a better idea."

"Don't turn around!" Evie reacted to her friend's warning by staying perfectly still. Valerie, who still had a menu, put it in front of her face.

They waited until the people Valerie saw started to rearrange chairs. When they were sure they would not be seen, they got up quickly and left the garden dining room.

Collin and Celeste showered and changed after being drenched. Celeste chose yet another set of expensive jewelry, gold, with diamonds. Heavy bangle bracelets, three rings, dangling earrings, and a necklace with three strands of gold and diamonds, each a different length.

"Does this go with the outfit, Collin?"

"Hmm? Oh, certainly. You look lovely."

"Of course I do. Now let's talk again about that necklace. It can be the same design, but she can add a ruby where that large diamond would have gone, and then I can have her make another set of earrings, with both diamonds and rubies…"

"Celeste! Do you think I'm made of money? I'm an attorney! I'm not a Rockefeller!"

"You're the one that found the ruby ring! I have to have something that will match it! I'm already making a sacrifice. I'd chosen a platinum setting. Now it has to be gold."

"Do you have any idea…"

"Show me you love me. And I'll continue to make you happy."

Collin shoved his thoughts down his throat while they walked to the winery for dinner. Inside, he looked through the door into the back garden and saw her. That jeweler. And the antique guy, too, and maybe his wife. He led Celeste to their table.

Collin didn't even take time to say hello. To Gema, he said, "Apparently, I'm in luck. If you haven't started on that necklace, Celeste would like some changes."

Gema looked startled, then quickly regrouped. "That's fine. I've gathered materials together, but I haven't started the work. Collin, Celeste, let me introduce you to Mem." She turned to Mem. "This is the couple we told you about. They're staying at the Inn and they've ordered a beautiful diamond necklace. I believe they purchased an estate piece from Frank as well."

Turning to Collin and Celeste, she said, "Do you want to pull up a couple of chairs and join us?"

When they were seated, Gema asked, "What changes would you like to make, Celeste?"

"I don't know if I can describe it to you now, but I want to add a ruby, so it will match the vintage ring. And then, of course, I would like to add drop earrings that have both rubies and diamonds. I might need a bracelet."

"Oh, yes. It would be best if I showed you some examples, and we can go from there. Would you be able to come in tomorrow?"

"How early do you open? We're going out on the lake."

Mem put her mouth to her hand. "On the lake? Tomorrow? Who agreed to take you out in this weather?"

Collin made a face. "We had an agreement with the goofball that owns The Escape. We heard that was the best one in the area, but he backed out."

"He certainly backed out because of the weather," said Frank. "He has some experience being on that lake when the weather is less than optimal."

"It's just a little rain. Anyway, he returned the deposit, so we found another boat. Brad's something or other."

"Brad's Buoys & Gills?"

"That's the one."

"You may want to reconsider…"

"No. We're going. We came here to go fishing; we're going fishing. Anyway, about the jewelry…"

"Oh, sure. I'll be there by 8:00."

Clark and Bryce left Kim at Mo's Tap. She sat at the bar and talked to Ian and the bartender. Ian was a handsome guy. They figured she would try to hook up with him. There was a lot of fire in that cousin of theirs.

Monte had been another story. They should never have let him drink that sixth beer. Or the fifth. Perhaps they should have stopped him at the first, to be honest.

Clark and Bryce hoisted an arm each around their shoulders and half walked, half carried Monte to the Inn, dropping him into bed fully clothed. Seeing the view from the deck doors, they stepped out.

The sun had started its long, slow summer setting, reflected from behind the massive build-up of storm clouds. Lightning flashed miles in the distance. It was wild and beautiful.

Bryce said, "Wish we had this view from our room."

Clark responded with another train of thought. "I got some texts from Ryan tonight. He's not sure Courtney will vote with us. He's really leaning toward Kim."

"Why?"

"It seems he loves the idea of supporting young entrepreneurs."

"Well, that's a bummer."

"Yes it is. We need to get his vote."

"We could do it another way."

"How?"

"What happens to Kim's shares if she isn't around anymore?"

There was silence for a few seconds, then Clark answered. "You know, the problem is that the first thing that came to mind was that I should answer your question. Worrying about what you mean by that suggestion was only a second thought. So I guess I'm ready to talk about it."

Silence again. Then Bryce said, "So, do you know what happens to her shares?"

If she doesn't have a husband, and if she hasn't made a will, the shares come to us. That's the way Dad and Uncle Franklin wrote their wills."

"How much do you get, and how much comes to me?"

"They didn't want to play favorites. I have twenty; I'd get twenty. You have nineteen; you'd get twenty one. We would be equal shareholders."

Bryce said, "Huh. Anything can happen out on that trail."

"You're right. Anything."

"I was thinking that maybe Monte would help us. She's paying for this trip, but she's not giving him everything he wants. Like that bicycle. Maybe we could soften him up, take him shopping, get him that bicycle, and suggest how we might make life easier for him."

"He'll never go for it."

"What if he thinks the shares will go to him?"

The two men were silent for several minutes. Finally, Clark said, "Anything can happen on that trail."

After one last look at the light show, the two men went inside and across the hall to their own room.

They were unaware their conversation had been overheard. Annie and Chris, tired and needing to get up early, had gone in to bed. Mr. Bean went with them. Tiger Lily, Little Socks, Kali, Ko, and Mo remained on the deck to watch the light show. They heard every word.

Kim and Ian moved to one of the private settings at Mo's Tap. Sitting close to one another, they talked about themselves, getting to know one another. Ian wasn't what you would call promiscuous. He was a single man who was more commitment-phobic than his good friend, George. Being responsible for community events, the kind that brought in tourist traffic, allowed him to meet a variety of women. With whom he would always be honest. It wasn't his fault if they sometimes forgot after the first night or two.

Kim watched his eyes and his face as they talked. Animated, warm, intelligent, open. Something she hadn't had in a long time. She sometimes got lost in the conversation, thinking of her current relationship with Evan. It was a relationship of convenience. It started when she received the shares from the death of her parents. He was there. Always. Just there. Always. Always. She was smothering. But she couldn't do anything about it right now. She needed his vote, and she needed his presence to secure at least one, and it would be best if there were both, of the remaining votes.

But for this week, she was away from his ever-present weight. For this week, she would open up to this man, and she would enjoy herself.

By the end of the evening, she had moved on from her plan to enjoy his company for the week and was planning a wedding, maybe on a cruise boat in the middle of the lake....

13

Henrie made breakfast for a crowd. He had power food for the bikers and midwestern big breakfast food for everyone else. It was Thursday morning. The Chelsea Grand Prix was two days away, but the weather was a disaster.

Storm clouds. Wind, interspersed with high straight-line wind. Rain, sun, rain, sun, and more rain. Then sun. Rip current warnings for the beach. Storm warnings for watercraft.

Isabel appeared for breakfast early, hoping to have a word with Henrie. He sat with her as she ate and she filled him in on the conversations she was having with Carlos.

Henrie offered sympathy and promised to talk to Annie.

Henrie poured a to-go cup of coffee for Isabel. As he poured, the bikers came into the dining room. Henrie became aware that several cats were under the Seven Cats Detective Agency table. Hisses and low growls emanated, unusual behavior toward guests at the Inn.

Isabel heard the noises as well. She looked down at the table and noticed a tail — a Jack Russell terrier tail — sticking out from under the cover.

Isabel rose from the table and said, "Henrie, I saw a couple of carriers on the back porch, and a wagon. Would it be alright if I used them to take Mr. Bean and Tillie to the Confectionary? It will keep them dry."

At the mention of her name, Tillie poked her head out and looked hopefully at Henrie, then Isabel.

"Certainly." He looked down. "Children, go now. Do not make Isabel work to get you into the carriers."

Tillie came out from under the table and looked around. She didn't see Mr. Bean. Isabel called for him. He didn't come. Henrie looked under the table and counted little cat heads. He was not there. He stood and said to Isabel, "Please use a carrier to take Tillie. If the little boy is not already at work, please let me know."

Henrie poured coffee for the bikers. As he placed the pot back on the burner, he pulled his cellphone out of his pocket, ostensibly to answer a text. He turned and brought the phone to his eyes, looking for all the world like an elderly man with very bad vision trying to read the small print. Henrie pushed a button. No one noticed the small click, as he immediately said, "I will have to read this with my glasses." The cellphone went back into his pocket.

Kim asked, "Henrie, is the car available today? I thought we might go to a sporting goods store, look for a better bicycle for Monte."

Monte stared hard at Kim as Henrie answered in the affirmative. Clark and Bryce stared at her as well.

Bryce finally said, "You're kidding."

"It's a rough course. Ian and I talked about it last night. It's not fair. He needs a decent bicycle that will handle the course. It's my money, not yours, and you don't even have to come along."

Bryce looked at Clark. Clark turned to Kim. "No, we'll come along. Nothing else to do."

About a half hour after the bikers left and much later than he expected to see them, Henrie greeted Collin and Celeste. It seemed they came from the entry door, not the stairway. Yes, there were traces of "storm" on their clothing. Again, he offered coffee. Again, he poured.

As they filled their plates, Henrie rearranged platters, made a trip or two to refill condiments, and made a fresh pot of coffee. He noticed a designer yachting outfit for her, short shorts and a tiny but expensive tank top, a light summer sweater and three-inch stiletto sandals, designer yachting clothing for him, a light jacket that may or may not repel water and casual Docker sandals.

He went to the kitchen. He could not help but overhear their conversation.

"Really, Collin? Yesterday, you were happy to buy that necklace for me. But today? What happened?"

"We spent five thousand on the ring, and the necklace was going to be another three thousand. And now, with the changes you want, and the additional pieces, I'm going to spend nearly twelve thousand dollars! Come on, Celeste, I'm not made of money."

"Obviously. If you had money, we'd be in Tahiti, not the upper Midwest."

"Maybe this wasn't such a good idea, and maybe I'll just go back to that store and tell her not to make the jewelry. And tell that guy to put the ring back in the case."

"And maybe I'll call your wife and let her know where you really are this week."

"Then you'll never get anything from me. She would take it all, and then some."

Silence.

"Well, maybe I could do without the bracelet."

Silence.

"Let's stop one more time and make a final decision before we go to The Marina. When we get out on that lake, we'll feel a lot better."

"You might feel better. I'll feel like a drowned rat. That boat we were going to go on had a nice area out of the weather. What about this one?"

"You saw the picture. It looks nice. He isn't going to feed us, though, so I had the winery pack a few bottles of wine and some cheese, sausage and crackers. You can sit inside, read your book, and relax. You'll probably have a better time than me."

Henrie was ready to go to the dining room to offer umbrellas when he heard Celeste say, "Let's drive. It's too wet to walk. We can drive to this Brad's boat, too."

Henrie nearly tripped. Brad's? Brad's Buoys & Gills? She was in for a rude awakening.

His guests finished with breakfast and out the door, Henrie, in a very un-Henrie-like gesture, left the clean-up for a few minutes while he grabbed an umbrella and hurried to Sassy P's. He had a photograph to show Minnie.

Ray, dressed in a slicker, and Jock, soaking wet, stood on the pier. In front of them stood a man who didn't seem to care about the weather. Waves lashed at the pier, rendering the slickers useless. Ray wanted to get inside, but he had to deal with this yahoo.

"Brad, forget that I don't want you to use The Marina. You can't go out in this."

"You cain't tell me what tado, Ray."

"It's dangerous out there. Your boat can't handle that lake."

"I ain't gonna go out on the lake. I'm gonna go to the cove up the ways here and put in. They can caitch all the fish they want."

"How are you going to make it out of the harbor? And you risk going against the rocks in that cove."

"That don't worry me none. You and me is not the same. I'm not a chicken."

Ray closed his eyes and shook his head. He looked up and said, "You need to tell them the dangers."

"I need the money. I ain't tellin' 'em nothin'."

Ray turned on his heel and walked swiftly back to the office. Jock ran ahead, happy to get out of the wind and rain.

When they reached the office, Cheryl, Rays' wife and the owner of The Marina, said, "A couple of women called here asking about that charter."

"The one Brad is taking?"

"Yes. They called yesterday, and they called again this morning, asking if we knew if they got another boat."

"Why would they think…"

"They said this man was stubborn enough that he would find whomever he could to go out, just so he wouldn't be told he couldn't do something."

"You talked to both of them?"

"One talked, the other kept telling her what to say."

"Ex-wife."

"Wife, more like it."

"Really?"

"That's what it sounded like. I think this guy's 'wife,' the one he scheduled the fishing trip with, isn't really his wife. I think the one giving instructions to the woman who called is his wife."

"How could you tell?"

"Trust me, I could tell."

"Is she here in town?"

"I don't know. It was a cell phone."

"What did you tell her?"

"That Brad's rattletrap of a boat was sitting here in our harbor – I made a point to tell them he was here illegally – and it looked like he was going to pick some folks up. Told them he would probably set in somewhere close, not go out on the lake, just in case they were worried."

"Were they worried?"

"They laughed like the dickens."

Ray laughed. "I hope it's his wife, and I hope she's in town. That guy needs to learn a lesson or two."

Ray and Cheryl watched from the office as Collin and Celeste, dressed in designer yachting gear, boarded Brad's boat. Brad got it started and maneuvered away from The Marina, struggling against the waves.

Cheryl shook her head. "Forget about the danger. What do you think that woman is going to do now that she knows Brad's boat is filthy, smells like dead fish and leaks like a sieve?"

Ray chuckled and turned to change into dry clothes. "Before I forget, call Pete and put in a complaint. We need to get this one on file, too."

Annie entered the kitchen as Henrie put the last of the dishes away. He had changed clothes, his others getting drenched from his early morning run to see Minnie.

Annie carried Sassy Pants, who normally only allowed herself to be held for two seconds. Today, she was subdued and seemed happy to be carried.

"Did everyone come down for breakfast?"

"Not everyone. I didn't see the women from the carriage house today. How is the little darling this morning?"

"She's quiet, but awake."

Tiger Lily, Little Socks, Kali, Ko and Mo emerged from the Detective Agency. They wanted to check for themselves that Sassy Pants felt better. Sassy Pants reacted to their meows and squirmed to get down. Annie put her on the floor. "Kali and Ko, you keep an eye on her today. She'll be staying home with you."

Kali and Ko nodded gravely and nuzzled Sassy Pants into the library and toward their windowsill seats.

Annie turned back to Henrie. "I let Monte know last night that I know he did it. Without saying it."

"Good for you. I took a photograph this morning and showed it to Minnie. She said yes, Monte is the culprit."

"I'll have to decide whether to press charges. I should, but I don't want to do it while they're still here."

"Wise idea. We can talk to Pete but hold off until after the Grand Prix."

"So, the women didn't come down for breakfast? Maybe they didn't want to get out in the rain. And speaking of that, I'm going to get that covered wagon from Bloomin'

Crazy and take the rest of the cats to work. I'll do it now, before she needs it for our flower deliveries."

"Isabel took Tillie in a carrier, using the other wagon. I have not seen Mr. Bean this morning. And speaking of Isabel, she and Carlos have decided the best option is for him to go to Mexico."

"Go to Mexico? And do what?"

"Carlos believes he can appeal to the better nature of the, um, criminals involved."

"You've got to be kidding. Will she go with him?"

"No. The plan is for her to stay here, continue to work at Bon Vivant, and cover at the Confectionary while Carlos is away. She does not want to risk being unable to return."

"When will he leave?"

"He is checking flights today and will leave as soon as possible."

"I won't rest until he's back safe." Annie leaned against the counter. "Anything else I should know?"

"You should be aware the couple that Ray turned down is out on the lake as we speak with Brad's Buoys & Gills."

Annie laughed. Then she caught herself. "I shouldn't laugh. I should be afraid for their safety."

"But it is fun to think about the lovely time they will not have."

"You're right. What about the bikers?"

"The cats are safe for the time being. They took the car to look for a new bicycle for Monte."

"How nice for him. And how nice for us. I'll breathe easy, at least through lunch."

Henrie poured a last cup of coffee for himself. "Remember, the Inn will be full as of this evening. The wedding party and their guests will arrive late this afternoon."

Annie paused. "You haven't seen Mr. Bean this morning?"

"No."

"Neither have I."

Annie looked down at Tiger Lily. The big girl's face was inscrutable.

Valerie and Evie took turns watching from their upstairs window. They experienced some confusion when the couple got into Collin's car and drove east, toward town.

They waited and were soon rewarded by seeing the car come back down the street. It went past the Inn and through the public parking lot toward The Marina.

Valerie and Evie dressed carefully that morning. They would get wet. Very wet. The weather was a combination of warm muggy heat, rain, and winds that would chill them.

Their bags were packed with water and easy-to-eat foods: energy bars, chopped fresh veggies, blueberries and strawberries. And three additional items.

While Evie took one of her turns on window-watch, Valerie drug the red bag from under the bed and selected the items to add to their bags.

Now, their prey was on the way to a boat and a really bad day.

"Ready?"

"Let's go."

At the entrance to the state park, Evie paid their entrance fees while Valerie researched the maps and brochures.

"Here," she said. "They have a map of the walking trails. Let's take a look before we go out in the rain."

They sat at a table in the park's reception area and spread out the map. Valerie's finger traced a trail that went toward the lake in a curving and winding fashion. At one point, the trail went very close to the lake.

The topographical information was light. They couldn't tell the elevation of the trail or if rocks were present on the outer edge. They could, however, see the lake's inlet.

"This is it. I'll bet we can tell when we get there."

"Yeah. That guy talked about tree roots and how thick the branches were, and it was right in between two curves, just like this shows."

"Let's go."

14

When Annie dropped the cats off at their places, she stopped first at Sassy P's, pulling the wagon in with all of the cats. "Stay in there. I'll just be a minute."

Annie told Minnie about the little girl, that she was feeling much better. "And I'm going to wait until the bikers are gone before making a decision about Monte. I doubt he'll come back in here, at any rate. I as much as told him I knew it was him."

At Mr. Bean's, she pulled the wagon in again. Tillie and Mr. Bean were in the window. "Where were you this morning, little guy?"

Mr. Bean came halfway to Annie, then stopped. He hissed at Tiger Lily when she popped her head out of the wagon. Tiger Lily hissed back.

"What's going on, kids?" Isabel came to the counter. Annie turned her attention in that direction. "Well?"

"He's taking care of a few things now. He got a ticket for tomorrow morning."

Annie stood, looking at Isabel for a long moment. "It will be okay, Isabel. It will."

"I pray so. Hey, Annie, Mr. Bean came over by himself this morning, in the rain. Is everything okay? The rest of the cats were still home..."

"I don't know." Annie reached down to pick up the little guy, who was not dancing, not smiling. She looked into his eyes, felt his nose, felt around his body. Everything seemed to be in place. "If you aren't feeling better this evening, little guy, we're going to go see Dr. Ralph."

Mr. Bean made no attempt to smile, snuggle or get down. Annie put him on the floor again. "Call me if you notice anything."

Tiger Lily hissed one more time as they left, and Annie hissed back. That startled the big girl, and she pulled her head back in.

She dropped Mo at the bar, dropped Little Socks at the yoga studio, and pulled the wagon into the Café.

The Café was filled with bored bikers. All had come to town early to walk, drive and ride the route. The area B&Bs, hotels and motels were filled with bikers. The streets, on any other day, would have been filled with bicycles.

Today, however, the streets were filled with bikers without a cause. They walked around town wearing slickers or trash bags with holes cut in for faces and arms. Rain boots were rarely in their luggage, so for the most part they wore sneakers. Sodden, sloppy wet sneakers.

Ian walked around the Café, drinking coffee and talking to as many of the bikers as he could. He was thankful for the rainy day. He needed a day of rest, and he enjoyed being able to meet the people who would participate in the Grand Prix. Several had done the cruise before; they were more than happy to share with Ian the positives and negatives of the course.

Ian kept an eye out for Kim, but she didn't appear at the Café this morning.

Annie worked at the coffee bar; Trudie helped servers on the floor. Tiger Lily was in her glory. She loved a crowded Café. That meant that people had to stand in line to wait for a table, and while they did, they usually gave her pets and told her how pretty she was.

Tiger Lily's friends were here today, as well. Cyril and Jock rested behind the hostess stand while Pete and Ray had lunch.

Tiger Lily turned her back to the Café for a while to talk to the boys. *"What's happening in town? It's too wet for us to get around and talk to anyone."*

Cyril yawned. *"Nothing is going on. You'd think, with all these bikers, we'd have a lot of business. Fights, petty thievery, fender benders. Nope. Nothing. Boring, boring."*

Jock had a different story. *"You know that couple staying at the Inn? The man and woman?"*

"Yes. They wanted to go fishing. We heard Ray wouldn't take them."

"He didn't, but they got a goofball named Brad to take them out. They're on the lake in this mess."

"Brad? Brad's Buoys & Gills is just a guy named Brad? It's not a…a shop or a fleet or…you know…more than just a Brad?"

"Just a Brad, and his boat is a disaster. Cheryl said it smells like dead fish and leaks like a sieve."

Tiger Lily laughed. *"The woman is kind of prissy. I don't think she's going to like it."*

"She's real prissy. And he tries to pretend he's a big shot. I hope they don't catch anything but pneumonia. Just so you know, Cheryl thinks the guy is married to someone else, and she thinks that woman might be in town."

"Really? Where is she staying?"

"I don't know. Wouldn't it be funny if she was at the Inn, too?"

"I think I'd know if she was. Oh, I should tell you about the bikers."

"What bikers?"

"Four bikers are staying at the Inn. One of them pushed me to the floor. And then he scared Mr. Bean and Tillie. The worst thing, though, is that he forced Sassy Pants to drink sake, that strong stuff at Sassy P's. She nearly died."

"No!" Cyril and Jock were on their feet, looking around at the bikers.

"They aren't in here. The guy pushed me in here, and I think they're embarrassed to come back. But if anyone is going to commit murder this week, it's probably them."

"Murder of cats or people?"

"People. Well, a person. They were talking about something I didn't really understand last night. Two of the men. It sounded like they had some kind of problem with the woman, something about votes and sharing, and they thought they might get the mean one to help them. His name is Monte. They said 'anything can happen on that trail,' like they might ask Monte to hurt her or something."

Cyril stomped his front foot. *"Why didn't you say something as soon as we got here?"*

Tiger Lily was a little embarrassed she had not thought to tell Cyril right away. She answered defensively, *"I was greeting my guests! Anyway, I've told you now. I don't know if there is anything you could do about it."*

"*You're probably right. You need to point them out to me, at least.*"

"*Me, too,*" added Jock. "*I'm not doing anything this week, not until the rain stops. I can help.*"

"*They left the Inn today in the car. The woman, her name is Kim, is going to buy Monte a new bicycle. I don't know when they will get back to town.*"

"*Well, if we're around when they are, point them out. What about the other guests? Your guests are always good for a little excitement.*"

"*I think that's about all. The goofy couple, the mean bikers, and a couple of women that go to the beach all the time. And Isabel. But I don't consider her a guest. She and Carlos have some kind of a problem, and he'll go to Mexico to fix it.*"

"*What kind of problem?*"

"*Something about his family. They can't come here to live because some bad people don't want them to go. I don't understand it. If you want to go somewhere, you should just go, and if they don't want you to go, you go anyway.*"

"*What does Mr. Bean say about it? Carlos probably said something.*"

Tiger Lily gave an offhand reply. "*Nothing.*"

Annie stopped at the hostess stand on her way out. The Café was still full. "I'm going to the library to do some research. I'll be back to take you home in the covered wagon. Take some time to consider your behavior before we get home today."

Annie left, holding an umbrella and her bag with her laptop and supplies. She had enough information about Lake Scott, and she had no more excuses.

She headed for the genealogy section first. She located the librarian in charge of the section. "I hope you can get some information from my home library. If I give you the names I know, and some dates or time frames, would you be able to pass it on?"

"I can try. Where is your hometown?"

Annie gave him the information. It was a small community in another state. If she were to go there, the drive would take several hours.

"They could be small enough not to have a genealogy section, but they probably have librarians skilled in research. Now, what are those names?"

"The last name is Mayes. The man I want to learn about is Darrell Mayes."

Annie gave him the dates she was given by her mother: his date of birth, the year he graduated from high school in her home town, the year he graduated from the same college her father attended, the date, place and manner of death.

"I have the names of his parents here. All I know about them is that the father died in the late 1970s and the mother in the early 1980s. They still lived in my hometown when they died, so hopefully the library – or someone – will have information."

"Can you tell me anything else?"

"Yes. Darrell was one quarter Cherokee. His father was one half Cherokee. They moved from his father's hometown just before Darrell was born, somewhere in Arkansas."

"You might be in luck. I'll find what I can from the library in your hometown, but in the meantime, you can use one of the library's computers to search the Cherokee ancestry site. It's well-maintained. Once we get some basic information, you might find everything you need there."

"Great. How about learning, you know, the history of the Cherokee nation?"

"We have books, and you can start with a simple computer search. Do you need help with that?"

"No, thank you. I supposed I can just Google the Cherokee site?"

"That would be the easiest."

"Thank you. I'm going to start with the history."

"Annie, might I ask who this man is to you?"

Annie told a partial truth. "He was a friend of both my parents. His children know nothing about his background, and Mom wanted to do something about that. But, you know, she's my mom. She didn't have a clue where to start."

Annie moved to the computer section, sat down and logged on.

She learned more than she could imagine, and she marveled that the education system left so much out of the history books. As it was, she skipped around, making note of some specifics but not – yet – really digging into the history. That would come later, when she knew where to focus.

Annie learned that much of what is known about pre-18th-century Native Americans comes from records of Spanish expeditions; contact with the Cherokee was noted in the 1540s. She found two main theories of Cherokee origins. In one theory, the Cherokee migrated to Southern Appalachia – in areas that would become Georgia, North Carolina, South Carolina and Tennessee – in late prehistoric times from the north. Another theory is that the Cherokee had been in the Appalachian region for thousands of years.

Late nineteenth century researchers recorded oral traditions with the help of tribal elders. Those traditions tell how the Cherokee migrated to Appalachia from the Great Lakes region in ancient times.

Huh, thought Annie. In a sense, perhaps the Cherokee have now come home.

During the French and Indian War in the 1750s and 60s, the Cherokee sided with the British. At the start of the Revolutionary War, in 1776, the Cherokee sided with the British again, but they also engaged settlers on their own. The Cherokee-American Wars were fought, off and on, small-scale and large-scale, until the 1790s, ending with the signing of the Treaty of Greenville. This treaty established the system of annual gifts of money and supplies to Native Americans. So began the institutionalized influence and control of government over the tribes.

From this time on, the government bought and stole land from the Cherokee. In Georgia alone, eight lotteries were held between 1805 and 1833 to distribute land seized from the Cherokee. In the 1820s, well before the forced migrations, tired of the continual loss of land, a group of Cherokee migrated to Indian Territory, to what is now Arkansas.

Gold was discovered in the Cherokee Nation in the 1830s. This was the straw that broke the camel's back. The government pushed to remove all Cherokee from their land in Appalachia. The removal to Indian Territory was an eight-hundred-mile journey undertaken during the winter of 1838-39. It became known as the "Trail of Tears." One fourth of the Cherokee tribe died during the journey.

Annie made notes to herself to continue research on the Trail of Tears when she had more energy. She knew enough about this subject to know the literature would be hard to get through. Honestly, the things that were done to these proud people were worse than repugnant.

At the end of the Trail of Tears, the Cherokee joined with the "old settlers" who had gone to Arkansas earlier, no longer a territory but a state. In the 1850s, the Drennen Roll was created. The roll contained names of Cherokee emigrants who were forced to move from the Cherokee Nation and the Old Settlers who moved voluntarily before the removal. Annie was heartened to know there may be a path for research, just as the librarian had stated.

Now residents of a southern state, some Cherokee were slave owners. Many enlisted in the Confederate Army; others joined the Union Army. In other words, thought Annie, they were much like other families during that period of time, divided by a few miles, temperament or political persuasion, and fighting to kill one another.

In the 1890s, President Cleveland appointed a commission, commonly called the Dawes Commission, to negotiate land ownership. In return for abolishing their tribal governments and recognizing federal laws, tribal members were entitled to apply for an allotment of land. The list of Cherokee who were finally accepted as eligible became known colloquially as the Dawes Rolls.

To put another spin on the ability for Cherokee to hold land privately, in order to do this, the Cherokee had to give up land that the tribe already owned communally. The topper was that the government would decide who was eligible to own land. And it might not be them.

Annie's research then led her to the Henderson Roll, a list of close to two thousand persons of the Cherokee Nation in North Carolina, Tennessee, Alabama and Georgia.

Annie finally sat back. What did she have, really? She knew more than ever before about the Cherokee Nation and public policy regarding native tribes in general. She had a lot of notes of items that would have to be researched to a greater degree: the Trail of Tears, the Drennen Roll, the Dawes Rolls, and the Henderson Roll.

She could do this, but she would put it away for now and wait until the librarian gave her additional information about Darrell's parents.

Annie was emotionally exhausted. She walked slowly toward the library entrance, paying little attention to her surroundings and unable to turn off the thoughts running through her head. Sassy Pants, her natural father's ancestry, the Trail of Tears and the horrors that surrounded that winter's journey.

She almost ran into Geraldine.

Annie stopped short of stepping on Geraldine's foot. Geraldine stood at the desk of the genealogist. "I see you are looking up Indian ancestry. Is this a personal search?"

"It's a search that I am making. Personally. Have a good day, Geraldine."

Annie moved on, unable to keep from hearing Geraldine's words to the genealogist. "So, the golden girl is hiding a secret from us."

Too late, Annie remembered the genealogist was married to Geraldine's sister. Rats.

Outside, Annie pulled out her cellphone to call Jenny. When Jenny came on the line, Annie told her of the most recent contact with Geraldine.

"I can't keep her from going to the library, Annie."

"I know, but can you do something? I don't know, something about forcing her to live up to the spirit of the restraining order as well as the geographical confines?"

"I don't think there is anything I can do, but I'll put through a motion, at the very least, on your established volunteer activities. And I'll mention today's incident. It will probably go nowhere, but the record will contain this attempt to invade your privacy."

Valerie and Evie crept from the state park to the rocky ledge overlooking the cove. They were in luck. A boat was there, anchored, barely maintaining itself above water.

Valerie crept closer. With the wind, she probably didn't need to whisper, but she didn't want to assume the wind wouldn't take her voice downhill. She kept her voice low.

"This can't be them. The boat's a rattrap. He wouldn't be caught dead in it, and she wouldn't be caught dead within fifty yards."

"That woman said it was awful. Let me see."

Evie kept low and crept close. She started to laugh so hard, Valerie worried she would choke. When she got her voice under control, she said, "It's them! It's them! This is too good to be true!"

Valerie pulled the bag out from under her jacket. "Here. Hold the umbrella so we can keep them dry."

She worked with the items, put them in her pocket, nodded to Evie, and stood. Evie held the umbrella over Valerie's head, moving back as she nodded, then back in. One. Two. Three times. Valerie had perfect aim.

15

Henrie's afternoon guests arrived in the middle of a downpour. Kali and Ko announced their presence with a loud yowl – one each – at the front door. They could sense new people, new luggage and an air of excitement. Henrie got to the front door just as the wedding party opened it.

"Good afternoon. Welcome to the KaliKo Inn."

And thus began yet another welcome and tour.

The happy couple introduced themselves as Grant and Erika. They were drenched, having apparently strolled from their vehicle without an umbrella. Henrie couldn't help but laugh with them as they shook their bodies and wiped water from their clothing. He was thankful they did that on the front porch rather than inside the house.

Their friends, introduced as Tom and Denise, were in the same jovial mood. Denise said, "This is a great camera. It will stand all of this rain and more. I got some great video even though it's gray and wet out there."

"Did you get those women?"

"Yes, I did. They looked so happy, I couldn't help but take a video of them."

Grant asked, "What women?"

"Oh, two women crossing the street. It looked like they were going into that carriage house back there. They laughed and danced all the way. They were soggy wet and splashing through puddles."

"Like us?"

"Happier, even, if that's possible."

Thank goodness, thought Henrie. This group will make an excellent counterpoint for the bikers. What he said, was, "They were most certainly guests of the Inn. I am sure you will meet."

Henrie settled Tom and Denise in their room first. They were going to be in the back room, second floor, in the main house. Their balcony overlooked the state park's south side, and if they turned their chairs, they had a decent view of the lake and the sunset. If they didn't mind watching in the rain.

All four guests went to the carriage house as Henrie rolled the luggage cart, covered with a light tarp to keep the rain off. The guests still did not bother to cover themselves. Henrie donned a raincoat with a hood.

Denise's camera was out. She videoed the honeymoon suite for posterity. The accommodations were sumptuous, with a king-sized bed, cozy sitting area, full kitchenette and oversized bathroom. A walk-out deck had a hot tub large enough for four people. The deck was enclosed by a six-foot privacy fence.

While Henrie was outside, Kali, sleeping under a chair in the foyer, and Ko, sleeping under another chair with Sassy Pants curled into her side, heard the bikers come onto the front porch. They came alert but didn't move. The bikers did something on the porch. It sounded like they were putting another bicycle into the rack.

Kali took the time to sneak to the chair under which Ko lay, watchful and silent. She lay down so that Sassy Pants was sheltered between them. *"They must have gotten that bicycle."*

"Yeah. Like the guy deserved a present."

Then the four were inside. Kim wanted to get out of her wet clothes. She went directly upstairs. Monte, Clark and Bryce got coffee and sat in the foyer. Kali, Ko and Sassy Pants had a moment of horror when Monte sat on the chair underneath which they hid. He didn't seem to notice them. Clark and Bryce sat facing him and the second floor balcony. From time to time they looked up to assure Kim did not hear the conversation.

"So, like we said, we want to talk to you, and we didn't want to do it in front of Kim."

Monte looked at his cousins with suspicion. "So, what is it you want to talk about?"

Clarke started in a low voice. "Forget for a minute that you have the bicycle you've been wanting for months. Forget that you're here, all expenses paid."

Bryce chimed in. "Yeah. Instead, think about what it costs you. You have to beg for everything, kowtow to her every wish. You give up your dignity. She treats you like a little girl."

"A little girl. Isn't that how it feels? All the time?"

Monte said nothing. He continued to look at his cousins. Almost thirty seconds passed in silence.

"We want to make you a deal."

"What kind of deal?"

"We need to win a vote, and it doesn't look like we're going to get the job done. We need more."

"What do you mean, more?"

"We need Kim to change her mind, and she's not going to do that. In fact," Clark warmed to his subject but kept his voice low, leaning in to make his point, "she is going to take the entire company under if we don't stop it."

Bryce joined in. "That means no more money, not for us, not for Kim. Even the peanuts she throws your way will dry up."

"So what do you want me to do? She won't listen to me. If I tell her she's making a bad decision, she'll just tell me I don't know what I'm talking about. And for once she'd be right. I don't have a clue what you're talking about. I had no idea the company was in trouble."

"It's not in trouble now. It will be left behind if we don't modernize, and the way she wants to modernize will kill us."

"So, again, what do you want me to do?"

Bryce and Clark looked at one another, then back at Monte. They both leaned in. Bryce said, in a low whisper, "You know that place on the trail, at the tip of Lake Scott, where there's a sharp curve and a long way to fall?"

"Yeah. I know it. What about it?"

Bryce and Monte, still leaning in, looked at one another and back to Monte.

"We need you to, you know, do something that makes her get too close to the edge during the grand prix, and then you can, you know, help her over."

"Help her over? You mean push her over. She'd die!"

"That's the point."

"You want me to kill my sister? Your cousin? Over money? On Saturday?"

"Lots of money. Remember, she owns the most shares. Even if the two of us put our shares together, she can overrule us."

"Yeah. Where do you think those shares will go? Huh? When she's gone? Who do you think gets them, and the money that comes along with them?"

"Well, I'm her brother, so I guess I get them."

"That would be a good guess."

Monte shook his head. "You guys are something else, you know that?"

"Will you at least think about it?"

"What's there to think about? I'm not going to hurt my sister."

"Remember that car you said you wanted? Didn't she go buy one for herself after you pointed out how great it was?"

"And that trip to Greece. All you had to do was say you wanted to go, and where was she the next month?"

"And how often have you had to ask her for money to take a woman on a magical weekend trip? And how often did she actually come through for you?"

"When are you going to stand up and demand what's yours?"

"At least think about it."

Clark and Bryce, backs to the door, turned to look at Henrie as he came in, shaking off water and rolling a luggage cart. When they turned back, Monte was already up and halfway to the stairs.

As the rain poured down, Ian and the teens gathered in the community building at the town park. If they couldn't ride today, they were still going to work out.

He had given Brendan a routine to do on his own this morning, and he knew the young man had followed through. Ian not only threatened to call parents, he actually called them. Brendan's mother confirmed that morning that he was in the basement using their gymnastic equipment to do the required exercises. "And he's pretty vocal about not liking it...or you."

Ian didn't have access to that equipment, so the kids were doing laps. A lot of laps.

They were running too hard to talk during the hour they had together, but by the time they left for home, most were muttering unkind things under their breath.

16

Isabel and Annie met at the Confectionary, Annie pulling Tiger Lily, Little Socks and Mo in the covered wagon and Isabel with Mr. Bean and Tillie.

"Stop at the winery with me. We'll have a glass of wine to end this soggy afternoon."

Isabel was happy to accept. Inside Sassy P's, two cats and a little dog jumped out and ran around in circles for several seconds, unsure where to go to have the most fun. They finally decided on the back garden dining area, close to the edge, dangerously near the raindrops.

Annie and Isabel sat at a café table. Mr. Bean pawed Annie's leg until she reached down to pick him up. She put him on top of the table and he sat, head down, facing Annie and Isabel. He looked down and to his left at the floor. Tiger Lily sat, looking up. He hissed. She licked her lips and moved just a little. He moved closer to the other edge of the table.

Tiger Lily readied herself and made the jump to the tall table, stopping herself before she barreled into Mr. Bean. They sat, looking at one another. Tiger Lily leaned over and licked his left ear. She leaned back. Mr. Bean looked at her, then turned his head slightly, and she leaned in to lick his right ear. Eventually, the two lay in a pile, moving around until they were curled into one another. The little boy took several deep breaths and allowed himself to go to sleep while the big girl licked his forehead.

As Annie, Isabel and Minnie watched, mesmerized, Annie gave a sign for two (glasses) and mouthed "special."

When Minnie brought the glasses, Annie spoke softly, so as not to interrupt her no-longer-quarreling children.

"Do you think this is the wisest course of action?"

"I think he's right. There is no way around it except for him to approach it head on. Maybe, if it comes down to it, he can buy their way out."

"That can't be legal."

"It's not, but it's reality. He won't make the offer at first. He'll see if he can reason with them, and if not, just follow his heart. He will not approach his mother and sisters until he has secured their safe passage. Then, if he secures it, he will go to his mother's home, pack up the van he'll rent at the border, and drive back to the border. That will be the dangerous time. The time that they are still in Mexico, driving, giving those criminals time to think about it."

"What if he doesn't succeed?"

"I think the worst could be that they demand more money from him every month to keep his mother safe. I will gladly give up some luxuries – things that you in America think are necessities – for their safety."

"I asked George to drive Carlos to the airport tomorrow morning. Henrie will be in the middle of breakfast, but George doesn't have to be at Mo's that early. Let him know if you want to ride along."

"Thank you, Annie. I suppose I have to start thinking about the wonderful possibility that we need to find someplace for Daniela and the girls to stay. Daniela can probably stay with Henrie, and if it's alright with you, we can sleep three to a bed and the girls can stay in my room."

"We'll find a place for them. If all goes as you plan, we will probably have another room or two available, perhaps even the upstairs to the carriage house. Don't worry about that."

Annie's cell phone rang. She looked. It was Chris. She answered.

"Sorry about dinner, Annie, I have to go out."

"In this weather? Well, I guess that's typical. What's up?"

"One of the worst captains in town, with probably the worst boat in town, didn't make it back to The Marina as planned, and Cheryl can't raise them on the radio."

Annie got a cold feeling in the pit of her stomach.

"Brad's Buoys & Gills?"

"That's it. How did you know?"

"Two of my guests are on that boat."

Kim waited in her room for Ian to call. They had enjoyed one another's company last night. So much, in fact, that she did not return to her room until shortly before breakfast. She was sure he would call.

She begged off when Clark called about dinner, saying she had "things to do." By 8:00, she grabbed her cell phone and went to Sassy P's, looking for wine and company. Or only wine. Or maybe company. She wasn't sure.

She found...Ian. She heard that laugh in the back of the room. She looked around the corner and saw him with that woman who ran the yoga place. At least, that was who it looked like. They appeared to enjoy one another's company immensely.

She turned, stood at the far end of the bar, purchased a bottle of wine and returned to her room, brushing past two women she'd seen before.

Inside the door, door closed, Valerie and Evie looked at one another and said, at the same time, and in the same dramatic flair, "Well, excuse me!" They laughed. Stopped. Looked at one another. Laughed again.

When they were seated, they asked for a table in the back corner of the room, "behind that potted bush, please." They positioned themselves so Valerie could see into the room. "Seriously, I don't think we'll see them. I got that propeller. That boat won't get in until someone finds it!"

Evie, suddenly subdued, said, "Do you think they'll be alright?"

"Of course. That cove is pretty sheltered. Even if the boat doesn't make it – did you SEE that thing? – they were close to that rocky shore on three sides. He can swim, right?"

"Well, yes.... Let's not talk about them. Did you call your friend?"

"I did. Your appointment is confirmed for 9:00 Monday morning. That will give you time to get the kids off to Bible School. Then your appointment. And then we're having lunch. We're going to celebrate!"

"Thank you again, Val, for everything. For this time, for paying the attorney..."

"You'll pay me back for that attorney. You're going to be a rich woman. Well, not rich, but comfortable. He's going to have to pay for your home, everything for those kids, including college, and he's going to have to give you an allowance, and let's not even discuss that 401K. You're getting half. At least. And the rest of those assets that he squirreled away. My friend will be able to find them. Trust me."

They heard laughter from a table behind. Valerie turned. An attractive young man and woman sat at a café table. They looked like a couple, but then they didn't, as two other women joined them. Women from the Café. Now it looked like four friends. Just friends.

Evie looked in their direction, wistfully. "That's what I want."

"What's that?"

"A man who will just be a good friend. I've never had that. I left college and found me a man that would be my master. I want a friend."

"You'll have one, my friend. You'll have ten. Starting Monday morning."

Clark and Bryce borrowed the Inn's car and drove to Marsh Haven, pulling Monte into the car with them. "Come on. We need to discuss this in private."

Monte's facial expressions and his silence were unreadable on the drive. At a bar in a seedy part of town, they sat in a back booth and ordered beer and burgers. After the server delivered the beer, Clark started to say something. Monte stopped him. "I'm in."

"What?"

"I'm in. I been thinkin'. You're right. All I get are crumbs, and I'm worth more than that. I'll get all those shares, so that will make me your boss. Only I don't wanna be the boss, okay? I'll have all the shares, and I'll only come to meetings when you tell me you have to have my vote, and I'll vote the way you want. You just make sure your accountants or your whoevers give me a check every week, or every month. That's all I want. I'll leave you alone."

Clark and Bryce looked at one another, then back at Monte. Bryce raised his beer. "Anything can happen on that trail." Clark responded with, "To the tip of Lake Scott."

17

Unaware of the drama involving the Coast Guard and two missing guests, the wedding party, in dry-ish clothes, at least for a minute, walked The Avenue in the rain.

As they walked up one side, then down the other, Denise kept her camera in hand. She was the designated photographer, after all, and she planned to film everything.

From the north side of The Avenue, she would film the south, from the south side, the north. As they walked past each storefront, she would aim the camera through the windows and catch what she could.

They started, of course, at the Inn. Denise stopped first in the median and turned to get a video. She caught a picture of the women she had seen before. They were on the second floor of the carriage house, looking out. Her eyes met the eyes of one of the women. She smiled, waved, and moved away from the window.

They started to walk again; Denise got a long view of the north side of the street, catching the name of each storefront. They crossed to that side and walked to each one, aiming the camera through each window. On occasion they caught sight of a customer or someone working in the store and they waved, to get a wave in return on the video.

At Bloomin' Crazy, they stopped just before the shop closed for the day. Clara, always happy to be on camera, posed. "You must be crazy, taking video of a soggy wet town. I'm getting ready to close, but if there's something you need, I'll help you."

Grant said, "We ordered flowers for our wedding this weekend. The moonlight wedding on The Escape?"

"Oh, that's you? Let me show you what I'm working on."

Clara took the group to her work area in back.

"You know that Ray painted his boat a couple of months ago? Rainbow colors?"

"Yes, we've seen the pictures."

"Well, since you didn't have a theme, I went with the boat."

Clara showed the group the flowers in the glass-fronted refrigerators. Every possible color in a variety of flowers.

Erika held her hands to her breasts and sighed. "Denise, get a picture of these, please." She turned to Clara. "I don't care how these get put together. It's going to be beautiful!"

The group moved on until they got to Soul's Harbor. Grant looked at his watch. "It's still early. Let's go across the street and get some supper. We have time."

Denise took a long shot of the south side, and they crossed over. She focused on the window going into the Café. "Wow. This is nice. Lunch here tomorrow."

"We're going to eat there tomorrow night. It's fine dining on Friday and Saturday night."

"We can still eat lunch here."

"Or at the winery."

"If we eat at the winery, we'll start drinking."

"And the problem would be?"

By now the group was in front of the yoga studio, closed for the day. They could still see inside and noticed bright silhouettes of women in yoga poses, a mirrored wall, orange accents, and a curious thing, black pillows on the windowsills.

Erika said, "I hope they're open tomorrow. I want to go in and ask what the pillows are for."

They got to Mo's Tap but Denise said, "Before we go in, let me just finish taking this video."

She went quickly down the sidewalk, filming inside Mr. Bean's, now closed, and the Winery, still open.

When she got back to the group, she said, "Okay. We'll have dinner here, but we have to stop in for a bottle of wine on our way back to the Inn."

Erika said, "Hey, don't forget, we have a counseling session with Pastor Teresa before we can go to the winery."

Grant looked at Erika. "Maybe we can ask her to go to the winery with us."

They laughed and entered Mo's for dinner. This was going to be a great weekend!

Annie and Cheryl sat at the radio console, coffee cups in hand, staring out the window into the darkness. This was the week of the summer solstice, and it stayed light into the night. Tonight, though, the sun had been obscured by clouds, just beginning to break up. They could still see the tall, white lighthouse and hear the waves break against it, but barely.

Cheryl said, "At least we're going to have a break in the rain."

"Yeah. The wind will still be with us, though, and the rip currents."

Ray walked into the room. "Anything yet?"

"No, no word since they said they found them."

"How bad will it be, Ray?"

Ray didn't want to worry Annie, but he didn't want to lie to her, either. "It's rough out there, and Chris found them in that cove, right where I told him they would be. It's surrounded by rocks. They can't get the Coast Guard boat in there; they'll be going in with a smaller boat. That will be easier to manage, in close quarters, but they have to get those idiots off the boat and onto the smaller one. Then off the smaller one onto the cutter."

"I have to charge for and pay an innkeeper's tax. Is there an equivalent idiot's tax we can be charging?"

"Only in our dreams."

The radio came to life. They could hear Chris reporting to the Coast Guard station. All were onboard, all safe, and they were on their way home. Then they heard, "Call Pete and ask him to meet us at the Station. These folks were the victims of an attack."

"Oh, boy. Once again, my guests are victims of a crime. I'll bet someone was after Brad, and they just got caught in the middle."

Cheryl looked at Ray, then Annie. "I'm not so sure that's the case, Annie."

"What?"

"This morning a couple of women called asking about this couple. I'm positive one of the women is his wife, and this guy is off on an affair."

Annie just stared at Cheryl. Then they both burst out laughing. Finally, Annie was able to say, "He sure knows how to show a woman a good time."

18

Pete left Brad in the main room of The Marina, covered in a blanket, while he talked to Collin and Celeste in Ray's office. "I have to ask you the same questions I'm going to ask Brad. Who do you know that would want to harm, injure or even kill you?"

Collin took the lead. "No one. We're just here on vacation." Celeste nodded in agreement.

"Tell me where you're from. Let's see, it's Collin and Celeste Curtis, correct?"

"Yes, sir. We're from…." Collin told Pete the name of the small town where he lived. "I'm an attorney…" He gave Pete the name of his firm. "I do mostly corporate and civil law, but in a small town, as you probably know, we all do a little bit of everything. I get the occasional criminal case, but nothing major."

"Can you think of anyone or anything connected to your law firm that could lead to this?"

"No, sir. I just can't. Honestly, I think someone has to be after that man that claims to have a boat for hire. That's a monstrosity. If we could have seen clearly this morning – if it hadn't been raining – we never would have gotten on it."

"Did you board here, at The Marina?"

"Yes."

"Did you ask him to meet you here, or did he, Brad, make those arrangements?"

"He told us to come here. I remember, because we already knew this place, so we didn't have to ask for directions."

"And you're staying at the KaliKo Inn. Have you seen anyone you know, or have you met anyone that stands out to you?"

"No one I know, and really, we've only met the people at the Inn and at that antique and jewelry place. Spent quite a bit of money there."

"Do you keep cash in your room?" Mentally, Pete kicked himself for not asking Henrie to secure the room.

"No. No cash. All debit or credit. Had to go to a bank machine to pay this idiot. He doesn't know how to accept that kind of payment."

"Did anyone see you get the cash?"

Collin and Celeste looked at one another, then shook their heads.

Pete turned to the woman. "Mrs. Curtis, do you work outside the home?"

Celeste looked at Collin, then back at Pete. "No. We have children. I'm too busy with them."

"How many children, how old?"

"Um...two..."

"Three. You're tired and cold, dear. Let me answer. Three, officer. They are, um...well, good grief, you'd think I would know the ages of my own children. Well, the oldest is in high school. He's a sophomore, no, a junior this year. And the girl, well, um, she might be a freshman by now, and there's the youngest boy, he's in sixth...no...seventh grade now. It's hard for a man to keep up, you know. The woman always takes care of these things."

Pete leveled his gaze at Collin. Then Celeste. Then Collin. Collin stared back. Celeste kept her eyes down.

Pete cleared his throat, asked that they remain in the office, and went into the main room.

"Brad. Let's talk."

"Somebody needs ta pay me fer my boat! It's a crime dadgumit! It's a crime!"

"Yes. A crime. Tell me what happened."

"They was up on the bluff."

"They, who?"

"They, I don't know who. I couldn't see. Wasn't lookin' up nohow. That first 'un…"

"First, what?"

"I think it were a grenade or somethin' like 'at, anyways, that first 'un come down an hit the water in front a the boat."

"In front? You were in the back?"

"We wuz in the back, me and the mister, and the lady was inside."

"So the first one hit in front of the boat."

"Yeah, then the second one hit the water to the side of the boat."

"Which side?"

"It hit the side that were closer to the mister."

"But in the water; it didn't hit the boat."

"That's what I said, ain't it?"

"So a third – grenade – came down?"

"Yessir."

"And it hit…"

"Right thar at the tail end of the boat, where the propeller comes out."

"Still some distance from you?"

"Yeah, well, it were closer to us. Then I looked up an saw 'em."

"Saw who?"

"Heck, I don't know. I saw two folks."

"And you didn't recognize the people?"

"I couldn't SEE the people. It wuz rainin' to beat the band!"

Pete followed up with questions about Brad's business. Who had cause to be angry with him, who might have a grudge. Brad could come up with no names, but Pete, knowing Brad and knowing the town, mentally made a list of at least a couple dozen. Brad's boat was, without a doubt, the least hospitable boat-for-hire on all of the Great Lakes.

"Tell me, Brad, Ray and Cheryl tried to raise you on the radio today and earlier this week. Has your radio been on the fritz, or are you ignoring it."

Brad hedged on the answer. It was not legal for him to do either.

"Uh…it were workin' alright an' all. Ifin people wuz tryin' to reach me, I wuzn't awares."

"I'll check it out."

"Well, you kin come check it next week…"

"The Coast Guard is taking custody of it for now. They've already locked onto it to tow it in. The lake's calmed down some."

"They ain't got no call…"

"It's a crime scene, Brad."

"Well, what ifin I tole ya, tole ya we jes had motor troubles, an then it wouldn't be no crime."

"That ship has already sailed, Brad."

Cheryl noticed a break in the conversation and motioned to Pete. He joined her in the corner by the radio. "I think Mr. and Mrs. Curtis are not Mr. and Mrs. Curtis."

"I wondered about that. What do you know?"

Cheryl told him about the telephone call, and her suspicion that his wife might be in town. Pete considered this. That would account for their confusion about children. Collin, an attorney, would probably be aware Pete would check up on him.

He returned to the office. "Mr. Curtis."

"Yes?"

"Would you care to introduce me to your lady friend?"

Annie and Henrie had a pot of coffee on, waiting for Pete, Ray and Chris. Henrie had placed sandwiches and a carafe of coffee in the guest room, assuming the couple would be wet, cold, hungry and unfriendly.

Chris arrived first and went directly to the liquor cabinet. Ray came next, after dropping Brad at his home, going via land rather than lake. Ray asked Chris to pour him one of what he was having. Jock dropped to the floor at his feet.

Annie heard Pete before she saw him. Rather, she heard Celeste. "Unfriendly" wasn't going to begin to describe her tone.

"You can find somewhere else to sleep tonight! I will never get the filth off my body! My clothes are trash! The stink alone! I. Never. Want. To. See. You. Again!"

She stormed up the stairs.

She stormed halfway down. Annie heard a "thud," and she was back up the steps.

Henrie and Annie went to the foyer, where Pete stood, bland faced, with Collin, red faced, disheveled, filthy, reeking of fish and boiling angry. "Get me a room!"

"I am sorry. Our rooms are taken."

"Well, then, give me a key to that apartment upstairs!"

"That apartment is not available."

"A cot in the gosh-forsaken apartment, and a bathroom! With a shower! Come on, man!"

Henrie stood. Impassive.

"Then give me a cot in the hallway, and direct me to a bathroom…"

"I am sorry. I cannot accommodate that request. The room rented to the two of you is available to the two of you. Otherwise, one or both of you will be required to go elsewhere. I dare say, the town's resources are strapped with the Chelsea Grand…"

"Oh, for heaven's sakes. Alright!"

He stormed up the steps, pounded on the door and demanded to be let in. Eventually, according to the sounds coming from the second floor, she complied. Not without treating the entire Inn to bloodcurdling words, possibly in French, as Annie didn't recognize all of them.

In the kitchen, Henrie poured the coffee down the drain and poured – for himself, Annie and Pete – one of what Chris was having.

Cyril, who had stood guard beside Pete during the encounter, nudged Jock. They went into the library, looking for their friends.

Tillie couldn't stand to be alone with all the excitement. She joined the others in the library. They pooled their knowledge.

Tiger Lily said, *"So, there is a wife in town. Is it possible we've seen her? Think about it, guys. She could have been in any one of our places, the Café, Lil Socks', anyplace. Anything?"*

Little heads shook. No one knew anything.

Tiger Lily looked at Mr. Bean, still quiet, still a little apart from the rest. *"I have to make a public apology."* Faces turned in her direction. Mr. Bean looked down. *"I was mean to Mr. Bean. He volunteered to do a job for the Inn, and I promised to save his snack. Then I ate it, and, well, I didn't properly thank him for doing the job. Neither did the two of you."* She looked at Kali and Ko, who looked down. *"He went out in the rain. You didn't have to."*

Kali and Ko, faces down, said, together, *"I'm sorry." "I didn't want to be mean or anything."*

Mr. Bean continued to look at the floor, but he said, *"Okay."*

"Do you accept the apology from all of us?"

"I guess so."

"Good. Because you're a valuable member of this team. First of all, we need to hear about Carlos."

Mr. Bean looked up. *"Carlos?"*

"Yes. Tillie said he's going to Mexico. Did he say anything to you?"

"That must be what he meant. He picked me up today and carried me around for a while, and he said he hoped he would see me again, but if he didn't, I was to take care of Isabel and Tillie."

"What?"

"He was real sad, maybe a little scared. Sometimes I get confused with those feelings."

A tear slipped down Tillie's face. *"He said he might not be back?"*

"He didn't say that exactly, just that he hoped he would be back."

They were silent, considering this. Cyril brought them back to the point. *"I'm sorry about Carlos. I really am. But we have to focus on the wife. What about those two women that go to the beach all the time. Could one of them be the wife?"*

"Did you see anything in their room, Mr. Bean?"

"No. Well, I saw stuff, but nothing that would be important."

Ko looked at Kali. *"What about that bag?"*

"What bag?"

"*That red bag. The one that belongs to the women?*"

Mr. Bean perked up. "*Yeah. I saw that bag, and I smelled it, too. It smelled like…well, it smelled like it could be dangerous.*"

"*That's not too descriptive,*" said Cyril.

"*I don't know how else to say it. Maybe you can smell it.*"

"*How? The cat doors are too small for me to get in.*"

"*Well…I don't know…won't Pete have to investigate?*"

"*He won't have any reason to go into that room. Tell me again where the bag is, just in case Pete has a reason to be in there.*"

"*It's under the farthest bed, up by the headboard. When I saw it, it was in the middle.*"

Tiger Lily looked around. "*Everybody think real hard. Can you remember ever seeing those two anywhere at the same time as the not-married couple?*"

Everyone thought about it. All the little heads shook again.

"*Well, we're just going to have to keep our eyes open on this one.*"

Cyril asked, "*What about those bikers? Have you seen or heard anything more about them?*"

"*Yeah!*" "*Oh, yeah!*" said Kali and Ko together. Kali ceded the conversation to Ko.

"*Did you hear what Monte did to Sassy Pants?*" Jock and Cyril nodded.

Kali told the rest of it. "*Today, they came in after buying that bicycle for Monte, and when Kim went upstairs, the other*" *two told Monte they wanted him to kill her out on the bicycle trail on Saturday, during that grand prix thing."*

"He's going to kill his sister?"

"He didn't say he would."

"He didn't say he wouldn't. They said they wanted him to do it, or help them do it, I'm not sure exactly which, at the tip of Lake Scott."

"Yeah. There's a curve, and a long drop down. They want to get her there and push her off."

"How can we stop them?"

Jock looked at Cyril. *"Is there any way you can get Pete there?"*

"Not that I can think of. Can you get Ray on the trail?"

"Saturday? Probably not. He has that wedding at night, and the people are going to go cruising before that. We'll be busy all day."

Everyone turned to Little Socks. She finally realized they were staring and said, *"What?"*

Tiger Lily said, *"Can you burgle the rooms?"*

"And look for what?"

"I don't know. Clues. All we need is one good clue."

"I've gone into rooms with less information. It won't hurt to try. They're rarely there, anyway. I can do it tomorrow. I'll go late to the yoga studio."

"While you're at it, burgle the room of the not-married couple and the women in the carriage house."

"Anything else?"

Tiger Lily looked at Little Socks, completely ignoring the scornful tone of her voice.

"No, thank you. That will be all."

As he prepared to leave, Pete said, "One more thing. I'm coming back in the morning. Collin is sure his wife isn't in town, and I don't know why I did it, but I agreed not to contact her until tomorrow morning. I'm coming here, and he's going to call her on speaker, so I can hear what she has to say. Cyril! Come on!"

19

Friday morning dawned with sunshine and medium-strength straight-line winds. The waves were not as high as the day before, but rip current and small craft warnings were still out.

James and Ava argued with Laila. "Please, mom, it's going to be beautiful. All the kids are going to the beach today."

"We won't go into the water, we promise, really, really promise."

Laila finally gave in. Had James told her about the incident with the rocks, had she known Ava paid no attention to her warnings and to her brother's supervisory status, and had she known James was covering for Ava, she would have said no, no, a thousand times no.

As it was, both Ava and Clarice – enjoying the same silence from Ginger – escaped grounding-for-life.

James and Ava said, "Thank you!" at the same time. James called Ginger to learn she and Clarice had received the same permission. Victory!

For the second morning, Henrie did not see Valerie and Evie for breakfast. He did not worry about them, as the wedding party had seen two women – apparently them – the afternoon before.

Henrie saw Isabel off to the airport; she accompanied as George drove Carlos. He promised to check on Jerry to assure all was in hand within the hour.

He fed the bikers early and sent them off with packets of energy bars and water. He was polite, but not warm, and he made sure the children were in safe places, either in the library or off to work, before they left the table.

The not-on-their-second-honeymoon couple was still in bed. He would keep breakfast warm until 9:00. After that time, the couple would be on their own. After all, he had fed them the night before.

Henrie called Jerry, assured himself all was fine, and sat down with a cup of coffee. He had no one else about which to worry. With the possible exception of Annie.

Annie had been in a strange mood this week. She seemed happy; she laughed at things that were amusing; she became angry at things that were appropriately maddening. However, she was not exactly herself.

Perhaps it was the full moon, now waning gibbous.

Perhaps it was extended worry about Sassy Pants.

Perhaps it had something to do with her mysterious trips to the library.

As soon as Celeste left the room, Collin picked up the telephone and called Gema's Creations.

"Gema, Collin Curtis here." ... "I'm fine, fine." ... "But there is a wrinkle." ... "I need to cancel that order." ... "Yes, everything, the necklace, earrings and bracelet." ... "Well, yes, I'm sorry about that. Surely you'll find someone else..." ... "I most certainly expect to receive the full deposit..." ... "We'll see about that. We'll just see about that. And tell that idiot antique dealer to put that ring back in the case!"

Pete sat in the foyer, drank coffee and waited patiently for Celeste or Collin to make an appearance. Cyril lay patiently at his side, Kali and Ko nestled into his belly. Celeste stormed down the stairs. She headed for the front door, a woman on a mission.

"Ahem."

Celeste turned. "Are you waiting for me?"

"You or Collin. You're here. I'll take you until he comes downstairs."

"I have to run an errand. You'll have to wait."

"Someone may have tried to kill you. The errand will have to wait."

"But if I don't get there this minute…"

"The errand will have to wait."

"Will this nightmare ever end?" She stood, waiting for him to acquiesce. Pete did not.

Okay, then let me get breakfast. We can talk in the dining room."

"I'm afraid you slept through breakfast. Henrie serves for a long time, but there is an end to everything."

"At least let me get some coffee."

Celeste went to the coffee station, and while the water heated she scrounged in the refrigerator, coming out with two left-over mini-croissant sandwiches from the day before. She put them on a plate, finished making the coffee and joined Pete in the foyer.

"So what do you want to talk about?"

"Tell me about Collin's wife. What does she look like, what does she do, and what problems would she cause if she knows about this liaison?"

Celeste rolled her eyes and shook her head and shoulders, like a dog shaking off water. "Okay. She's about my height and size. Not really. She's at least twenty pounds heavier. She's not nearly as pretty as me. She doesn't have any sense of style. She wears, well, she wears used clothes. She shops at Goodwill! Tacky, tacky, tacky."

Pete breathed in deeply and said nothing.

"She's always taking care of those kids. Her nails are a wreck. She doesn't style her hair. Oh, her hair is mousy brown, stringy and, oh, it's more than shoulder length. Maybe just past her shoulders. She usually wears it up in a ponytail, because, well, because she's so tacky."

Celeste took a bite of sandwich and a drink of coffee. "She always has a book in her hands; she drives a rattletrap car; she never wears jewelry. Does that describe her well enough?"

"I believe you have described her perfectly."

Last night, Pete assumed this woman's distress caused her to behave in a manner he couldn't describe as anything less than unattractive. This morning, he determined she had no redeeming qualities.

"You mentioned the children. There are three, correct?"

"Yeah. Three kids. Disgusting rug rats."

"Disgusting? How?"

"They're always doing something, some sport or activity or other. Collin is forever having to go somewhere to watch them in some play or some game or some other such thing. Disgusting. You'd think they would be able to handle it without him. He should be off supporting them, not watching every little home run."

Pete nodded his understanding. "And tell me, do you know what would happen if she would learn about this liaison?"

"Would learn? Would learn? You made it pretty clear that she was going to learn about it! I'll tell you what will happen. She'll divorce him and she'll take him for everything he's worth. She'll take the house; she'll get alimony; she'll get at least half his pension; he'll have to pay for everything for the kids, from knee socks to college. He won't be free of her until the last one of them graduates. And then he'll still have to share his pension. He'll have to live like a pauper."

"And that bothers you?"

"I guess, a little, but I'm done with him. I'll find someone that has something to give me in return for my company. He won't have a penny. Are we done here?"

"Certainly. Thank you for your time."

Celeste nearly ran out the door, leaving it open as she ran down the steps and turned to go up The Avenue.

When Collin finally came downstairs, Pete offered to help him make coffee and look for leftovers in the refrigerator. Collin sighed and accepted the offer.

Kali and Ko slipped to the second floor to let Little Socks know the coast was clear. They stood guard at the top of the stairway, just in case.

Pete started the conversation with the obvious. "Let's make that telephone call to your wife."

"Really? You want me to get a divorce, right?"

"Just make the call."

Collin sighed again and brought out his cell phone. He didn't think to tell Pete the one convenience he allowed his wife was a cell phone. When he needed her, he needed her. She had to keep the cell phone with her at all times. As he dialed, he thought to himself that Pete didn't need to know she didn't exactly have to be at home to take the call.

Collin put on the speaker so Pete could hear. One ring, two, then, "Collin, is everything okay?"

"Yes, Evelyn. Why do you ask?"

"You never call when you're on a business trip. How's it going?"

"It's going well. I may be home a little early, maybe a day early, on Sunday. Is everything okay at home?"

"Sure. Nothing new."

"The kids okay?"

"Yes. They're at vacation Bible school this week, so they're gone all day."

"Oh, that's right. I forgot. Well, I just thought I'd check in. I'll, um, I'll let you know if I leave early."

"That would be great. I'll need to know if I have to take more out of the freezer."

"Okay. Well, then, good-bye."

"Bye."

When he hung up, he looked at Pete. "Satisfied?"

"For now, at least about that. Tell me what would happen if she were to decide to divorce you."

"There are two ways that could happen. She could decide to divorce me because we aren't happy, or she could decide to do it because I've been having an affair. If we just aren't happy, the judge won't throw the book at me. If it's because of this affair, let me tell you, I'll be living on skid row for the rest of my life."

"Do you think your wife suspects you're having an affair?"

"I don't think so. I've been pretty circumspect."

"Who handles the finances?"

"I do."

"And the credit cards that have your extra expenses? Do those bills go to the house?"

"They come to my office."

"There's no way she could know about it?"

"No way. She's not the sharpest knife in the rack."

Pete suppressed his distaste. "Okay. I guess we're finished here. Be sure to give me a call if anything comes to mind."

Kali and Ko, still on guard at the top of the steps, made sure Little Socks got out of the room. The two big girls walked serenely down the steps and followed Pete and Cyril to the kitchen.

As Pete refilled his coffee cup from the pot in the kitchen, he said, "Tell me again, Henrie, about the other guests here."

Henrie told Pete about the other guests, when they arrived, where they were from, their purpose for visiting Chelsea, and everything he thought might be important.

Pete lingered at the kitchen counter. He stared at Cyril. Cyril stared back. Finally, he turned to Henrie and asked, "Could I see everyone's card? What they write out when they sign in?"

"Certainly." Henrie walked to the desk, opened a drawer and pulled out a handful of registration cards. "Here are the current guests."

Pete looked at them, one at a time. He went fairly quickly through most of them but lingered on the two women. "Tell me a little more about these two women." He showed Henrie the card.

"Yes. Valerie and Evie. They are from Muncie, Indiana. They vacation together every year. This year they are here for the sun and the beach."

"In June?"

"They seem to have a good time. According to another guest, they laughed on their way to the carriage house yesterday. Through the rain and puddles."

"That's where they're staying?"

"Yes, on the second floor. Do you suspect them?"

"I'm a police officer. I suspect everyone. I think Muncie is not far from Union City, where Collin and Celeste live. Only Valerie's address is given, not Evie's. Collin called his wife 'Evelyn.' You pronounce her name Ev-y rather than Eve-y. Evie could be short for Evelyn." Pete paused, then resumed. "Maybe I'm making a mountain out of a molehill." Pete looked down. Cyril tapped his right foot furiously.

"Perhaps, but you must follow your instincts. You certainly have my permission to conduct your investigation on the premises."

"Thanks, Henrie. I think I'll do that. And thanks for the coffee and for making sure Annie didn't make it."

Henrie smiled as Pete turned to go. Cyril and the cats followed. As soon as they got outside, Kali and Ko led the way to the carriage house.

At the landing, Pete knocked on the door and identified himself as a police officer. A redheaded woman dressed in a swimming suit and cover up answered the door, mouth open.

"Police? Really? Can we help you?"

"Yes. I'm investigating an incident on the lake that involved guests of the Inn. I'm interviewing all of the guests, just to see if they heard or saw anything that might be helpful. May I come in?"

"Sure. Your dog can come, too. I see you brought Kali and Ko."

"They're acting as my guides today. I can't seem to go anywhere without them."

"Well, come on in. I'm Valerie. This is Evie. We were just getting ready to go to the beach, so pardon our swimwear."

"That's not a problem." Pete stepped in and looked casually but carefully at Evie. She wore her hair in a stylish short cut. She was brunette with auburn highlights, about the same height and weight – perhaps ten pounds heavier – than Celeste. Her fingernails and toenails were carefully manicured and painted bright red.

Pete noticed several outfits thrown on the third bed, probably the unused one. They looked stylish. Not tacky.

Valerie and Evie motioned Pete to the seating area and they took an easy chair and a rocker. They didn't notice that Kali and Ko had worked their way under a bed and that Cyril, from the side of the bed they couldn't see, was on the floor, nose under. Kali and Ko, working together, pushed the bag closer to Cyril so he could ferret out all the scents.

Valerie started the conversation. "So, what was the incident? How can we help?"

"A couple staying in the main house was on the lake yesterday. The boat they had chartered anchored in a cove about a mile up. It was a sheltered cove. They really had no business being out because of the weather, but the cove afforded some safety. While they were anchored, someone from up above, coming from the state park, threw three grenades. At least we believe they were grenades."

"Oh, no! Were they hurt?"

"No, they weren't. It's not clear if the intent was to harm them. If so, the attacker was incredibly inept, missing the boat twice and hitting the boat near the propeller with the third throw."

Valerie said, "That sounds awful! How can we help?"

"Have you met the other guests of the Inn?"

Valerie and Evie looked at one another as they spoke. "Let's see, we've seen the woman that's getting married..." "Isabel." "Yeah, Isabel." "And we met her fiancé, Carlos, but he's not a guest." "Have we met anyone else?" "I don't think so." "Just Annie and Henrie." "Oh, except those folks that came yesterday. They were outside when we got back." "Yeah. But we didn't talk to them."

They both looked at Pete. Valerie said, "I guess we aren't very helpful, are we?"

"That's alright. It's amazing how guests here can come and go and never interact. Tell me about yesterday. Where did you go, what did you do, who did you see?"

"Let's see," said Evie, "we ate breakfast up here – we have groceries – and then we decided we didn't want to stay here, even with the rain."

"Yeah. We went for a walk."

"Where?"

"The state park."

"Did you see anyone while you were there?"

"No, just the guy that sold us the tickets to get in."

"Where did you go while you were in the park?"

"We took one of the walking trails. Wait, I have the map."

Evie walked to the table by the door to get the map. As she opened it, she prayed she could come up with a reasonable lie. She saw it. A trail that went in another direction and didn't intersect with the trail they actually took.

"Here," she said, putting it down on the coffee table in front of Pete. "We took this trail, it's the Interior Number One."

Valerie stayed out of this conversation, letting Evie take it.

"Do you need to know what time we got there?"

"That would be helpful."

"Was it about noon, Val?"

"I think so."

"And we were there until, well, the new guests saw us. It might have been around 4:00 or so."

"So you were on this trail for about four hours."

"That sounds right. We took our time, stopped a few times to eat and drink some water."

"How far on the trail did you go?"

Evie looked at the map and saw the trail was a circular one, wrapping back around to the entry.

"We went all the way, see how it winds around and comes back to the entrance?"

"Did you take any other trails?"

Evie looked again at the map. "I think we went off on this one. It wraps around and comes back, too."

"It must have been uncomfortable out there, with the rain and the wind."

"We got wet, but we dressed for it, and we knew it was going to be a wet day. We just didn't want to stay inside all day."

Pete carefully noted the routes Evie pointed out. His next stop would be the state park.

"And you didn't see anyone else, except the employee at the center." This was a statement more than a question.

"That's right."

"Well, ladies, thank you for your time. If you hear or see anything that might help, please call me at the police station, or tell Henrie or Annie. They can get in touch with me."

Valerie walked Pete to the door. He turned and called Cyril. Cyril stood by the bed and barked once. Kali and Ko sat beside Cyril and stared intently at Pete.

"Cyril, come."

Cyril barked.

Pete moved to the bed and took hold of Cyril's collar. He gave a gentle tug and Cyril, reluctantly, rose and walked to the door. He whined all the way. The cats didn't want to stay with the women in the room, so they dashed between Pete's legs and out the door.

"I'm sorry, ladies. Sometimes they can be a little rude. Thank you again."

Pete closed the door behind himself. As he walked down the stairs, he thought how likeable these women were, and how much he was going to hate pinning the act on them.

And what was the act? A prank? An assault? Attempted murder? He didn't know what they had tried to do and why they had done it, but they were guilty. He knew it.

Valerie and Evie looked at one another and sighed deeply.

"Quick thinking with that map, Evie."

"Thanks. I hope we're in the clear. No one saw us, so no one can contradict what we said."

Valerie glanced down at the floor. "Oh, no, look."

She pointed to the floor under the bed. The red bag was at the edge of the bed, where Cyril had stood and barked.

"Those cats must have pushed it out. Let's put it in the armoire. We can lock it."

"And let's be thankful cats and dogs can't talk."

"Do you think we need to go out the back way? We can go around the porch and walk from the private beach."

"We don't need to do that. Today's a much better day than yesterday. Surely they're out on a boat somewhere. They won't see us."

Valerie and Evie picked up their beach bags and danced down the stairs. They talked and laughed their way to the beach. One more day in the sun, then they would return home ahead of Collin. On Monday, Evie would meet her divorce lawyer, someone Valerie knew in Muncie. Someone who would not be swayed by her husband, the big fish in a small pond.

In the median, straight across from the Inn, Valerie asked, "Are you feeling the freedom?"

Evie raised her head and laughed, sun in her face and wind in her hair.

On the second floor, in their room facing The Avenue, Collin and Celeste argued.

"Why did you have to cancel it? If it's too much money today, put something down. We can get a piece at a time until we have it all."

"I am not spending that kind of money! Period! I'm through! Let's just pack up and go home."

Collin stepped onto the balcony to cool down from the argument.

He watched two women on the median. One had a familiar walk. Then he heard her laugh, and he saw her face as she lifted it into the wind. Evelyn.

20

Pete walked into the reception area of the State Park. He went to the desk and asked the staffer if he had worked there the day before.

"I sure did. What an awful day. The first day I don't bring my book and I didn't have a single thing to do all day."

"Did two women come in?"

"Oh, yeah. I did do one thing. Sold them tickets. Crazy, those women."

"Why do you say that?"

"Not even the campers were out. They stayed in their campers or tents all day, the weather was so awful, but these women wanted to go for a walk!"

"Do you know which trail they took?"

"Sure. I watched them go. Nothing else to do. They went on the trail that goes around the outer edge of the park."

"The outer edge?"

"Yeah, the one that goes close to the lake."

"Does it go to the beach?"

"No, it goes almost to the edge of that rocky cliff, you know, the one that people pull into to go fishing or swimming?"

Pete picked up a map and gave it to the staffer. "Can you show me the trail?"

"Sure. It's this one."

The staffer drew his finger along the trail.

"Show me how they would come back if they go out on this trail, and how long that would take."

"Well, they could take one of these feeder trails to come back, or they could just turn around at some point and come back, but if they took this trail – the outer trail – all the way, they would be out for hours, all day."

"Did you see them come back?"

"No, well, I saw them when they walked past the building, but I didn't see which trail they came back on, if that's what you're getting at."

"Yes, I guess that was it. As far as you know, no one walked out there besides them? No one that could have seen them or met them going or coming on the trail?"

"Nope. Like I say, the campers stayed dry, and no one else came in."

Pete stood outside the building for a couple of minutes while arranging for Marco to walk the trail to look for evidence.

For one last morning, Ian gathered his teens for two laps around the vineyard. Only two, because they would face serious headwinds for a significant portion of each lap, and he didn't want to tire them out. He rode with Brendan.

As they made the turn for the second time, they were joined by four more bikers, three men and a woman. As they kept going, the woman came close. "Hey, Ian."

He turned. "Kim! I haven't seen you around. Well, not since..."

"Yeah. Not since. Except that I saw you last night."

"Huh?"

"With your girlfriend? I saw you last night."

"I wasn't…"

"Yeah. Just wanted to let you know we could have had something sweet. You could have been a rich man. Not happenin' now, though. See ya."

Ian watched her spin off, putting on the speed, as he slowed down.

Brendan asked, "Hey, man, you got woman troubles?"

"I didn't know I had a woman to have troubles with, but apparently…."

Brendan laughed. "Hey, Renee and I are going to cut off here and get home. We both have to lifeguard today." He signaled to Renee who was riding behind them. The two teens left the pack.

Ian called out, "Be safe out there. See you tomorrow. Get a good night's sleep."

He didn't hear Brendan say to Renee, "Can't believe he's got woman troubles. What woman would have him, anyway?"

The Café was busy again today. The wedding party stood at the hostess stand while they waited for a table. Denise took the opportunity to video Tiger Lily at the hostess stand.

Tiger Lily, always happy to oblige tourists, especially nice guests of the Inn, preened, purred, and made sure to show Denise the beauty of a tabletop hop. While Denise aimed the camera, Tiger Lily jumped to the table at which Collin and Celeste sat.

Celeste, in a loving mood, stroked Tiger Lily's back and allowed her to make a suggestion on the menu. Tiger Lily placed a paw on the caprese salad with fresh mozzarella. "Thank you, Tiger Lily. I think I'll try that."

Denise had moved in close to take the shot, receiving permission from Celeste with a nod of her head.

Tiger Lily purred, turned to give a starlet cat smile to the camera and returned to the hostess stand. What joy! Pete and Cyril waited there!

Cyril trotted behind the stand to see what food had been placed by servers while Pete, taking care to look casually around the room, noted the loving picture that Collin and Celeste made. Interesting.

The wedding party was seated as soon as Tiger Lily returned to the stand. They sat at the corner where the north and east windows met, a perfect table for a day with sun and beautiful clouds.

Denise looked around and snapped still photos of the Café. The table at which they sat had a ceramic top, with three colorful cats at play. All of the tables were similarly painted, but in different designs.

She stood and walked around to get a better angle for the camera. Each table was different; there were cats, dogs, tropical birds, other animals and outdoor scenes of every variety. The chairs were colorfully painted and cushioned, none of them matching at any one table, lending to an air of casual chic. The walls were mint green with the exception of an accent wall behind the coffee counter and server station. That wall was bright purple.

She returned to the table and said to Erika, "You know, this is really a cute place, but I can't imagine it as a fine dining restaurant. Are you sure that's what it is at night?"

"Positive. Trust me, it's going to be a gourmet dining experience."

"Dining, maybe, but atmosphere? I'm not sure."

"Let's just wait and see. Look, they have chicken salad with apples, pecans, Greek yogurt and rosemary. Oh, and asparagus lemon risotto. Look at this! Hawaiian chicken kabobs! I can't choose!"

"You won't be able to fit into your dress."

"I don't care. I'll buy a kimono!"

Clarice and Ava waded into the water. They looked around. No one paid attention.

"Just a little further. Come one. It'll be fun!"

Valerie and Evie, stopped once again in their effort to get into the lake, splashed their feet at the edge of the water. Two lifeguards were on duty today. They were vigilant, blowing their whistles whenever anyone waded further than ankle deep. Rip current warnings were serious business.

Valerie and Evie watched the teens on the beach. Older teens played volleyball. Without the opportunity to get into the water, several volleyball nets were in use.

Younger teens played ring toss or threw Frisbees, edging ever closer to the water, coming back only when the lifeguard, an older sister or brother or the occasional parent interceded.

Evie sat down at the edge of the water. "I know it's warmer on the sand, but I miss being in the water. I want to pretend I'm swimming."

"Okay. I'll sit." Valerie sat.

Then they heard it. A scream. One of the young teens was in the water, caught in a rip current. Another teen struggled as well. She was the one screaming. Evie and Valerie heard, "Help!" just as the lifeguards blew their whistles loud and long for everyone to get out. The lifeguards jumped down, rather than use their ladders, but Evie and Valerie knew they would never get there in time.

Valerie and Evie did what they did so well. They ran into the water until they could run no more, then they jumped in and swam. The two stayed together, knowing they were safer in twos than alone.

When they reached the first teen, Evie swam on while Valerie took the teen in her arms and started to kick toward shore. They were at the edge of the rip current. Valerie was a strong swimmer, but this teen thought she was going to drown. She spooned the teen into her, but she fought, and fought. Valerie heard the wave runners come up. One passed her by, and the other stopped. The lifeguard was unable to get to the girl; she struggled too hard. She jumped in. Between the two of them, they got the girl to the wave runner. Once the girl had a hand hold, she calmed down. The lifeguard climbed back on, pulled the girl up, and then Valerie.

Evie continued on. She was caught in the current now, but she was a strong swimmer. She stayed above water and kept moving toward the young girl, who kept going under. When Evie reached the girl, she grabbed for Evie and struggled. With difficulty, Evie turned her around in the water, spooning her into her stomach, and started to kick backwards toward the shore.

She felt it happen. She was caught. She was making no headway and the girl continued to panic. They were not going to make it. She didn't even know this girl, but if it had been her daughter and a total stranger, she could only hope the total stranger would rescue her daughter. Or at least try.

Just as she thought she was going under, a strong hand grabbed her by the shoulder strap of her swimming suit. A lifeguard was there, on a wave runner. He pulled Evie until she could reach the handles at the base of the wave runner, and then he reached for the girl, pulling her onto the seat.

When Evie caught her breath, she saw the girl, belly on the seat of the wave runner, coughing up lake water and sobbing. The lifeguard kept one hand on her back and reached his other hand to Evie.

She shook her head and pointed to the handle. She was too tired to talk, but he got the message. He turned and drove slowly back to shore, pulling Evie, who now held on with both hands.

Now, Evie was ready to go home.

Ginger positioned herself at the lifeguard station, wanting to flirt. Brendan was having none of it today. She found an infinite number of excuses to stop by, but he finally put a stop to it. "Ginger, it's dangerous out there today. I have to keep my eyes on the lake. I'll call you tomorrow after the race, okay?"

Miffed, she joined James. He was more interested in talking to Traci than consoling her, but he did try to soften the rebuff. "He's got a job, Ginger."

She wouldn't be pacified. "I wasn't interested in him anyway."

"Yeah, right. Come on. Join us for this game. Take that space beside Traci."

One game turned into three. James heard the screams when everyone else did. He did a quick scan of the younger teens on the beach but didn't see Ava or Clarice. Then, panicking, he looked at the girls in the lake. It was them!

Screaming Ava's name, he tried to run the water's edge. He didn't realize that Traci held onto his arm; Billy and Eddy had grabbed him as well. In a daze, he noticed another small group of teens holding onto Ginger in the same fashion. Through a fog, he heard voices saying, "You can't do anything…" "There's nothing you can do…" "Look, someone's on their way…" "Brendan and Renee…"

Finally, James sank to the sand. He watched the rescue unfold in sheer terror, barely taking in one scene after another. He saw a woman reach Ava and turn with her to come back to shore, but they weren't making headway. Eyes focused on Ava, he saw a wave runner get close. Someone jumped into the water…is that Renee? And then, thankfully, Ava was on the wave runner. His vision slowed down, and he watched while they came to shore.

When they were almost in, his teen captors let go of him, and he ran into the water to meet them. Once he had Ava in his arms, all he could do was say, over and over, "You are in so much trouble!"

The wedding couple posed for pictures and videos courtesy of Denise. They had moved to the median. Tom directed them in a series of poses for stills and action for videos at the game tables and on a couple of the benches.

Erika pointed to the lighthouse. "Let's go out there. We have the lighthouse in the background; let's make it a real prop."

As Denise picked up her bag, she noticed activity coming toward them from the city park. "What's up?"

Grant walked a little way toward the park. "Looks like some kind of parade." They turned at the sound of a siren. A police car drove quickly from the town circle to the end of The Avenue to meet the parade head on.

The parade was led by two all-terrain vehicles coming through the sand, driven by teens in lifeguard uniforms. When they reached the public parking lot, they sped up, met the police car and parked in front of The Clinic. Two women were already outside with stretchers.

The woman from the grocery store and a police officer ran to the all-terrain vehicles to help the girls off. Another car sped down the street, and what looked to be the mother of one of the girls jumped out to join the group.

Most of the attention was on the girls. They were seated, then laid back on the stretchers. The main characters went into The Clinic. Denise kept rolling video, catching everything.

When she heard the third all-terrain vehicle, she swung her camera in that direction. Someone was driving the women who stayed on the second floor of the carriage house from the beach to The Avenue. The women made the driver stop at The Clinic. Denise could tell they were saying they could walk the rest of the way.

The lifeguards, now exiting The Clinic, approached the women. Each one gave each of the women a deep hug before waving and going back to the beach.

The women hugged one another, smiled, then laughed, and headed toward the carriage house. They smiled happily at the camera and waved.

Denise said, "We're going to have to meet these two. I'll bet they have a great story to tell." They left for the lighthouse, Denise filming as she walked.

21

It was Friday night on The Avenue. This was one night the cats could count on being left alone. Their humans went somewhere to eat – these days it was the Bon Vivant Grille – and left them with plain old food in their dishes.

It was hard to take, sometimes. Humans had all the fun.

Tonight, Ray and Cheryl dropped Jock off at the Inn, so even he wouldn't be able to get table scraps from the restaurant. Unfortunately, Cyril would not be able to come. Laila's daughter, Ava, and Pete's daughter, Clarice, had a close call in the lake today. After tending to a mutual errand, the two families would stay home tonight.

Tiger Lily could imagine that once the joy of knowing everyone was safe wore off, somebody was going to be in big trouble. It might roll uphill, also, and hit James and Ginger.

The lake could be a dangerous place, but it was wild and beautiful and oh, so inviting.

The cats and Jock were in the apartment on the third floor of the Inn. They had to stay in, unless they left Jock alone, because he couldn't use the cat doors. When they heard Simon Finnegan and Oscar McMurphy call from the foyer, Sassy Pants ran downstairs to invite them up.

Little Tillie was behind them when they entered the apartment.

Tiger Lily, from the windowsill in the dining room overlooking The Avenue, said, *"We need a bigger windowsill."*

"I'll stay on the floor with Jock," offered Tillie. *"That will leave more room for Fat Cat and Scaredy Cat."*

Scaredy Cat looked at Tillie. *"I really like my new name better."*

"I'm sorry. I'll try to remember to use it. But you know, when I met you, you had a different name. It's hard for me to think of your new one."

Jock stomped his foot. *"Let's hear what the cat burglar has to say about burgling the rooms."*

Little Socks was in the middle of the long windowsill. Everyone turned to look at her.

"I went into the room of that couple first. I didn't have a long time there, because that man, Collin, came upstairs as soon as he was finished talking to Pete. I only found one thing. His bag — the one that he uses for his personal stuff — had a picture in it. I grabbed it and brought it up here."

She jumped to the floor and ran to the dining room buffet. She wriggled underneath and came out with a photograph held between her teeth.

She jumped to the top of the dining room table and dropped it on the middle. Eight cats jumped to the table; one little dog jumped to a chair and put his front legs on the table. Jock walked around to the center and stood, front paws on top of the table. Annie didn't seem to mind the scratches her furniture gained over the weeks and months. Which was a good thing.

Little Socks had to move the picture a little, so everyone could see it.

"Do you see what I see?" she asked.

Mo said, *"Trill."*

Kali and Ko, absent mindedly, translated for him. *"Five people." "A mom, a dad and three little kids."*

"*Look closer,*" insisted Little Socks.

Sassy Pants was the first to see it. "*Dat man. Heze dat Collin, but younger an wiff hair on his lip. And dat woman. She looks like one of de carriage house womans, but she haz hair dats longer.*"

They all leaned in.

"*I'll be darned,*" said Tiger Lily. "*A young couple with young children. The missing wife. That's Evie. She's been here the whole time. Did you have time to go into their room?*"

"*I did, and the most important thing is that the bag wasn't under the bed anymore.*" Little Socks threw an accusing glance at Kali and Ko. "*Someone pushed the bag to the edge of the bed, and they left it where the women could see it.*"

She turned and gave them a full stare. "*Could you have been any more obvious?*"

Together, they defended their honor. "*We had to get it to Cyril!*" "*Cyril had to smell it!*"

Jock said, "*Cyril could probably have smelled it from the middle of the bed. You probably didn't have to move it.*"

"*But we had to put it where Pete could find it!*"

"*Yeah, Pete needed to find it….*"

He saw the big girls look down at the floor, crestfallen. "*You were doing what you thought was right.*"

Mr. Bean said, "*What did he smell? Did he tell you?*"

Kali answered for the two of them. "*He said it smelled like grenades. He's had some bomb training, and he knew the smell. Pete said someone threw three of them, but Cyril thinks he smelled more in there. It smelled like something was still inside.*"

Jock said, "*And he couldn't get Pete to take a look?*"

This time it was Ko. *"He barked a couple of times and tried to stay there so Pete would come look, but Pete got him by the collar and we all had to leave."*

Tiger Lily looked at Little Socks. *"Could you smell it? Do you think it's still in the room?"*

"I think it might be in that locked cabinet, the thing they call an armoire. Why do they give such silly names to things?"

Sassy Pants answered. *"Its cuz they likes to make tings sound big and portant."*

Little Socks bopped Sassy Pants on the nose. *"It was a rhetorical question. You weren't supposed to answer."*

"Wots a torical question? Why you aks question and not want answer?"

"Not torical; rhetorical." She bopped Sassy Pants on the nose again. *"Learn English!"*

Tiger Lily jumped in between them and faced Little Socks. *"I'll do the bopping around here."* She lowered her head and gave Little Socks a meaningful stare. *"Don't forget how special she is."*

Tiger Lily, with the look and the words, reminded Little Socks that they shared a secret, that Sassy Pants kept Little Socks alive when the two were kidnapped. The other cats had not been told.

Little Socks broke the stare and huffed. She looked everywhere but at Sassy Pants and said, *"I'm sorry."*

Tiger Lily took a deep breath and said, *"Anything else from their room?"*

"One more thing." Little Socks jumped down and went under the buffet one more time. She had a business card in her teeth. She threw it on the table.

Everyone looked at it.

"Can anybody read yet?" asked Tiger Lily.

Solemn shakes of the head all around. The room was silent for several seconds.

Oscar McMurphy said, *"So, you have a picture, and you have something that nobody knows anything about, because no one can read."*

Simon Finnegan added, *"And what do you do with them? You're cats. You can't just walk up to Annie or Henrie or Pete and tell them about it."*

Mo said, *"Trill!"*

Sassy Pants translated. *"Sometimes we can, cuz sometimes we gives dem sumpin' an dey knows wot to do bout it."*

Mr. Bean said, *"We can leave that picture somewhere that Mommy will find it, and she'll see it's that woman."*

"But she won't know where it came from, and she might not recognize Evie."

"Maybe we can leave it where Hilly will find it, outside that man's door, and then they'll know it was his."

"But Hilly doesn't see all the guests. She might not know it's Evie, and she might just put it back in his room, or on that table outside his room. He'll see it and put it away."

The room went silent again.

"Well," Tiger Lily started, *"no one was hurt. She probably didn't mean to hurt him or she would have done it already."*

Kali said, *"Valerie and Evie are leaving tomorrow."*

Ko added, *"Yeah, and the couple, Collin and Celeste, are leaving Sunday. We probably don't need to give Mommy any clues."*

Jock nodded. *"But don't lose them. You never know when a clue might come in handy."*

Little Socks took the picture between her teeth and Mr. Bean took the business card. Together, they stashed the clues underneath the buffet.

When they returned, Tiger Lily looked at Little Socks again. *"What about the bikers. Did you find anything in their rooms?"*

As she jumped to the floor, Little Socks said to herself, *"Why didn't I just bring it?"*

She came back with a piece of paper. There was writing all over it. Some looked straight, some looked sideways, and some looked upside down, but she couldn't be sure.

Tillie said, *"This looks like notes and doodles."*

Sassy Pants kept clear of Little Socks when she asked, *"Wots doodles?"*

Tillie answered. *"Doodles is stuff people write when they're talking on the telephone to other people. They're writing notes, but sometimes they doodle at the same time. The doodles can be nonsense, or sometimes they could mean something."*

"How do you know about doodles?" asked Jock.

"My former humans, you know, the mean ones, they took notes and doodles, and sometimes they would find something important. One would say, 'We need to do this,' and the other would say, 'Where do we go,' and the other would say, 'I don't know, I wrote it down.' And then they would look at whatever the writing had been done on, and they would turn it this way

and that, sometimes upside down, and they would find what they needed."

"So this could be important. Good work, Little Socks."

Tiger Lily asked, "Which room was it in?"

"The two men, Clark and Bryce. The ones that want Monte to kill Kim."

"This could be really important."

"Do you think they would leave an important piece of paper out where Kim might see it? Especially if it had to do with killing her?"

Tillie, the doodle expert, offered an opinion. "Sometimes doodles are in code. If she saw it, she might not be able to read it."

"If we can't figure out a way to save her, we're going to have to figure out a way to get this to Pete and let him know where it came from."

"If it comes to that," said Little Socks, "at just the right time, I'll take it back into the room and drop it."

"Good idea. Jock, any ideas on saving her?"

"No. I'll be on the boat all day. I don't know anyone that can get to the tip of Lake Scott and keep big men from pushing her over the cliff."

Tillie said, "I'd go, but I don't know where it is."

Simon Finnegan and Oscar McMurphy said together, "We do."

Simon Finnegan explained. "Before our old humans dumped us, we drove to the tip of Lake Scott. We know right where that curve and the cliff are."

Tiger Lily looked at them closely. *"You were in a car. If you go back, you'll be on foot. Do you think you can find it?"*

"Yeah. As long as we can find the lake, we can get there. It will take us a long time, though."

Jock said, *"I think you'll need to leave tonight. Can you take care of yourself? Catch food, find water?"*

"Sure. We're good at camping."

"Will Holly and Jolly be scared if they can't find you?"

"No. Sometimes we stay out all night, because we're used to it. They're real happy to see us when we get home, but they've never locked us in because of it."

"Well, then. That's the best plan we have."

"Trill!"

Kali and Ko said together, *"What plan?" "What kind of a plan is that?"*

Mr. Bean added, *"So far, there's a plan for Fat Cat and Scaredy Cat to go to the tip of Lake Scott. And do what?"*

Oscar McMurphy said, *"We'll discuss it on the way there, but I can tell you we'll need a lot of luck. There are lots of bikers, not just these four."*

"Yeah," said Simon Finnegan. *"We're going to have to figure out how to keep her from being thrown over without getting run over ourselves."*

"Or thrown over."

"Yeah, and that."

The two cats looked at one another, then at Tiger Lily. *"If we do this, can we be detectives, too?"*

"*Henrie's responsible for the sign, and I don't know how we'd tell him to change it. In our hearts, you'll be detectives.*"

Privately, Tiger Lily thought that if she had known it was that important to them, she would have called them detectives before. Without them, Little Socks and Sassy Pants could have been lost forever.

22

Pete and Janet were so happy Clarice was safe, they held off all discussion of discipline until morning. Laila combined it all. As she held Ava and sobbed, she choked out, "You are both grounded until you leave for college."

Annie and Henrie raided the refrigerator at the Inn. Annie took a hearty supper to Laila and her three children while Henrie took a lighter supper – supplemented with items gathered by Minnie at Sassy P's – to Pete and Janet. Annie didn't stay long at Laila's. She saw with her own eyes that both Ava and James were okay and made sure Laila was calm before she left. She had another task.

Annie trotted up the steps to the carriage house second floor entrance and knocked. Evie opened the door to her. Annie beamed. "I hope the two of you brought little black dresses, because you are eating at the best restaurant in town tonight. Everything, a five course meal, wine before, wine during, and after-dinner drinks all included. And your room has just been covered as well. You won't pay us a dime for your stay here."

Evie and Valerie were exhausted but exhilarated at the same time. They looked at one another and at Annie. "Really," started Evie, "you don't need…"

"I do need. You rescued two children who are as important to me as anything. Ava lives across the street; her mother owns the grocery store. And Clarice, well, she's the daughter of the Chief of Police."

"Oh, my."

"Yes, my. I know you're leaving tomorrow, but I'm sure you can count on a visit from the girls' parents in the morning before you go. They are so grateful."

Valerie and Evie looked at one another. They understood one another completely. There was nothing to lose. Collin was a goner. It didn't matter if he saw them. He would find out soon enough.

Their smiles were broad as they turned back to Annie. Evie accepted on their behalf. "We'd be delighted."

Collin and Celeste dressed in their best evening clothes. Given their designer duds, this would be a wowzer moment for Chelsea. This vacation was not going to be a bust after all. Walking on cloud nine, plans made and committed to, they prepared for dinner at Chelsea's finest restaurant.

The wedding party met for before-dinner drinks at the honeymoon suite. As Tom and Denise knocked on the door, Evie and Valerie were coming down the steps. They were dressed, literally, in little black dresses with strappy high heeled sandals and – of course Tom and Denise couldn't see this – silky black lingerie. They felt good from their heads to their toes.

As they reached the bottom of the steps, they turned to pose for Denise's ever-present camera.

Grant and Erika opened the door. Erika gushed, "We heard! You're heroes! Are you going to celebrate tonight?"

"We are. We're going to the Bon Vivant Grille, on the house. Isn't that fantastic?"

"Come join us for drinks first. We're going there, too."

"Drinks? It sounds like we'll be drinking a lot when we get there."

"Oh, but you can have an aperitif first."

Grant beckoned them to come in. "We have a bottle of champagne on ice. We're celebrating all weekend, so come on, join us."

It was almost an hour before the six came out of the honeymoon suite, dancing to the music that had played while they drank champagne.

The wedding party was seated at the same table they had at noon. Valerie and Evie waited at the hostess stand – minus Tiger Lily tonight – to be seated. In just a minute, Isabel, looking like a million dollars in a short black dress, approached them.

She smiled and said, "I'm so happy to see you. Your meal is on the house, and I'm seating you at one of our best tables.

Denise did not even sit down before bringing her camera up. She intended to film every single minute of this weekend. Before focusing on the space, she filmed Valerie and Evie as they followed Isabel to a table. Midway, she caught the women as they smiled and gave finger waves to a couple at a table.

Denise focused on the couple. Oh, the couple she had filmed earlier. And now she knew they had been attacked yesterday. We're all guests of the Inn; everyone knows everyone else. They smiled and nodded as Valerie and Evie walked by.

Denise turned to scan the room. The Café, now Bon Vivant, had a completely different look tonight. Linens in every color of the rainbow covered the enamel table tops. They were hemmed to allow Tiger Lily's ledges to stay visible. The napkins were also in rainbow colors. The wedding party's table of four had a blue tablecloth and napkins of green, purple, orange and yellow.

Pendant lights, each colorful and unique, were turned on, kept low to provide ambiance. The flowers were also different. Denice had noticed the pretty purple bouquet in a crystal vase earlier today. Tonight, the vase was filled with flowers of every color. It was as if the wedding celebration had started a day early.

Ian texted his group to call a team meeting. No one sassed him for it; they knew better. Ian had rules. One of his rules was that he was the coach, and no one, no team member, could question his authority. Even if it was a night off and even if they had dates. He knew no one would have a date tonight. They were preparing for the Chelsea Grand Prix tomorrow morning. He had told them. No dates.

Jessie and Eric were the first to arrive. Quiet kids, they were typically the first to arrive, the last to leave; the first to help, the last to ask for help; the first to notice others, the last to be noticed by anyone. They sat with Ian at a table in the middle of the dark room. Ian said nothing, so they said nothing to one another.

They watched as the rest of the team straggled in. The last to arrive were Brendan and Alena. They walked in, sullen, as only teenagers could be, mirroring the sullen faces of everyone else. Ian made eye contact with everyone around the table. His face had never appeared so stern.

"We have a problem here, kids. Someone has behaved in such a way as to cause a great deal of notice. People all over town have started to talk. We can't have that. Not on our team."

The teens had begun to look around the table at one another, not knowing what to think, who to distrust. Who was doing what? What would Ian do? Would he disband the team? Cut out the bad apples? Who were the bad apples? Would they be able to compete tomorrow?

Ian stood. "Sit here. I'll be back."

He walked into a side room. They sat. The longer he was gone, the more agitated they became, but no one spoke. They didn't know what to say. Bill and Eddy started to lean in to one another, probably to talk. They sat back with the side door opened. A light came on in the back of the room, and Ian returned, followed by several people and the town's big police dog.

Their parents! Their families! The families of the two girls that were in trouble on the lake today! It was a party!

Ian stood to the back of the room throughout the celebration. He had done nothing but get them together. Tonight was their night. Tomorrow, they needed to be ready.

Annie, Chris, Henrie and Clara, blue because she faced a weekend without Ramon, dined together. Ray and Cheryl, who had expected to meet Pate and Janet, offered two chairs to Boone and Hilly. Terrence and Jerald were at another table, joined by Jennifer and Marie.

Felicity and Trudie, for the last month finally free of having to help at the Bon Vivant Grille, were at another table. George and Candice joined them, having taken the night off, leaving Mo's Tap in the capable hands of other staff.

Every table was filled. Unlike the opening weekend, which had table seating at specific times, people came and went on their own schedules. As Annie watched, rarely was a table empty for more than the time it took to bus and reset it.

The Bon Vivant Grille was still on probation, in a sense. It opened for business – Friday and Saturday nights only – two months ago. The opening had been auspicious, plagued by a grill fire, a murder on the second floor and paparazzi intent on making headlines at Annie's expense. The food, though, had been outstanding.

The raucous opening had contributed to attendance even now. One could hardly get into the restaurant without a reservation. Annie and her friends came every weekend, some on Friday, some on Saturday, some both nights.

Annie and the management staff of Bon Vivant, Cookie, Georgia and Isabel, would have to make a decision in the next two months. There were at least three options. Close, knowing they had given it a good run; remain open on weekends, using Tiger Lily's Café as a base; or remain open, but in a new location with additional hours. Annie was open to every option. The profits, community support, staff support, and of course input from her entire management team would be taken into consideration.

The menu was limited. It changed every week, providing a farm-to-table fine dining experience. The menu rotated as local foods became available. Cookie was a fastidious and creative chef. His commitment to excellence was one reason Annie believed the restaurant would live on, in some form, for many years.

Tonight, as always, six entrees were on the menu, including one vegetarian and one vegan option. Annie had worried about the bread and dessert selections. The Confectionary provided these items, and Carlos was in Mexico. Annie put that out of her mind. She had vowed not to worry about Carlos until it was time to worry. She needn't have worried about the breads and desserts, though. Jerry and Isabel worked together to come up with some luscious options.

Jesus had come through with wine selections for the weekend as well. George stocked a cooler with artisan beers, picked by Cookie to pair well with the entrees on the menu.

Guests chose their meal by marking a card. They were to choose one item in each category: appetizer, soup, vegetable, starch, entrée and dessert. Additional selections – at an additional charge – included wines before and during dinner and an after dinner drink. Coffee and tea were served during or after dinner, per guest wishes.

Annie and Henrie – and Chris with some additional insights – told Clara what she had been missing by not living at the Inn.

"So we have, once again, several scenarios playing out for the weekend."

"Are you counting Isabel as one of those scenarios?"

"No. Well, not really. She comes and goes, and most of her goings are right here on The Avenue, and then there's Tillie. It's more like she's a part of the family."

"But you have those bikers, and they're family, right?"

Henrie's formal tone always gave a spark to the conversation. It did again, as he said, "I believe two of the men are brothers, and the nasty man and the woman are brother and sister."

"Speaking of the sister, have you seen that sparkler on her hand, Henrie?"

"I have. It was not in evidence when they checked in. I must ask Gema if she sold an emerald and diamond ring. I would like to know the cost as well. I believe it would have fed five families for a year."

By now, the four had received their appetizers. Between the four, they chose vegetarian summer rolls wrapped in rice paper with a tangy peanut dipping sauce; shrimp mixed with tomatoes, jalapeños, onions, cilantro and a vinaigrette dressing; grilled peaches with fresh mozzarella and basil wrapped with a strip of prosciutto; and tomato basil bruschetta.

Chris was well trained. He cut his bruschetta in half, ladled half to Annie, and received half of her shrimp.

"We need to do that, Henrie."

Henrie accommodated, while he went on. "And our evening last night was made all the sweeter by the dulcet

tones of our on-our-second-honeymoon-but-they-really-
were-not couple."

"By the way, did you notice them today?"

"Yes. In the morning, they were quite finished with one
another, but by the afternoon…"

"Honey couldn't pass between them."

"Yes, something like that."

Chris asked, "What happened?"

"I suppose they came up with a reason for a divorce that
would not cost money."

"I thought the same thing. I wonder what it could be."

Clara offered, "Maybe they thought they could come up
with some dirt on his wife."

"The long-suffering little wifey-poo who keeps the
home fires burning? With three children?"

The soup arrived. San Francisco summer chili made
with black beans, summer squash, onions, tomatoes, corn,
jalapenos, quinoa and spices; tomato soup made with olive
oil, basil, pepper and garlic; creamy parmesan polenta; and
a cold pickled beet soup with radishes and dill, served with
wedges of hardboiled egg. To share this, Annie and Chris
used their own spoons in one another's bowls. Henrie
looked at Clara and gave his head a small shake. She
huffed, and pulled a slice of lemon poppy seed bread out of
the basket. Annie grabbed a cinnamon brioche.

"I have to complain about Cookie." Three spoons hit the
table while everyone looked at Annie. She continued to eat
her brioche while she said, "He always serves portion sizes
to prevent gastro-whatever-can-happen-when-overeating.
I always want one more bite."

"This is a marketing ploy. Want more? Come back next week."

The vegetable dishes were easy. They could have chosen steamed, but they chose grilled. Two servings of yellow summer squash and two of a vegetable medley. For a starch, Annie and Chris shared farfalle salad with dill, goat cheese, onions, tomatoes and spinach, and a simple garden potato salad. Henrie and Clara ordered the same thing. Quinoa salad made with red peppers, tomatoes, cucumbers, corn, black beans, nectarines, shallots, lime and cilantro.

"The wedding party doesn't have anything sinister going on. Look at them. Young, happy, in love with one another and with life."

"I wish I could be a bug on that wedding boat tomorrow."

"I'll bet, with your flowers, that it will be lovely."

"Ray offered a tour last week. Have the rest of you been on since it was painted?"

Chris said, "You'd think I would have been, but with all the times Ray and I get together, I've not been on it once since then."

"I went on, to see what I had to work with when I made up the flower arrangements. It is so pretty. Even all of the interior spaces are painted in Annie's colors. And each bedroom has a color of its own. Ray's stateroom has two colors, red and purple."

Cookie seemed again to outdo himself with the entrées. Annie and Chris shared grilled skewers made with firm tofu, potatoes, eggplant, peppers, onions and

pomegranate-peach barbecue sauce; and grilled pork
tenderloin with baby arugula and peaches. Annie enjoyed
watching Henrie work his way around baby back ribs with
blueberry chipotle barbecue; Clara had the grilled
Hawaiian chicken with pineapple.

"What about those women, Annie? You have a bad guy
– at least bad with cats – but you have heroes this time,
also, and don't they look fine tonight!"

"They do. And they are having the time of their life.
People won't leave them alone! I don't think they've taken
two bites without someone coming up to say thank you or
congratulations."

For dessert, Annie refused to share. She had dark
chocolate one-layer cake with raspberry sauce. Chris and
Henrie ordered peach tarragon pie, and Clara had lemon
blueberry sorbet.

Throughout the evening, Annie would glance
surreptitiously at the staff. Isabel, capable and competent,
seating diners, and waiting, serving and bussing if needed.
Only those who knew her knew the worry in her heart.

Cookie, who from time to time would exit the kitchen,
glance around the room and approach a couple of tables to
thank diners for coming and ask if they needed anything.
She smiled at this, and occasionally he caught her eye to
wink. They had decided together that he had to overcome
his terminal shyness and force this behavior. He did it
often enough that almost every diner witnessed it, if not
having been approached themselves.

She could see into the kitchen as Georgia, Cookie's
main assistant in the kitchen, triaged orders and assured
plates went out on time, appropriately garnished and in

concert with the rest of the plates at the table. She was a more than capable cook, but Cookie counted on her to tell everyone – including him – what to do and when to do it.

The table ended their evening with coffee and Kir, a digestif made with white wine – Jesus selected a pinot grigio – and creme de cassis, garnished with orange.

When they finished – finally – there was nothing left to do but go home and roll into bed. Annie and Chris were quickly joined by seven cats and a little dog. Tillie's mommy would be home late, and she didn't like to sleep alone.

23

Annie overslept. What else was new? It was Saturday and she had nothing to do. No place to be. No one who cared, apparently. Not even the cats. Chris was long gone and the cats were downstairs with Henrie. Or maybe they had gone to work. She didn't know.

She made a cup of coffee, took a shower, dressed, made another cup of coffee, glanced at the clock and said, "Oh no!" Annie ran down the stairs and into the dining room, slowed down to say good morning to the guests at the table, and ran into the kitchen.

"Henrie, I'm late…"

"For Mem's training session. There is not a thing you need to do here. Have a good morning."

Going back through the dining room, she asked Isabel, "Do you want to go to Mem's session with me? The healing power of tea? It starts in two minutes."

Isabel said, "Let me grab my bag."

While Isabel grabbed her bag, Annie looked at Celeste. "I don't know that Collin would care for the session, but would you like to go? It's just on the other side of The Avenue."

"No, thank you. I'm going back to that darling little jewelry store to see if my necklace is still there. And then we're leaving. A day early, but I talked him into it. We'll find a cozy place on the way home."

Celeste leaned over to nuzzle Collin behind his left ear. Annie smiled and scratched the back of her head to cover her gag reflex.

Mem had set all the tables on the teashop side of her business – the front – with mismatched china teacups and saucers. Each table had a teapot, steam rising from the spout.

The tables were filled by the time Annie and Isabel arrived. Mem brought two folding chairs from behind the counter. They squeezed in with Clara, Diana, Holly and Jolly.

Annie whispered, "Who's minding the stores?"

Each whispered back the name of a part-timer. Diana whispered, "Ginger."

Mem, standing at the front of the room, said, "Ladies, and I see a few gentlemen, we're going to talk about the healing powers of tea. And let me tell you this from the start. Some teas have healing powers when you drink them, and some will heal you just as well when you do not."

Mem, for dramatic flair, picked up a china teapot and poured a dark tea into her cup, holding the cup low and the pot high.

She put both on the table. "Throughout the room are pots of a variety of teas. Please do not help yourself until I give you permission. For this session, I will intersperse information about teas and the benefits of drinking them with other ways to use tea.

"First, let's talk about how to make the perfect cup of tea. Tea is not something you drink casually. No, you choose the best leaves, you wait – patiently – for your water to come to the right temperature, you steep the tea for just the right amount of time. Each tea requires a different water temperature and a different steeping time."

Mem looked around the room. "As you drink your tea," she demonstrated with the cup she had just poured, "breathe in the flavor and allow the steam to warm your face. Sip slowly. Savor every moment."

Mem set the cup down. "Let's talk about water and timing. If you plan to brew black tea, water should come to a full boil, but then you must let it cool for one minute. If, however, you plan to brew green tea, never let it cool before pouring the boiling water over the leaves.

"Never, never, ever use hot tap water to brew your tea. And, allow me to say, you should never, never, ever heat your water in a microwave. Use a proper stove."

Clara turned to Annie and whispered, "She's talking about me. It's a good thing I have to leave early. Much more of this and I'll be offended."

Mem continued her lecture. "I can see some of you begin to nod off or become otherwise distracted. Before I get into the specifics of black tea, let's do something fun. Clara, did you wonder why I put a bowl and stack of washcloths at your table?"

"I thought that you thought I might spill."

Laughter emanated around the room as Mem smiled and said, "Well, that, too, but really, I hope I have enough washcloths for everyone. This will really wake you up."

Mem walked to the table and poured the tea into the bowl. "This is chamomile tea. It has been allowed to cool a bit, so it is warm, not hot. Before you came in, I put three drops of lavender oil into the pot."

Mem soaked a cloth in the bowl and wrung it dry. "Try this, Clara. Put it over your face. Breathe deeply."

Clara put her head back and placed the cloth over her face. She breathed in deeply. With the cloth still over her face, she said, "Oh, my. This feels so good. What's it doing to me?"

"Beside the fact that you will feel much better once breathing in the chamomile and lavender, when you remove the cloth, your face will actually be brighter."

"I could stay under this for hours, but Mem, I'm sorry. I have to leave." Clara made no move to take the cloth off her face or to stand up. "In just a minute, I'll really leave. Really."

Mem looked around. "Gather round, everyone. I'll hand you a warm cloth."

Annie stood back, allowing others to go ahead of her. As she stood, she heard a loud whisper. Annie turned to look. It was Geraldine's sister, the wife of the genealogist.

In a stage whisper, the sister said, "Have you heard that Annie is looking into her Indian ancestry? I hear it's Apache. Or was that Comanche? I wonder which one of her parents was less than forthcoming about his or her heritage."

The woman to whom she spoke used the same loud whisper to reply, "No wonder she has the temperament she does. I hear Indians can be, well, let's say a bottle short of a six pack."

The women slid into line to get a chamomile mask behind Annie. Mem handed a warm, damp cloth to Annie. As she reached for another cloth to prepare for Geraldine's sister, she tripped – from a standing position – and accidentally pushed the rest of the clean, dry cloths to the floor.

Clara chose this moment to leave. She accidently stepped on the clean cloths. Suddenly all feet and thumbs, she couldn't seem to do anything but step on them as she tried to pick them up.

Diana, with a to-go coffee cup in her hand, leaned over to help Clara and accidentally poured the entire cup onto the cloths.

Diana, Clara and Mem stood and stared at one another, appropriately aghast. Mem turned to the women and said, "Oh, I'm so sorry. All of my cloths were out here. I have nothing left for you."

Annie had just put the warm cloth over her face, hiding a smile, when she heard the siren. It was, of course, very close, as the Police Department was just at the end of the street. Annie expected to hear the siren die off as it drove away. Instead, it got louder and stopped not so far from where they were, on the other end of the street. Her end of the street.

Annie took the cloth off her face, turned around to look out the window, and saw Pete run to the carriage house and up the steps, Marco right behind him, gun drawn.

Jennifer and Marie looked down together as their cell phones went off signifying text messages. "It's Gina at the police station. Annie, we have to go to the Inn. Someone's either injured or…."

Annie finished the sentence. "Dead."

24

The wedding party's big day was here. Late this morning they would board The Escape for a luxurious trip going nowhere.

They would dine – yes, they could say dine, everything would be formal – in the sun, stop for a swim, and make use of the cabins and facilities to shower and dress. The black tie ceremony would be followed by another meal worthy of the occasion.

They would be joined for the day by the Captain, his dog, the pastor performing the ceremony, and two people to cook and serve.

After a quick call to the Captain, Erika turned to her fiancée and friends to say, "Yes! He said there was enough food, drink and everything else for two more people. Let's go upstairs and invite them to come!"

Erika and Denise ran up the stairs to the second floor. They noticed the door stood open just a touch, not enough to see from the street but enough to remain unlatched.

To keep the door from opening, Denise took hold of the knob as she knocked on the door. There was no answer.

"Valerie! Evie! Are you in there?" No answer.

"I'll bet they just didn't get the door closed. Let's take a quick look, just in case."

"I know, stick your camera in and take a picture. If we see anything, you know, compromising, we can erase it."

Denise stretched one arm into the doorway and snapped a photo. The women giggled as she brought the camera out and pulled up the photo. They looked at it together. And screamed.

Annie ran to the Inn and stood with Henrie on the sidewalk directly in front of the carriage house.

"Both of them?"

"I do not know, but I assume so."

"Who found them?"

"Erika, the bride-to-be, and her friend, Denise. They went to the room to invite Valerie and Evie to join them for their cruise and moonlight wedding."

"Oh, my. I guess their day just took a turn for the worse."

"Yes."

Henrie looked down. Little Socks stood at his feet. She had used a paw to tap his leg. Now she sat back, expectant. A photograph with several holes in it – probably cat tooth marks – lay at her feet.

Mr. Bean stood beside her, a similarly-marked business card still between his teeth.

Henrie leaned down, took the card from Mr. Bean, saying, "Thank you, young man." He then picked up the photograph and nodded his thanks to Little Socks. The two waited at his feet expectantly.

Annie stared at the two cats, then at the items in Henrie's hand. The photograph was self-explanatory. It was a much-younger Collin and Evie with three children.

"The missing wife."

"We must tell Pete." Henrie drew out his cellphone and sent a text to Pete. In a minute, Pete came out the door. He looked at Henrie and Annie, then trotted down the steps. Without a word, he accepted the business card and photo. He looked at the photo for only a few seconds before asking, "Where are they?"

Henrie answered. "Collin and Celeste left shortly before the women were found."

"Were they headed home?"

Annie said, "Celeste said they were going to find a 'cozy place' to stop on the way."

"Then why leave early? Chelsea and the Inn are cozy."

"She said she talked him into it. She didn't say why."

Annie watched as Denise came out of the honeymoon suite, camera in her hand. She walked toward the Inn, probably on her way to her room.

"Pete, you might want to get that camera. Denise has taken photos and videos of everything and everybody since she got here."

Pete didn't answer Annie, but he crossed the lawn in big strides and called after Denise. Henrie and Annie watched the conversation. Pete spoke. Denise's hand went to her mouth as her face made a classic "oh no!" pose. Pete spoke some more. Denise looked down at her feet and handed the camera over.

Denise turned and continued to the Inn while Pete got on the radio. Within minutes, a police officer arrived on foot. He took the camera and trotted up the street. Annie watched as he went into CyberHealth. Pete was headed back upstairs. Cyril waited at the landing.

Annie turned to Henrie. "I'll bet they're going to download or copy the photos and let her keep the camera."

Henrie looked down at Mr. Bean and Little Socks. "I do not want to know what the two of you did to come into possession of these items. However, I will tell you that your mother and I are very proud. Very proud."

Mr. Bean beamed. Little Socks blinked and washed a paw.

Annie turned at some activity in the direction of the park. "Oh, look. The ten-milers are done already. I wonder when our metric century bikers will be home."

"We have seen so little of them. They appear for an early breakfast – well before you arise – and they stay out all day. I hardly think I will recognize them."

Felicity, Trudie and Teresa walked together down the sidewalk. All three wore stunning sun dresses and low sandals. They stopped to ask about the activity.

"The wedding party may be a bit subdued," said Annie. "The women found Valerie and Evie, and...well...the KaliKo Inn has another murder to add to its resume. Actually two."

"Oh, my. We'll try to keep them focused on the positive."

"You all look fantastic. I don't think I've ever seen you this well-dressed."

Felicity said, "It's black tie, but we have swimsuits in our bags. If we have time to take a dip in the lake, Ray said we can use his stateroom to put ourselves back together."

"I want to hear everything. We need ideas for Isabel and Carlos."

"Speaking of Carlos," Teresa turned to Annie, "have you heard from him?"

"No. I was with Isabel, and as of an hour or so ago, there was no word."

"Is it time to worry?"

"No. No. We are not going to worry. Not worrying."

Trudie said, "Ladies, we have a boat to set up." They left, walking toward The Marina and what promised to be a lovely Saturday afternoon and evening on the lake. Annie watched as they met Clara on her way back, a wagon in tow. Probably empty. The flowers must be on board.

Clara stopped when she reached Annie and Henrie. "Were they both murdered?"

"I think so. And guess what. Evie was the missing wife."

"No! Is Pete putting the screws to that husband?"

"They're gone."

Clara shook her head. "Hey, I'm sorry I had to leave the tea seminar. I would have loved to find an excuse to pour tea over the heads of those two women. What was up with that?"

"It was nothing. Just Geraldine's family doing what Geraldine can't do for herself."

"What did they mean, your Indian heritage?"

"Who knows?"

A look passed between Clara and Henrie. This would be tucked away for later.

Clara took a last look at the carriage house and crossed The Avenue to Bloomin' Crazy. Annie and Henrie stayed on the sidewalk. They talked briefly to the wedding party as they left for The Marina, offering both their condolences and their congratulations.

Pete finally came downstairs, a large clear plastic bag in his hands. As he got closer, they saw a red cloth bag inside the plastic one. He stopped. Cyril trotted over to his friends, the cats and Tillie, who waited on the lawn.

"Cyril sat down at that armoire and refused to move until I unlocked and opened it. I'll bet if I had paid attention to him yesterday, I would have found this bag under the bed."

"What's important about the bag?"

"There are a couple of grenades, and packing material for three more."

"So they did throw the grenades. Do you think they were trying to hurt them?"

"I don't think so. The little bit I know about them, I think they just wanted to scare them, or ruin their vacation. I called the attorney, the one on the card. Evie had an appointment with him Monday morning. He's a divorce attorney. Valerie confirmed the appointment again, after the grenade incident. So, no, I don't think they intended more than what happened."

Pete shook his head. "I didn't get a chance to thank them. I heard it was Evie that pulled Clarice out."

Annie and Henrie nodded their heads, wondering at the sheer luck that she had been there. That both of them had been there.

Henrie got as much of an "ah ha" look as he could manage. "Pete, I recall Isabel telling Valerie and Evie about the rocks. I do believe they walked there, two days in a row, and that they climbed the rocks at some point."

"They could have figured out that's where the boat would go, and they could have figured out how to get there from the park."

Annie turned as Laila walked up. "Pete," she said softly, "are they both gone?"

"Yes, they are."

"I didn't get a chance…."

Annie put her arm around Laila. "I know."

Pete's officers finished their work. They came down the stairs carrying large bags that probably contained evidence.

"Is there anything else you need from us, Pete?"

"I'll come over and make sure I have Collin and Celeste's information, and Marco will look at their room. I doubt we'll find anything, but we have to look."

Cyril told the cats and Tillie about the bag. *"Pete found some grenades, and he got the camera from the woman that took all the videos. He called the man on that business card, too. Good call, picking that up, Little Socks."*

"Who was he?"

"He was going to help Evie get a divorce. He didn't think Collin knew about the appointment. He knows Collin. He told Pete that Collin was a pompous so-and-so, but he didn't think he would do anything like this, murder his wife, even for money. He would have had another plan. Some kind of plan to keep her from getting any money."

Tiger Lily told Cyril about the bikers. *"You'll probably get called to go up there. Make sure Fat Cat and Scaredy Cat are okay."*

Cyril nodded gravely.

Little Socks started back toward the house. *"We have to stay on the front porch and watch. As soon as we know those men have been caught, I have to put that piece of paper where Pete will see it."*

"Let's hope — when they're caught — that she's still alive."

As the cats turned to walk away, Cyril called after them. *"Kali and Ko, you were very smart to focus on that bag and to tell everyone about it. If not for you, we wouldn't have looked more closely at the women, and Pete wouldn't have everything he needs to find their killer."*

Kali and Ko, not used to being the smart ones, smiled gratefully at Cyril and walked to the porch with their heads and tails held high.

25

Ian made sure his team got to bed early Friday night, even after cake and punch. They were at the head of the pack starting out. He wanted them to pace themselves and not be concerned about "winning." Not this time. There would be time enough for that. Another year, another race.

They had not had the opportunity to bike over the rough areas of the state park's hiking trails, but Ian made them walk it about ten times in March and April. Their bicycles were ready for the rough terrain, and their minds were prepared. Ian coached them then and now to take it slow.

As they made their way through this section, single file, they were passed by many bikers, including one group of four that was rude. After that group got past – Ian noticed that Kim didn't even look as she brushed past – Ian took time to make sure everyone heard him, taking a few times to tell it, that a key to great sportsmanship is being a good sport before, during and after each event.

For this race, he kept the team together. They started together; they would finish together. They would race…well…another year.

Throughout the race, opportunities for teaching presented themselves. For example, the fact that they started early, slow and careful at the beginning had them close to the winning slots at the end. They passed everyone that had passed them earlier with the exception of the four rude bikers.

Ian wasn't so sure he wanted to catch up to them. He thought it would be best to stay as far away from Kim as he could.

The northeast tip of Lake Scott was about the halfway point for the metric century route. Kim, Monte, Clark and Bryce had walked this route and knew it would be one of the roughest parts of the trail. They were aware some bikers in past years got off to walk their bikes around the last curve. The trail became more narrow and rocky at this end of the lake. At the curve, someone falling from the sheer drop would land on nothing but more rock fifty feet below.

The four planned their strategy before taking off at the starting line. Clark and Bryce insisted they put on speed in the beginning to establish and maintain a lead that would keep them out of eyesight of the group. "That way," said Bryce, "they won't see us and they may forget to try to get ahead of us."

As long as they were ahead, and as long as the trail allowed, they stayed two abreast, Kim and Monte in front, Clark and Bryce a few yards behind. After the danger point, they would take off on their own, race to the finish line, and take first, second, third and fourth places.

As they neared the tip of the lake and the dangerous curve, Monte began to lag behind, putting Kim in the lead. As she got to the curve, caution took the better of her and she dismounted to walk the bicycle around.

As she did, she looked back toward Monte. His bicycle was on the ground and he was right behind her. He came at her fast, grabbed her left arm with his left hand and used his right hand on her back to propel her over the rocks.

Kim had a couple of seconds to react; she dug in her feet and went low, knocking Monte off balance. From out of nowhere came a horrifying sound, like wild animals fighting to the death.

Monte screamed and let go of Kim. She turned to see two cats on his back and neck, claws dug deep and teeth clamped to his ears. Monte tried to pull them off. It looked like he would succeed. If he did, he could throw them over the cliff. The cats seemed to sense this, and they jumped down to attack his ankles.

Clark and Bryce reached them, and as Kim tried to yell, "He was going to kill me!" they threw their bicycles to the ground and came after her. Clark reached her first, grabbed her right arm and would have thrown her, but instead he yelled in pain, turned and bent to rid himself of the cat whose claws were dug into the small of his back. Sharp teeth dug into his side.

Bryce had difficulty reaching her as well. One of the cats had climbed onto his back and was now on top of his head, scratching his eyes and forehead. Blood flowed freely from the wounds.

Monte started toward Kim again, ears and neck bloody, but he was a few yards from her.

Kim saw bikers coming around the last curve. It was Ian and his group of teens. She screamed as loud as she could, "They're trying to kill me!"

Ian's took in the situation at once. Kim was off her bicycle and in distress, believing the men to be – could that be correct – trying to kill her. It must be correct, because the three men mounted their bicycles and took off around the tip of the lake.

His disaster training kicked in. "Renee, you, Eric and Jessie stay with her. Get her down the hill when she's ready."

He turned to Alena. "You wanted a race. Go catch them."

Alena's smile was wicked. She and the other teens took off, barreling down the hill as only teenagers bent on adventure could manage. Ian followed, careful to stay at the back of the pack of raging teens, but close enough to handle any situation.

Kim collapsed, surrounded by three helpful teens. As she caught her breath, she stared at the two cats. They sat on the lake side of the trail, calmly licking blood off their claws. One of the cats, the biggest one, looked up at her and made eye contact. She could have sworn the cat smiled.

Pete was still at the KaliKo Inn. While Marco searched Collin's room, Pete called the state police to put a be-on-the-lookout notice on the couple and their cherry red sports car.

His cellphone rang just as he hung up. Ian was calling from the SAG stop close to the north end of Lake Scott.

Pete called upstairs to Marco, "We have to go. Lock that door and come on."

He turned to Henrie and Annie. "Don't let anyone in that room. I think we have a situation at the tip of Lake Scott."

When Marco hit the bottom of the steps, he and Pete walked quickly out the front door. Annie followed them to the porch. "What now, Pete?"

Pete kept walking and answered over his shoulder. "Some volunteers at the SAG stop are holding three men, said they tried to kill a woman at the tip of Lake Scott."

"Three men? And they tried to kill a woman?"

Pete stopped and turned back to her. "Yeah. Mean anything?"

Annie put her head in her hands as she sank into a chair. "I'm sure you're going to find out they are guests of the KaliKo Inn."

Pete looked at her. "Lock their rooms."

The humans didn't notice when Little Socks slipped down from her chair and inside the Inn.

Tiger Lily called after Cyril, *"Find them. Bring them home."*

The SAG stop was situated at the point the route left Lake Scott and followed public roads. When Pete and Marco arrived, they saw three men on the ground, hands and feet zip-tied. They were bloody about the face, neck and arms. A group of teens encircled them, walking about and laughing amongst themselves. Pete recognized all of them. He nodded, but walked past to approach Ian, who stood to one side with one of the girls, Brendan's little sister, Alena.

"You didn't tell me you hurt them."

"They mostly looked like this when we caught up to them."

"How'd they get hurt?"

Ian laughed. "They said it was two cats."

"Cougars?"

"Cats. Regular cats."

Alena said, "They're just bullies, is all. They can dish it out, if it's just one girl, but with a group of us, they couldn't take it."

"Did you help catch them?"

"I got the first one. I wanted the one in front, but no one could get by until someone took out the slow one. That one." Alena pointed to a man Pete would later know to be Monte.

"How'd you take him down?"

"The way Ian taught us, you know, if we were alone and someone was trying to get to us. Before I took off after them, I got my spoke wrench out. And, you know. When I caught up to him, I jabbed it into his rear wheel. Too bad. Looked like a brand new bike."

Ian smiled. Pete smiled. Alena smiled.

"How'd the other two go down?"

Ian answered. "Essentially the same way. Once Alena and Monte were out of the way, the rest of the group pretty much surrounded the other two."

"Monte?"

"That would be Kim's brother. Kim's the woman they were trying to hurt. Or kill. Whatever." Ian pointed to the tent behind the SAG table. "She's in there, if you want to talk to her."

Pete nodded his thanks and turned to Marco. "Better get those guys into an ambulance and start getting statements from the kids. I'll talk to her. Maybe take her back to the crime scene."

Ian nodded toward a golf cart. "You can take her up using that. I'll go with you, if you'd like. The kids and I got there just as she got away from them."

Pete nodded again. He walked to the tent and ducked inside. He recognized Kim, having seen her around town a time or two. It didn't look as if the cats touched her. "I'm Pete, Chief of Police."

"Kim. Kim Jax."

"Do you want to talk first, tell me what happened, or do you want to ride back to the scene and tell me there?"

"Let's go back there. It will be clearer in my mind."

With Ian driving, Pete, Kim and Cyril took a ride to the tip of Lake Scott. At the tip of the lake, Pete asked Kim to take him through it. He turned on a tape recorder, and as she pointed to the locations – where she stopped to walk her bicycle, where Monte tried to push her over, where she was standing when Clark and Bryce attacked her – he took pictures.

The scene was not preserved. Ian confirmed that all the bikers that signed up for the metric century had gone through the SAG stop. Not counting his group of teens, at least seventy bicycles had tracked through the scene.

Pete's eyes were drawn to Cyril. Normally, Cyril would have sniffed out as many clues as possible from the scene of the crime. Instead, he sat close to the lake with two cats.

Kim looked at Cyril and the cats. "You might not believe me, Chief, but I think those cats saved my life. I think they knew what they were doing."

Pete looked closer. The same two cats had been at the scene of the catnapping last winter. Correction. At the scene of the rescue. They now belonged to Holly and Jolly. How did they get here? Pete closed his eyes and shook his head. Two more cat detectives. That was all this town needed.

Eventually, Pete exhausted his search for evidence. He, Ian and Kim walked back to the golf cart. Pete called Cyril, who stayed with the cats. "Bring them with you. We'll take them home."

Simon Finnegan and Oscar McMurphy stood and strolled regally to the golf cart, jumping on the back and looking for all the world like a prince and a princess in a parade.

Simon Finnegan and Oscar McMurphy got to the Inn in time for snacks. Today, Henrie served egg salad. Portions had been spooned into individual dishes for the cats and Tillie. When Henrie saw the two feline guests, he added two more dishes.

Fat Cat said, *"The lady's okay and the men are locked up. We're hungry!"*

Several cat voices clamored for information, but Tiger Lily shushed them. *"Let them eat first. They've had a long, hard day, and it started last night."*

Finally, when they had their fill of egg salad and healthy drinks of water, Fat Cat told their story. Scaredy Cat filled in as she thought appropriate.

"We walked all night to get to the tip of the lake. It wasn't hard to find, but sometimes we had to stop and ask if we were going in the right direction."

Sassy Pants perked up. *"Who talked to you?"*

"Oh, you know, squirrels, chipmunks. There were some cats, but they wouldn't talk to us."

"They were what you call feral."

"Wot's feral?"

Tiger Lily bopped Sassy Pants on the nose. *"Let them tell the story, then you can ask questions."*

Sassy Pants got a hurt look on her face. She rubbed her nose with a paw and sat back.

Fat Cat picked up the story again. *"Anyway, we got there and found places to hide. I went to the far side of the curve so I could see down the trail, and she,"* motioning with his head to Scaredy Cat, *"stayed at the tip of the lake. When the first set of bikers came into view, I could tell right away it was them. I waited long enough to see that they were pretty far ahead of the rest of the bikers, then I joined Scaredy Cat – I mean Oscar McMurphy – at the tip."*

Scaredy Cat nodded. *"We talked about what to do. We got behind one of the rocks to hide."*

Fat Cat continued, *"When they got there, the lady, Kim, got off, I think to walk her bicycle around the curve. It's really dangerous. That guy, Monte, was ready for her to do that. He got off his bicycle before she did, and he got up behind her and tried to push her over."*

Scaredy Cat laughed. *"We got him good."*

"Yeah. He'll probably have scars on his ears. He tried to throw us over the cliff, but we were ready for him. We jumped off and grabbed his ankles."

"Yeah, and then those other two came, and I got one of them on his lower back. He had some love handles, and I put a few holes into them."

"I got on the other one's back and shoulders, and I got his face real good. I may have gotten his eyes."

"We were going to have to go after that first one again, but those other bikers came with Ian and they chased them away."

"We sat down to wait. We knew Cyril would come, and we hoped he might get us a ride back to town."

"Yeah. That was a long trip. My paws have a few cuts."

"And we were tired."

"And hungry."

Tiger Lily looked at them with satisfaction. *"You're very brave."*

The cats looked up as Pete and Cyril came into the dining room. They had been so intent on the story, they didn't hear them come into the Inn.

Pete pulled out the dining room chair at the end of the table, the chair closest to the Seven Cats Detective Agency. Cyril sat down next to Tillie. When Henrie walked to the kitchen/dining door, he saw Pete staring at the companions.

Pete's eyes started with Cyril, and they roamed over Tillie, Sassy Pants, Mr. Bean, Little Socks, Kali, Mo, Tiger Lily, Ko, Simon Finnegan and Oscar McMurphy.

Annie came into the dining room. She stood, silent, behind Pete. By now, she and Henrie stared at the companions as well.

Pete looked at the companions as he talked. "I don't know how you knew something bad would happen out there. I don't know how you got out there. I don't know if Cyril was involved in this. I don't know how you got your hands on the business card and the photograph. I don't know how Cyril knew to make me find the bag that had the grenades. I just know that somehow, you are always there, always ahead of me."

Pete looked at Little Socks. She looked back, careful to let him win by blinking every now and then.

"Is there something I need to find in the room of those bikers?"

Little Socks stared at him. She blinked once.

"Make it easy for me. Just show me."

Little Socks stood and trotted to the stairway, turning once to see if Pete would follow. Pete did. So did Annie. Henrie followed with a pass key. Cyril nodded to his friends and followed as well.

Little Socks sat outside the room Clark and Bryce stayed in. Henrie, after unlocking the door, stood back to allow Pete to enter. As Pete slipped on rubber gloves, Little Socks went to the end of the bed and sat by a much-chewed piece of paper. It was a mess, with tooth marks and a combination of writing and doodles going every which way on the page.

Pete knelt next to the cat and the paper. He looked her in the eyes. "Anything else?"

Little Socks stood, placing one paw on Pete's knee. She leaned her face into Pete's and gave him a soft kitty kiss. Then she jumped over his legs and ran out the door.

26

Kim didn't know what to feel. She called her fellow board members to let them know what had happened and that charges of attempted murder would be filed against her brother and cousins. The last call was to Evan, who offered to call both the corporate attorney and a good private attorney.

"I understand the corporate attorney, but I'm not paying for a criminal attorney for the people that tried to kill me, even if they are family!"

From the other end of the phone, Evan said, "Not for that. The corporate attorney will take the company's best interest to heart. You need someone to represent you, so you can take control of their shares, or hand-pick the people you want to have them."

"Oh. Good idea. Thanks, Evan."

"Always looking out for you. Do you want me to come out there?"

Kim looked at Ian, waiting for her in the foyer of the Inn. "No, Evan, I'm fine. I'll be home in a couple of days."

Ray relaxed on the deck while the wedding party took a swim in the lake. Jock stood guard, ever vigilant for a swimmer in trouble. He barked once, and Ray opened his eyes to look around.

Teresa, Felicity and Trudie were up from their swim, taken on the shady side of The Escape. Felicity approached Jock, whose tail was in full motion, expecting a treat. What he got was a pat on the head.

Felicity yelled down to the wedding party. "Do you want me to film this?"

Denise answered. "Yes! Can you get at least three minutes?"

"Sure." Felicity picked up the camera and filmed, moving around the railing for several angles. After one minute of filming, a fifth swimmer was in the frame. Jock. She gave it two more minutes and turned the camera off, waved good-bye and went below to join Trudie and Teresa.

Ray leaned back again.

The mood of the wedding party upon boarding could be described as melancholy at best. Ray stopped the engines far enough out that land was only a distant glow on the horizon. There, they served lunch: lobster club sandwiches and spinach walnut salad topped with raspberries. Pinot Grigio and coffee were served. The mood lifted a bit.

As the women cleaned up from lunch, Ray powered back toward shore, putting into a semi-private bay for an afternoon swim. They had been here for a couple of hours now. It was about time to get everyone on board to get cleaned up for the ceremony, but Ray liked hearing the peals of laughter coming from the water.

A shadow fell over him. Teresa stood looking down until he opened his eyes. "Time to get them going, Captain."

"Alright." Ray groaned as he got up. Truth be told, he enjoyed his rest as much as he enjoyed hearing their laughter. Jock was back on deck, so he asked for his help. "Jock, call them up."

Jock obeyed, barking with abandon at the wedding party until they gave in and swam toward the platform and ladder.

While the wedding party showered and dressed below, Ray and Teresa put the makeshift chapel together and placed the flowers. Trudie brought the champagne bucket, decorated in flowers as well, as the crowning touch.

Ray, as captain, could perform wedding ceremonies. For this wedding, he stepped aside. The couple wanted their pastor to perform the ceremony, but their pastor was unable to come during the weekend they chose. Instead, their hometown pastor contacted Teresa, and through a process of several emails and telephone calls, the ceremony came together.

By the time the wedding party came up, dressed in formal clothing and deck shoes, Ray and Teresa were ready. Dinner was sufficiently prepared that Trudie and Felicity joined them in the chapel. Felicity once again took the camera, so Denise's participation in the ceremony could be documented.

Like Denise, she turned in a circle, making sure to capture everyone and everything in this temporary chapel.

Ray stood in the back, Jock beside him. Ray had a black tuxedo jacket over his summer captain's outfit. Jock wore a white bow tie around his black neck.

Felicity, Trudie and Teresa were dressed in black. The wedding party was dressed in a variety of colors. Grant wore a yellow tuxedo with red deck shoes. Tom wore an orange tuxedo with purple deck shoes. Erika wore a long, strapless dress made of flowered material with large purple, pink, red and peach tropical flowers. The dress was form-fitting; the waistline was cinched by purple satin; a slit came up her left leg to her thigh. Denise wore a short, strapless tie-died dress with a tight bodice and swishy skirt. The bodice was cinched in blue satin that ended in a bow.

As Felicity focused her camera on the feet of the women, Ray looked. Both women wore white deck shoes. How boring.

Ray enjoyed this group. Since their swim, their bright personalities had returned and it seemed everything was funny. They laughed through the wedding ceremony as both Grant and Erika messed up their lines.

After the ceremony, Ray served champagne to the wedding party in the "chapel." He and his helpers went to the galley to finish dinner. It would be served on deck.

Trudie said, "Ray, you don't have to help. All we have to do is plate the meals, and we're done."

"At least let me help carry things out."

"You and Jock are going to sit down and enjoy dinner. Hey, you can light the candles."

Ray went on deck and noticed for the first time how pretty the dining table was. Felicity had borrowed some of the colorful tablecloths from Bon Vivant. Through clever ways of folding and draping, all six rainbow colors were visible.

Another champagne bucket stood to one side, decorated in Clara's colorful flowers; eight colorful napkins waited, two at each place setting, folded into drooping but beautiful linen swans. Six candles were in one long brass candleholder. It was solid with high stems to hold the candles firmly. Flowers were woven around the base of the candleholder; only the fresh colors of the flowers were visible.

Two bottles of Zinfandel sat on a table to the side, open and breathing for the occasion.

Ray lit the candles and stood back to look at the effect. The sun was still bright in the sky; the moon was rising. The Escape still rested in the swimming cove, nose in, allowing persons on the deck to see nothing but water and sky. Dinner would be served slowly, and the party would watch the sun set over a calm lake. Eventually, Ray would take The Escape back to the middle of the lake for a moonlight cruise.

Before going below, Ray went to the stereo system to turn on Denise's iPod music shuffle, an eclectic blend of what seemed to be every type of music imaginable.

As Ray went below, the wedding party came on deck and poured more champagne for themselves. Denise was once again in her video and photo glory. She filmed the table, the champagne and wine setups, the music station, the view from the deck, the wedding party sitting down to dinner.

The first course was brie in puff pastry. Sometime later, Felicity and Trudie carried out bowls of Caesar salad and crusty French bread with seasoned olive oil for dipping.

The next dish was grilled mixed vegetables, served with a side of rosemary mashed potatoes. Finally, and Ray had to admit this was his favorite course, they served roasted pork loin with granny smith applesauce.

Sunset was almost upon them when Ray took the dessert course up, individual crocks of crème brûlée, the top layer of sugar seared to perfection. Felicity and Trudie followed him, clearing the table of all extraneous plates and silver. This allowed Ray to go forward to prepare The Escape to go home.

Jock padded after him, then stopped and turned. He sniffed the air and went to the railing. He looked into the trees in the distance. Then he barked once, twice, then set up a furious banter of barking, snarling and growling.

Ray, always vigilant when Jock raised an alarm, walked back to Jock at the railing. He stared into the tree line but could see nothing menacing. He turned and said calmly, "Why don't you all go into the galley, let me check this out. Tom, would you blow out those candles on your way, please?"

Ray took Jock by the collar to pull him back, but Jock broke free and continued his alarm.

Ray turned to see that almost everyone was in the galley; only Trudie and Denise were still on deck; Trudie encouraged Denise to stop filming and get below without success. Her camera was aimed in the direction of Jock's attention.

Ray said, "Denise, you have to…"

And the shot rang out. Jock wailed in pain. Denise filmed Jock as he went down, capturing Ray on camera as he pulled Jock to the deck and shielded him with his body.

And then…well, then all heck broke loose. Trudie and Felicity were back on deck. They shielded Jock and pulled him below while Ray got The Escape moving. As the engine had been turned off, a few minutes elapsed before The Escape actually moved away from land.

During that time, several shots were heard, and many of them found purchase on the boat. They seemed to follow Ray as he moved to the wheelhouse to start the engines. Ray did much of the work from a crouching position, worried more about what was happening to Jock than what might happen to himself.

He didn't realize Denise continued to film into the trees, staying low along the deck line.

As soon as The Escape was in motion, Ray reached for the radio and called The Marina. When they were safely on the lake, he yelled for Tom and Grant to come up. He showed them how to steer and showed them the landmark to steer for.

Ray went below. Bloody towels were strewn on the floor. Trudie held two more against the wound in Jock's shoulder. Felicity held his head in her lap. Denise filmed until her batteries finally died.

27

"But ask the animals, and they will teach you, or the birds in the sky, and they will tell you; or speak to the earth, and it will teach you, or let the fish in the sea inform you. Which of all these does not know that the hand of the Lord has done this? In his hand is the life of every creature and the breath of all mankind."

Teresa started her sermon with this passage from Job 12:7-10.

Sassy Pants, who usually did not like to be held, liked to snuggle in Annie's lap. She slept peacefully while Annie and Chris sat in the back pew of Soul's Harbor. Tiger Lily sat beside Chris, pressed up against his leg. The other cats took up the rest of the pew. Only Little Socks seemed to be awake enough to listen to the sermon.

Well, Annie and Chris were awake. Kind of. Saturday night had been long. Again.

Annie heard the passage from Job but little else. Her mind churned. Maybe she needed a vacation. Chris wanted to take her to meet his parents. That wouldn't be a vacation; that would be pure torture. She would be away from her cats and her friends; she would be among the filthy rich.

As Teresa wove a sermon around the Bible verses, Annie wondered if Terrence and Jerald would give her lessons in etiquette so she would use the right fork.

Chris reached over to pet Sassy Pants and let his hand rest on Annie's other leg. Annie put her hand on top of his and wondered what his parents would think if they could see them now. What would Miss Manners say?

Isabel sat in the row just in front of Annie. Tillie, tired of turning around to look at the cats, finally settled in for a nap beside her. Across the way, Janet and the girls sat with Holly and Jolly. Cyril was with Janet. He turned his head often, as if watching for Pete to come into the sanctuary. Simon Finnegan and Oscar McMurphy curled into Cyril's stomach. Annie thought the cats prevented Cyril from pacing.

After church, Annie invited everyone from The Avenue to bring food and drink to the beach. The day would be sun-filled and eighty degrees. Humidity was low. The lake was warming up. It would be a beautiful day.

At the Inn, Henrie handed a basket to Annie. "This is for Ray and Cheryl. There is a special treat inside."

Chris took the basket from her. "We'll walk it over and be back in time for the picnic."

"Very well. Isabel insisted on helping. She made fried chicken with buttermilk and taco seasonings. I made the potato salad and your favorite deviled eggs."

"We won't be late."

Tiger Lily and Mo walked with Annie and Chris to The Marina. Once there, they got into a boat owned by Ray and Cheryl and motored the short distance to their home, accessible only by water.

Tiger Lily and Mo jumped out and ran to the house. Annie said, "They know what's going on. I don't remember talking about it in front of them."

"You never know where they are, and their hearing is so much better than ours."

"It's more than that. At about the time it was happening, the cats all got attentive. Do you remember? They jumped to the window in the dining room and stared toward the lake. By the time we got the call, I could track it back to when they did that. They didn't come off the windowsill until you got off the phone and you knew everyone was safe."

"Everyone but Jock."

"But they knew they couldn't do anything about that. Did you see how they huddled together?"

"Yeah."

"I don't know, Chris."

They stopped walking. Chris turned to her. "You don't know what?"

"I don't think I can leave them here while I go visit your parents. Not for that long. I can't leave them for that long."

"You don't have to. I thought you knew I assumed they would come with us."

Annie looked at Chris. "Really?"

Chris shook his head. "You mean if I had said those words, 'the cats can come,' this conversation would have ended months ago?"

Annie smiled. "Maybe. Only one more thing."

"What's that?"

"Will you teach me how to use the right fork?"

Chris laughed. They started walking again. "We use a dinner fork and a salad fork."

"I can handle that."

"And then there's the dinner knife, the appetizer knife, a spoon, a soup spoon and an oyster fork. Oh, and a dessert fork or spoon. Or both."

While they walked and Chris talked, Annie's mouth dropped open and she stared at him.

Cheryl stood at the open door. She smiled. "Did Henrie send that?"

Annie snapped her head to look at Cheryl. "Yes. I gather there's a special treat inside."

"I know someone who is ready for that treat."

Chris and Annie followed Cheryl inside. Ray sat on a long, low sofa, Jock stretched out beside him, his large head in Ray's lap. Tiger Lily and Mo sat on the back of the sofa, their front legs trailing down the back of the sofa to touch Jock's side lightly.

"How is he this morning?"

"He's probably already addicted to painkillers, but he's happy."

Henrie went back into the Inn. He walked to the second floor and knocked softly on the room that faced the lake. He heard, "Come in."

He did. He saw a man and a woman at the deck table, drinking coffee and watching the goings-on below.

"Pardon me, Kim. Good morning, Ian."

"Henrie."

"I am certain you heard the festivities gathering below your window, and I am here to offer a formal invitation to join us. There is food and drink for all to enjoy."

Kim looked at Ian, then back at Henrie. "Would people be embarrassed that…"

"Tell me, why would anyone be embarrassed? They are very happy for your safety, and proud of the role our friend Ian played in your escape from certain disaster."

Ian smiled. "I love the way you talk, Henrie. What do you think?"

"What do YOU think?"

"The beach is going to be filled with cats and dogs…Henrie, how is Jock?"

"His brain is addled with pain-killers and the healing process has begun."

"Are those two cats down there? The two that belong to Holly and Jolly?"

"Not yet, but I expect they will arrive shortly."

"Well, then, Kim. We have to go down. We have to thank the real heroes for saving you."

Pete sat down in the interview room across from Collin. Collin was dirty and unshaven; his clothes were disheveled from a night in lockup. Even silk and linen will muss up given enough time and circumstance.

"What's all this about? They told me Evelyn is dead, and now we're locked up. I didn't have anything to do with it. I didn't even know she was in town. You know that."

"I know nothing of the sort, Collin. Let's just go through this."

"Yes, let's. I'm a jerk. I'm having an affair. That doesn't make me a murderer."

"Like I said, let's just go through this."

Pete pulled open his briefcase and placed a folder in front of him, leaving it closed. Collin looked at it with trepidation.

Pete asked, "Do you remember our last interview?"

"Yes."

"I believed you then, but you left something out. You neglected to tell me you were calling Evelyn on her cellphone."

"I had no way of knowing she wasn't home."

"I know that, but I also remember that you and Celeste were not getting along very well. Something happened to change that. By lunchtime, I saw the two of you at the Café, and a more loving couple could not have been invented by Harliquin."

Collin stayed silent. Until Pete didn't speak. And didn't speak. Collin finally said, "We made up."

"What caused you to make up?"

Collin's eyes shifted from side to side. He finally said, "She decided she'd been foolish, and we just made up."

"I see. Tell me, when did you learn that Evelyn was in Chelsea?"

"When they told me she had been murdered."

"They, who?"

"You know who. When I was arrested."

"Before that time, you didn't know Evelyn was in Chelsea." Pete's question was phrased as a comment.

"That's what I said, isn't it?"

"That's what you said." Pete phrased his next two questions as if they were comments. "And you stand by that statement. You are telling me the truth."

"Yes. Why would I lie about that?"

"That, Collin, is the sixty four thousand dollar question." Pete opened the folder and pulled out a photograph. It was a still from the video taken at the Bon Vivant, the one that captured Collin and Celeste, smiling, acknowledging a finger wave from Valerie and Evie.

Pete put the photograph in front of Collin and said nothing, waiting for him to respond.

"Well. Um. Well. Um. I guess I could have been mistaken."

"Mistaken?"

"Um. When was this taken?"

"I believe it was sometime after you realized Evelyn was in town – I note the absence of surprise on your face in the photograph – and sometime before you were arrested and feigned ignorance of her presence in Chelsea."

"Okay. Okay. Let me be honest, here. I know it looks bad, but believe me, I didn't murder her. I didn't!"

"Would you like to know what Celeste had to say about that?"

"You talked to her already?"

"I did."

"What did she say?"

"She said she is a very sound sleeper. She said if you got up during the night to do something, like walk across the lawn to the carriage house, she would not have noticed."

"What? She accused me of murdering my wife?"

"You are the logical suspect."

"I didn't! Maybe she did! Maybe I'm a sound sleeper, too, and maybe she got up and, and, and killed her!"

"There were a lot of maybes in that sentence, Collin. Why don't you just tell me what you knew, when you knew it, and what you did, starting from the minute following our interview."

Collin fumed, but he looked at the table, shook his head and began. He told Pete that he and Celeste had argued, that he walked to the deck, and hearing a familiar laugh, he looked down and saw Evelyn on the median.

He told Pete of the conversation he and Celeste had. "I figured that I could make it bad enough for Evelyn that she couldn't survive in our hometown, so, I figured if I leaned on her, she would back off a divorce and stay put."

"How were you going to lean on her?"

"I would have told everyone that she was a lesbian, and that she and her lover, Valerie, had been together since college."

"Who would care if that were true?"

"The kids would, her parents, her friends, everyone in town would. She would be a laughingstock, and I'd get custody of the kids and she would get nothing."

"In whose world are you living, Collin? How long has it been since being a lesbian would result in something like that? Especially since you were off having an affair?"

"But a decent affair, with a woman. That's different."

Pete shook his head. He realized this was going nowhere fast, so he changed tactic. "Tell me, since it's apparent you don't love her, why would you want her to stay in the marriage?"

"Someone has to take care of the kids, clean the house, cook, you know, and give the appearance of, well, the appearance of respectability."

"So you would have a house slave and she would continue to live in the lap of luxury. Shopping at Goodwill while you wear tailored linen, driving a rattletrap car while you drive the latest sports model, driving the kids here and there for activities while you go out to dinner, staying home while you go off on vacation with your latest girlfriend."

"The way you say it sounds pretty bad."

"How would you change it?"

"Well, well, I'm the man, and the man decides these things. She doesn't have a right to make those decisions."

"Didn't. She didn't have a right, is what you meant to say, right? But she was getting ready to make a decision, wasn't she, Collin?"

"She might have. I don't know. She didn't say anything about it."

"But she was a different woman in Chelsea, wasn't she. She was bright, lively, and," Pete tapped the photo, "she wasn't going to let you treat her like that anymore. Was she." It was a question stated as a comment.

Collin didn't say anything.

"Was she." Again, it was a question stated as a comment.

"No, she wasn't. I could tell from the minute I saw her from the deck. She found something. Something inside.

She was, well, it was more than the hairdo. She was different."

"So you killed her."

"I did not kill my wife! I did not! If anyone did, it was Celeste!"

"What reason would Celeste have to kill your wife?"

"I don't know. Maybe she thought, like you seem to, that the plan wasn't going to work. Maybe, I don't know. But I know I didn't kill my wife! Now I'm going to have to take care of everything, the house, the kids, everything. I never wanted that."

Janet sat on blanket with Annie and Chris. Pete dropped to his knees beside her. He barely had a chance to kiss her hello when Cyril bounded on top of him, knocking him to the sand, joyful at his return.

Eventually, Cyril tired of showing him affection and he ran back to be with Tillie.

"I've been working all morning. I need a vacation!"

"Poor you. What have you been working on?"

"Among other things, I had to drop Denise's camera off this morning so Mem could copy all the photos and videos. Again."

"Do you think you'll be able to see anything?"

"I already have. I took a look before dropping it off. There's something there. I hope the state police may be able to clean it up."

"How about the murders of Valerie and Evie. Have Collin and Celeste been picked up yet?"

"Yep. They weren't hiding; they were at a resort hotel about an hour north of here. I went to interview them this morning. Had to leave Cyril home. Some police departments are not as open about allowing dogs as others."

Annie and Chris laughed.

Janet said, "Cyril moped around all day until you showed up. So, do you think they did it?"

"Hard to tell. The sheriff's department sent the interview videos following their arrest. After seeing the interviews, I had doubts. They weren't told why they were picked up until they were on camera. Both of them, in separate interviews, looked genuinely shocked that the women were dead."

"What did they say when you interviewed them?"

"Celeste was all about Celeste. 'It's just like her to do this to me.' That kind of thing. I don't think she has the intelligence to kill someone without leaving evidence. But then again, it would be her style to do it, convince Collin to leave and think no one would bother to check her out. To save herself, she tried to pin it on him."

"And Collin?"

"I listened to his words and I watched his body language. From what I could tell, he didn't want a divorce and he didn't want to kill her. He didn't love her, but he needed to keep her around to take care of the house and kids. He needed someone to emotionally abuse so he could enjoy his affairs without being a bully. By the way, he didn't recognize that aspect of his personality. That was an observation."

"What a jerk."

"A jerk is right. That attorney that I called, Evie's divorce attorney, said Collin was pompous, but he didn't think he would murder Evie. He would have had another plan. Some kind of plan to keep her from getting anything. Collin pretty much confirmed that theory. He said he had a plan."

"What kind of a plan?"

"He was going to threaten to spread a rumor that she was a lesbian. He thought that would be enough to keep her under his thumb."

Chris said, "I have two thoughts. One: she could convince everyone that it's not true. Two: she could take the 'so what' attitude and let him say what he wants."

"Collin was pretty dense on that point. But...I have to say, he's kind of believable. I don't see him as a killer."

"So that means you've got to look further. Who will you look for?"

"Not a clue."

"At least the incident on the bike trail is clear cut."

"Yes, thank goodness. We still need to build a case, so we don't get totally into the 'we said, she said' scenario. That piece of paper we 'found' on the floor will help."

"Really? You were able to figure out those doodles?"

"Marco did. He was able to figure out which numbers were telephone numbers and track those back; and he also figured out they were working on a vote that would not go in Kim's favor. But they weren't going to make it, so they had to do something else."

"How did he figure that out?"

"Certain doodled words and figures, like a person in a hangman's noose, the words "Plan B," 'she's gotta go," that kind of thing. All done in a very artistic manner and doodled over, but he was able to pick it out."

"That's it? That's your case?"

"That and Monte. The sniveling weasel spilled his guts as soon as he found out his cousins had lied to him. They had convinced him all Kim's shares would pass to him if she died."

"That wasn't the case?"

"No. According to the corporate attorney, the shares would go to Clark and Bryce. Monte would be out in the cold. Actually, according to the attorney, they'll all be out in the cold if these charges stick. Kim will own it all. By the way, I'm tacking on an animal cruelty charge for Monte."

"Thank you!"

"Oh, hey, I've been so busy this week, I didn't have time to bring this to you."

Pete reached into a pocket and brought out a jewelry box. He handed the box to Annie.

"My ring!"

Chris leaned over to look. "Really? What happened?"

"The guy took the plea bargain, the judge agreed, everything has been signed, the rat is in prison for a year. We no longer need the ring as evidence."

"Thank you, Pete!"

"Not a problem. Now put that back on your finger where it belongs."

Chris admired the ring on her hand. Months before, Annie had been mugged and the ring stolen from her hand. It was found in the man's possession and was the only piece of evidence that could convict him. Annie had lived without it all this time.

Now it was back where it belonged. On her hand.

Annie looked around, wanting to have eyes on all her cats. They were spread out along the beach, some in shade, some in sun. Some on their sides; some on their backs. All of them in full-body-sand-catcher mode. She would have a mess to clean up tonight.

Ian and Kim arrived at about the same time as Holly and Jolly. Once again, Annie was glad her father had put a concrete walkway down one side of the beach. Holly was able to make it all the way down to the water on her own.

Simon Finnegan and Oscar McMurphy joined Kim on the blanket, curling into her lap. She held them close, one hand on the head or body of each cat.

Annie asked, "Kim, have you had an opportunity to talk to people at home?"

"Yes. The other board members and the corporate attorney will meet me early this week, when I finally make it home, that is." She glanced at Ian.

"We don't need that room for several days, but I expect Henrie has already told you that."

"He did. I won't stay long. I understand the prosecutor will need to talk to me, so there's a reason to stay."

"I'm sure there's only that one reason." Annie laughed and leaned into Chris.

Eventually, Holly said, "Pete, tell me again what you think these cats did."

Oscar McMurphy and Simon Finnegan jumped out of Kim's embrace. They ran down the sand to play with Cyril and Tillie. They didn't need to listen to Pete tell the story again.

Pete explained, again, that he was certain the cats had prior knowledge that Kim was in danger and that they purposefully walked that distance to save her.

Kim added, "They were there when I needed them. When it was over, they waited for Pete."

Holly and Jolly laughed. "Kim, we don't know you, but Pete, you need a vacation."

Annie and Chris smiled at Pete and Kim but said nothing.

Pete pressed on. "Then how do you explain their presence at the tip of Lake Scott?"

Holly answered. "They stay out sometimes. Sometimes they're gone for two or three nights. That may be where they go."

Kim added, "And how do you explain that, for whatever reason, they were where I needed them to be, and they saved me? They saved me, Holly."

Jolly said, "We're very happy you're safe, Kim, but they're cats. Just cats."

Holly added, "And thanks for giving them a ride home, Pete."

28

Annie was happy to see Isabel working the block party. Carlos had been gone for a week. Annie was on pins and needles. She couldn't imagine how Isabel was handling the situation.

The charity block party and fundraiser for this month was actually on the beach. It was a pirate-themed party, and Water.org was the charity. It conducted outreach in Africa, South Asia and Central America to provide safe water and sanitation.

The weather was perfect for the party, a late afternoon and early evening affair that focused on children and youth. Adults from the community, including most of the adults that lived or worked on The Avenue, were spread out on the beach, from Annie's private area to the far edge of the city park. They supervised games, lifeguarded the beach, served food and drinks and helped build gigantic sand castles.

The beach was filled with companions as well. Cats, dogs, rabbits and ferrets on leashes, turtles in containers, hamsters in cages, plus a few animals that were probably illegal but that appeared to be safely contained.

Tiger Lily and her siblings checked in with their managers. Tiger Lily found Felicity and Trudie at two different food and drink stations. She made sure they didn't need her help before moving on. She spent most of the evening at the truffle table. Jerry made rainbow-colored truffles that tasted like s'mores; they were called Tiger Lily truffles. She didn't understand what Jerry and Mommy meant when they said the truffles were not named for her. Certainly they were named for her, and she needed to be the truffle hostess.

Little Socks sat close to Diana for nearly an hour. She knew Diana would leave for vacation early tomorrow morning. She wanted to make sure Diana felt up to it. She never left the yoga studio in the hands of someone else.

Sassy Pants found Minnie. Jesus was working. Minnie and some other people threw wine bottle corks for Sassy Pants; she shared her new toys with her siblings.

Mo found Candice. She had a candle – a covered candle – from the Tap. She knew Mo wanted something special for dancing. Candice lit the candle and set it in the sand close to her feet. She knew when Mo needed a fix, he would come. And he did.

Kali and Ko stuck close to Henrie. They hated crowds. Henrie stayed in a food service tent and put a pillow behind the serving table for them. That put them close to the macaroni salad and Mommy's favorite deviled eggs. What fun! Both of them threw up a few times before the evening was over. Food overload.

Mr. Bean and Tillie sat together but away from the crowd. Carlos was still gone and Jerry was worried. Isabel was worried. Mommy was worried. They were worried.

As Annie threw toss-rings back into an area of play, she saw Isabel pick up her cell phone. Annie could tell it was either from or about Carlos. She started walking toward Isabel but picked up her pace when Isabel collapsed on the sand, head in her hands. By the time she reached her, Isabel's phone was off and she sobbed into her hands. Annie dropped to her knees on the sand beside her.

"Isabel, I'm here. What do you need?"

Isabel put her arms around Annie's neck and cried into her shoulder. Annie's heart was breaking; she didn't know how bad it was, but she had to wait for Isabel to talk.

Finally, sobs under control, Isabel said, "They're in Texas. They're on their way home. Everyone is fine."

Mr. Bean saw it first. Isabel crying, Mommy holding onto her. He bopped Tillie on the nose to get her attention and the two of them ran to be with them. They arrived just as Isabel told Mommy that Carlos was alright.

Mr. Bean and Tillie danced their little butts to the sound of the music playing over the wireless speakers and made their way to one of the children's play areas. Children and adults wore eye patches, had hooks for hands and parrots attached to their shoulders.

Ray and Cheryl managed a dig for buried treasure while a subdued but healing Jock looked on. Cyril missed the party; Pete was working late and this time, he didn't have to leave Cyril behind.

This worked in Jock's favor. Clara's boyfriend, Ramon, was home for the party, which meant his flirty, beautiful Bergamasco, Fiamma, was home as well. Fiamma attended to Jock's every need. Without interference from Cyril.

As night fell, late for the children on this last day of June, Terrence and Jerald set off fireworks from their new, oversized – perfect for a Great Lake – speedboat. Chris piloted their boat so they could concentrate on the display.

Annie, watching from one of the food service tents, asked Henrie, "Are they going to have any left for their own party this weekend?"

"They purchased two sets. I understand they spared no expense."

Finally, the party drew to a close. As Annie, her friends and staff cleaned up, Pete stopped by. Annie and almost everyone else cleaned; Pete poured a glass of wine.

Cyril trotted over to Jock and Fiamma to make sure Fiamma remembered him. And to make sure Jock didn't get all the attention.

Pete took a sip of wine. "We caught the guy, Annie."

"What guy is that?"

"The guy that killed Evie and Valerie."

"No! Who was it?"

"Brad."

"Brad?"

"Brad's Buoys & Gills."

"No! Why did he do it? How did you catch him?"

"First, how we caught him. You know those photos and videos from Denise? I was at a standstill. I had nothing else, so I went through them again. I saw Brad on The Avenue on Friday, the day after the grenades hit his boat. He was just sitting there for a couple of hours. Every time Denise's camera was on the median, there he was. Remember the rescue? This was the day the girls were pulled out of the water."

"How could I forget?"

"I'll never forget. But here's the interesting thing. When Valerie and Evie got to The Clinic, they talked to people for a little bit, then they walked to the carriage house. Brad watched them the entire time."

Annie just stared at Pete. "You caught him based on that?"

"I didn't have anything else. But the same day I realized what those pictures and videos could mean, the state police got back to me with some enhanced photos from The Escape."

"She got a picture of him?"

"She did. He was in the trees, and it was dark. There was one shot where the sunset sent a burst of light toward the trees. His face was visible."

"Why did he do it? Why the women? Why Ray?"

"It seems he was less than honest when he said he didn't see who threw the grenades. He looked up after the first one hit the water and he saw two women. He kept looking, because he could tell the second grenade was going to miss. He was far enough away from it that it didn't faze him. Then he knew the third one would hit, so he finally ducked. But he watched them long enough to get size, hair color, that kind of thing."

"But how did he know how to track them down, and why did he even care? Didn't he have insurance?"

"He didn't have insurance. He's going to lose everything for a lot of reasons, not the least of which was not being up to code."

"He couldn't blame that on them."

"He did. When we questioned Brad, Collin and Celeste at the Coast Guard Station that night, he picked up on the fact that Collin's wife might be in town and could be trying to make his life miserable. He staked out The Avenue, figuring, rightly, that he may just run into them."

"Blind, dumb luck."

"You got it. He figured Collin would be fingered for the murders, so again, he waited until the women were in for the night, and he, well, you know the rest."

"But why Ray? Why would he go after Ray?"

"Ray is everything Brad is not, and just like he blamed the women for his bad business decisions, he blamed Ray for having a good business."

"Do you have everything you need to put him away?"

"I do. He's looking at two first degree murders and one attempted murder. They might try to pin several attempted murders on him, because of the number of people on The Escape that night."

"And Jock? Can he be charged for hurting Jock?"

"We'll see. If it were up to me, well, you know what I think about that."

Annie and Chris sat up in bed. She had her laptop in her lap, engaging in a Skype conversation with Nancy, her mother. Chris read a book and dozed. Cats variously snuggled with Chris or Annie or jumped down to play. Every now and then, they would check in to see what was happening with Grandmommy, Grandpoppy and Uncle Honey Bear.

Only Tiger Lily was constant throughout the conversation. She sat just inside camera range. Uncle Honey Bear did the same. Annie could swear they communicated somehow with one another without making a sound.

Annie had a lot to tell her mother.

"I've made some progress on the Mayes family. Before and during the Indian removals, most of the Cherokee ended up in what became Arkansas. It's possible Darrell's ancestors were what they called "old settlers," Cherokee that went to Arkansas a couple of decades before the Trail of Tears. Or, they could be part of the Mayes clan that had to make that trek."

"Oh, Annie, I don't know that I want to hear about it. I might want to remain blissfully ignorant. But how did you find out that much?"

"The Cherokee developed a system of written language in the early 1800s. They kept census records throughout that period of time, including the names of all the old settlers and everyone who was on the Trail of Tears, those who lived and those who died. You can find it online now. All of it. Oh, there was a Mayes that served in the Confederate army; he was a slave owner. He could be an ancestor."

"Will you be able to find out for sure?"

"Maybe. I'm waiting on the two genealogists to get some more information, one from here and one from the home library. By the way, the one here is a relative of Geraldine, so don't be surprised if you start hearing gossip about me from your own library."

"Oh, Geraldine. What's happening with that lawsuit?"

"They're making noises about making a financial settlement, but that's all for right now. They haven't offered anything worth looking at. And my attorney is going to try to extend the restraining order, so Geraldine can't volunteer where I do."

"She didn't."

"She did. Signed up to work at the lighthouse museum."

"Has she had anything else done? Let's see…I've seen the boob job and the nose, lips, and possibly some liposuction. Is anything left?"

"She may have had her eyes lifted. She's looking wide awake these days."

"Never a dull moment in Chelsea. How's Chris?"

"I'm great, Nancy. I'm right here. Say hello to Sam for me."

"I will. Anything new with you?"

Annie moved the computer so Chris was visible to Nancy.

"Yeah. Annie's going to visit my parents with me."

"How delightful! When?"

"Soon. Very soon. I'm going to insist on it."

"Will Henrie take care of the cats?"

"Nope. They're coming along. Mom has a suite ready. They'll live like kings and queens."

"How wonderful. Bribery is the only way to get Annie to do anything."

Annie turned the computer monitor back to herself. "Thanks, Mom."

"You're welcome, dear. Tell me about Carlos. Have you heard from him?"

"Yes. He called Isabel this evening shortly after crossing the border. They're in Texas now and will be here in a couple of days. Daniela and both of the girls are with him."

"How wonderful. Will they become citizens?"

"Carlos is a citizen already, as you know. He'll make appointments for them as soon as possible. We'll have jobs for them as soon as they can legally work."

"You give them all my best. Oh, Sam is calling. I think he needs me. Well, we'll be seeing you soon. Tiger Lily, it was good to see you."

Tiger Lily touched Nancy's face on the screen before Annie signed off.

Tiger Lily prowled the house. Everyone was asleep. She walked past Sassy Pants to make sure she slept soundly. She put a paw on the little girl's cheek. Very softly. Just a light caress.

Tiger Lily checked on Mr. Bean. When he slept, he slept like a rock. Tiger Lily leaned over to lick his right ear a couple of times.

Little Socks opened one eye as Tiger Lily walked past.

Kali, Ko and Mo slept in a pile at the foot of the bed. Nothing would wake them.

Tiger Lily trotted silently to the first floor and slipped into Isabel's room. Tillie slept soundly as well.

As she turned to go upstairs, she smelled them.

Tiger Lily crept into the dining room and slipped her head under the cover of the Seven Cats Detective Agency. Simon Finnegan and Oscar McMurphy slept soundly on one of the pillows, contented smiles on their faces.

Silently, she said, *"Sleep well, detectives. Sleep well."*

Thank You For Reading!

The family of cats and the author hope you enjoyed reading this book as much as we enjoyed writing it!

About The Author

Kathleen Thompson was raised on a small family farm in Indiana. She has an undergraduate degree in Sociology from Manchester College (now Manchester University) and an MBA from Indiana University South Bend.

In a variety of towns and circumstances, she served as a probation officer, parole agent and juvenile residential counselor before moving into administrative, marketing and fund raising positions in human service organizations. Ms. Thompson took a break from human services for seven years to own and operate a bar and restaurant. Let's be honest; that's another type of human service.

While making plans to return to her rural roots, Kathi and her mother discovered an injured kitten at the family farm. The kitten, whose face was a mass of injuries, decided to make Kathi her guardian. She wrapped herself around an ankle, purred like a V8 engine, and wouldn't let go.

Against the advice of her mother, Kathi took the kitten home and to a veterinarian. The vet diagnosed road burn serious enough to take all the fur from the left side of her face, and the kitten – Tiger Lily – eventually healed and took a huge piece of Kathi's heart.

Tiger Lily was joined by the rest, rescue kitties, all: Little Socks (thank you, Aunt Mary); Kali, Ko and Mo (thank you, Connie); Sassy Pants (thank you, Ant Sherwy); and Mr. Bean (thank you, Pulaski Animal Center). Recent arrivals Speckles (thank you, Tennille) and Moriah (thank you again, Pulaski Animal Center) have joined the cast but will not live at the Inn.

Tiger Lily's Café rattled around in Kathi's brain – there isn't much else up there – for all of the years since, sometimes as an actual café and sometimes as a book. It was less expensive to write the book.

Connect with Kathi and her family of cats at their website: www.tigerlilyscafe.com, or find them on Facebook: www.facebook.com/tigerlilyscafemysteries.

Find us on the web: www.tigerlilyscafe.com

Find us on Facebook: Tiger Lily's Café, A Mystery Series by Kathleen Thompson

Text to join: Emails are sent every two weeks. You can opt out at any time. LILYSCAFE to 22828 (You may also sign up for the emails from the website.)

www.ingramcontent.com/pod-product-compliance
Lightning Source LLC
Chambersburg PA
CBHW062121170626
46813CB00002B/533